MW00680055

SHAKESPEARE'S
A NOVEL
Lady

SHAKESPEARE'S

A NOVEL

ALEXA SCHNEE

New York, New York

Shakespeare's Lady

ISBN 13: 978-0-82494-528-2

Published by Guideposts
16 East 34th Street
New York, New York 10016
Guideposts.org

Distributed by Ideals Publications, a Guideposts company
2630 Elm Hill Pike, Suite 100
Nashville, TN 37214

Though this story is based on actual people and events, it is a work of fiction.

Library of Congress Cataloging-in-Publication Data has been applied for.

Cover design by Peter Gloege
Cover photo Jitka Saniova / Trevillion Images
Interior design by Müllerhaus Publishing Group | www.mullerhaus.net

Printed and bound in the United States of America
10 9 8 7 6 5 4 3 2 1

DEDICATION

To my parents—words aren't strong enough
to express how much I love you.

"I love you more than words can wield the matter."
King Lear, Act I, Scene I

ACKNOWLEDGMENTS

First and foremost, I would like to thank my family for their constant and unrelenting support. From diapers to teenage moodiness to college life, you have always been there for me throughout the highs and lows. I would like to thank my mother and father, Lisa and Tim; my sister, Andie; and my brother, RJ, for living with me most every day. I appreciate every hug, every laugh, and every cup of coffee you brought me more than I can say. A special thanks to my grandmother Cherie, whose priceless wisdom I can always count on. I would also like to mention my extended family, who has offered me love in countless ways.

I'd also like to thank my editor at Guideposts, Beth Adams, who believed in this story from the very beginning, and my agent at Books & Such, Rachel Kent, who is always there with a guiding hand and positive attitude. Thanks to Rachel Meisel, who made sure I was well taken care of while Beth was with baby Gretta. I would also like to mention Tricia Goyer, who encouraged me to always continue writing in our middle school writing class and insisted that I dream big.

I want to acknowledge my friends, who made me laugh and walked beside me through every step. Whether I met you in ballet class at age four, studying Italian in Venice, or in Mrs. Goyer's writing class, you have each added a sweet ingredient to my daily life, and your care and support means the world.

I can't thank enough the countless friends I made at Mount Hermon for the love they bestowed on me throughout my first writers' conference. It would be impossible to name them all here, but know I am thinking of every single one of you who saw potential in my work.

Lastly, I would like to thank the Bard himself, who inspired me to create words of my very own.

PROLOGUE

ANY WRITER WILL TELL you that brilliance does not come from the head. It comes from the heart.

I learned this from the greatest writer the world has ever known. He whispered it in my ear as I lay in his arms. He told me as he looked over my crossed-out lines and empty pages. I see its truth in the little book he gave me. But I never understood what he really meant until it was too late and he was already gone.

Yes, I loved William Shakespeare. Yes, he loved me. No, it did not end well. William and I would never grow old together. We would never build a life together. Love doesn't always guarantee happiness.

He was so handsome. An actor. A writer. So passionate about his work that sometimes it seemed to be the only thing he could ever love. His words were my rival, and sometimes I felt I could never compete. But I loved William Shakespeare more than I loved any-one on this earth. I loved him more than Henry Carey, more than Alfonso, more than myself, even. He was my salvation from the life that had been chosen for me. He encouraged me to become more than what I had been destined to be.

Our love went against everything I believed in. A lifetime of doing what I believed was right was wiped away the moment he and I became lovers. I sinned against my queen, and I sinned against my God.

He wrote about me. He hadn't even done that for his wife. He wrote incandescent words about a woman who was captivating, beautiful, and mysterious—all things he told me I was. No one knew the identity of the woman in his sonnets, but I knew. When I read them, I knew he loved me, even all those lonely years later.

Because I loved William Shakespeare, I lost my honor, my name, my dearest friend, and my queen. I lost my best work, one of my greatest accomplishments.

Was it worth it? Was it worth it to love that man? That genius? Was it worth it to throw away my life for him?

You tell me.

The world doesn't remember my name, but they will never forget me. I am a part of his work, his sonnets. I am his lover, his muse, his Juliet. I am his Dark Lady.

PART ONE

Therefore my mistress' eyes are raven black,
Her eyes so suited, and they mourners seem
At such who, not born fair, no beauty lack,
Sland'ring creation with a false esteem.

—Sonnet CXXVII

England, 1587
During the Reign of Queen Elizabeth I
Greenwich Court

I remember Twelfth Night so clearly. I often reflect on it even now, when I am about to fall asleep. I can recall every detail. I remember what I wore, what I said, what dances I danced, the pageantry and singing. It was my first introduction to Queen Elizabeth's court, with its intrigues, absurdities, and dangers. This was the night my life really started.

My emerald dress flowed to the floor. A simple silver chain was clasped around my neck. I was perfumed and powdered; the brush's bristles tickled my neck and face. My hair hung loose down my back, as I was a young lady just recently come to court. This was a flag of my virginity, a proud display of youth. Lady Margaret lent me a silver netted caul, which we draped over the back of my head. What a contrast against my long dark hair, shining in the candlelight.

I remember the warmth of Lady Margaret's hands on my shoulders as she inspected our accomplishment. I detected a bit of pride in her sweet features as she admired me.

She smiled and said, "You look like a countess. And you deserve to be one."

Lady Margaret would know. She was the Countess of Cumberland. The title afforded her many fine things; Cumberland was a rich and fertile area. She was gowned in a subtle pink, her hair pulled back in an elaborate bun. She reminded me so of the fairies I used to create stories about when I was young...but I did not tell her this because it seemed childish.

Lady Frances stepped up to me and ran a hand through my hair. She was dressed in a royal-blue gown that was a perfect complement to her eyes. Her blond hair danced around her shoulders. She was gorgeous—the epitome of English beauty. A pang of jealousy went through my chest. We all knew her night would be filled with courtiers, dancing, and laughter.

She held my shoulders between her two hands and shook them. "There will be dancing, and food, and men!" she cried.

A knowing look passed between Margaret and me—the latter was what Frances was obviously most excited for.

The Great Hall was filled with sound that night. The music itself felt like a presence in the cavernous room hung with the queen's rich tapestries. A long, heavy table laid with endless settings for the queen's guests filled one end of the hall. Plates and knives had been scrubbed until they shone. Ladies clucked around each other and swarmed the high-ceilinged room, while men gathered around tables with wine, their glasses sparkling in the candlelight. The air felt thick with merriment.

Feasting was the evening's first event, and Queen Elizabeth had outdone herself. The queen's chefs had roasted a swan to perfection and painstakingly replaced the feathers before presenting the delicacy to her guests. There was rich roast duck for everyone, accompanied by the finest wine. We had the softest, most aromatic bread I had ever tasted and wild boar that had once roamed the queen's own forests. I could only imagine the hours Elizabeth's handmaidens had spent, organizing this grand feast.

The queen sat far in front of us, on a raised throne, so all could admire her. In my first audience with her, when I was presented, I could only think of how cold and distant she had seemed. It was obvious she was enjoying herself now, though. She wore a lavish, golden gown embroidered with beads and pearls, her favorite gem. She wore her wavy copper hair like mine—long and loose around her shoulders. Whether or not she deserved the honor, we were all willing to believe it that night.

No one abstained from drinking or making merry. Rowdy men poured themselves more ale while the women chattered. The Great Hall could hardly contain the splendor of the evening.

After we feasted, we danced. Lady Frances was immediately chosen by a young courtier with an eager smile. Lady Margaret was allowed to dance with her husband, the Count of Cumberland. They danced together with calm experience.

My eyes never left the dance floor as finely dressed figures twirled in time to the music, the ladies' gowns swirling around their slippers, the men's feet their metronome. Frances's hair flew out behind her like a banner, and we could hear her laughter floating above the tune.

I longed to join them. My hands ached to hold a handsome courtier's, and I couldn't help but sway to the music. It reminded me of the songs I would play for the countess in Kent. I missed her, but I was grateful to be here. The scene before me was all I had ever imagined of court.

There were so many handsome men in the room, I could hardly look at one before I drifted to another. But one man in particular seemed to stand out from the rest, perhaps because he looked utterly indifferent.

He stood slightly away from the other men near the large double doors with a glass in his hand. He nodded in time to the music, but he seemed to be buried in his own thoughts. His eyes darted in my direction, and he must have caught me staring at him. My own eyes went to the polished floor, my face burning in embarrassment.

"Who is that?" I asked Margaret when I had the chance to pull her aside. She was short of breath.

"Who?" She craned her neck to look. "That man?" She waved a hand. "A playwright, I believe."

"He's quite striking." I was surprised at the boldness of my words. Those sorts of things I usually kept to myself. But there was something about this playwright. He wore no finery or anything that might attract a young lady, and he seemed to be more interested in the music than in finding a partner to dance with. All the company he needed was himself.

I peered over at him. I felt my heart dance to the music when I caught his eyes again. He raised his glass to me from across the room. It was all the encouragement I needed.

I took a step forward, and then another, until I realized I was actually crossing the room to talk to him. I was almost there. His eyes again happened upon mine, and I swallowed. His dark brown hair was cut short, and I could detect a hint of stubble lining his jaw. He watched me, waiting for me.

Suddenly, I felt a tap on my shoulder. I turned and saw an older man with a bit of a hunch. The skin around his eyes was wrinkled, and his hair was gray. In his day he may have been handsome, but now he looked old and cantankerous, almost like a goat. I started to pull away, but then I noticed he was dressed well, in a red doublet and sparkling jewels. I knew he must be at least a duke, so I curtsied. He seemed not to notice my hesitation, as he reached for my hand and swept me onto the floor with an air of authority.

"Have you just arrived at court?" he asked, his voice crackling with age as we danced to the lively tune heavy with viols and harps. Dancing correctly was an art. A good dancer could impress while a poor one would be ridiculed. I tried to keep in step—to be as light as a butterfly and yet as sure as the ever-coursing Thames.

I nodded, afraid to speak. I searched my mind for the steps of the dance. Did I step backward or forward before the lift? He placed his arm around my waist and spun me around. I kept my balance and even managed to smile. Although my partner was not the prince I'd hoped for, I enjoyed the excitement of dancing.

"You are so different from the other young ladies at court," he continued. He placed his lips next to my ear. "The queen finds you rather enchanting."

I stepped away in time with the music. So this man had spoken with the queen. He must be more important than I originally believed. Something beat wildly in my chest; I realized it was my heart. The queen liked me. I wondered if she was watching me now.

The music's rhythm guided me, and I danced better than I ever had before. We stepped jointly to the right and the left and clapped, my dress brushing the floor behind me. My heart continued to pound. The queen approved.

"You remind us both of someone." He looked me in the eyes. I felt my face grow hot.

"Oh?" I asked. I tried to sound sure, but my shaking voice revealed my apprehension. "Who?"

"You were born long after she died, but both the queen and I see the resemblance you bear to the queen's mother."

Anne Boleyn? She was the woman famous for leading King Henry the Eighth astray from his wife. The Countess of Kent did not approve of her for that very reason. Anne Boleyn was said to be a witch—bewitching the king into making her the queen. I had heard that she had taken all sorts of potions to bear him a son, but the only child she had ever borne was Queen Elizabeth. The king commanded that the accused enchantress be beheaded at the Tower of London.

"Are you cold?" the man asked. His hand slithered farther down my back and he pulled me closer to him, as if to protect me from the chill.

He must have intended the remark about the queen's mother to be a compliment. I smiled as politely as possible and focused on the rhythm of the music. Thankfully, the song finally reached a sleepy end. After expressing my gratitude to the old gentleman with a curtsy, I quickly rejoined Margaret and Frances.

"Who is he?" I asked, keeping an eye on the hunched man as he made his way back to the queen's side. He whispered in her ear, and she nodded and smiled approvingly. Light caught on the crown nestled in her hair.

"Henry Carey, Baron Hunsdon," Frances answered. "He is the queen's first cousin and is in a very good position to take the throne. His wife remains in Hunsdon, I see."

"He compared me to Anne Boleyn," I said, finally airing the astonishment I had hidden from him.

The two ladies eyed me with surprise. Margaret sighed before leaning in closer to me. "Well, if he did compare you to her, it was meant in your favor," she finally said, her voice even over the sound of the music. "Anne Boleyn was his aunt and the queen's mother."

"She was a witch," I whispered as softly as possible. I matched Margaret's hushed tone.

Margaret took my hand and squeezed it tight. Her motherly, plump face calmed me, but the tightening of her lips told me that this was not a moment to be taken lightly.

"Listen to me." She spoke with urgency. "You must never say that again. If you are overheard calling her that, it will not be looked upon kindly. The queen is very sensitive regarding her mother."

Frances tossed a length of golden hair over her shoulder and spoke in agreement. "Her Majesty is rather thin-skinned."

"She has reason to be, Frances. Would you like it if your mother was called a heathen and an enchantress?" Margaret scolded. As she reproached Frances, not a single hair moved on her head. I nodded. I understood. The queen's ruthlessness was infamous. If I was expelled from court, I would have nothing at all.

Our conversation was interrupted by another young courtier who fancied Frances.

"Would you care to dance?" he asked, extending an eager hand. He wore much finer clothing than the playwright, but he was no less handsome.

"I would be delighted," Frances agreed, taking his hand. She winked at me as he began to lead her to the floor. Margaret and I watched as, once again, Frances's young man possessively placed his arm around her waist and her laughter filled the air. She had danced with all the handsome young men tonight, while I was forced to dance with the elderly baron.

Later into the evening Henry Carey asked me to dance once more. I agreed, though I had been hoping someone a little younger would ask me, like the man I had been admiring earlier. The two gentlemen were conversing earlier. Perhaps the baron could introduce me to the playwright.

We did not speak while we danced; he seemed to have said all he had to say. The baron had to be at least thirty years older than me. My first ball was not going the way I had hoped it would. But the music was lively and the spirits high, so I tried to focus more on the music instead of his hand on my back. I glanced around the crowded hall. Several young ladies were dancing with older men, so I felt less embarrassed.

Something caught my eye over the baron's shoulder. Couples began moving to the sides of the room, making room for something to pass through—and then the queen emerged in the space made for her. Courtiers surrounded her, wearing jewels and linens almost as fine as her own and twinkling in the candlelight lighting the hall. Though the queen had been an avid dancer in her youth, she now walked about the dancing couples. My breath quickened as I realized that her focus was on me. I could feel her hawkish eyes watching my every step of *la volta*, one of the most difficult dances and the queen's favorite.

I kept my eyes down so as not to offend her or cause any disrespect. Only when she came to the baron's shoulder did we dare to stop and look to her—for she was addressing us directly.

"A charming couple." Her voice was loud enough to be heard throughout the Great Hall. She gave a nod to her cousin, sharp, concise, and final, before she crossed to the next dancers.

My heart raced. She had accepted me. But it dropped as I

realized what this meant. I knew there was no way I could refuse the baron's advances now.

A FEW DAYS LATER, after Twelfth Night was over, we heard a knock on the chamber door. This was not uncommon. Many courtiers had come to see Frances after the ball. The ladies-in-waiting had been catching up on the court gossip. We sat around the great room, our dresses gathered into wide chairs and bright silver needles in our hands. Laughter punctuated the conversation as each lady shared details others had missed. I played my harp to pass the time and amuse the others. My fingers halted in midair at the knock, waiting to finish the song I had begun.

I was surprised when a timid maid approached and announced the caller to be Henry Carey, asking to speak to me.

I hesitated then told the maid to let him in. He strode into the room and glanced around it, looking for me. I met his eyes, and he continued toward me until he reached my side and sat on the bench beside me. I leaned aside, inching away from him. I grasped my harp in my hands, as an abandoned song still waited to be conducted.

"Play something for me, Lady Bassano," he said, motioning toward my handheld harp with a spotted hand.

I nodded curtly and began plucking at the strings, a familiar melody soon playing out. I played him a simple song I'd learned when I was younger, a lullaby my father had sung to me. It was the only thing I remembered about him. For a few moments, the song took me away from the discomfort of entertaining the baron. I forgot I was sitting next to an old man who had taken a liking to me because I looked like his aunt, a witch. The notes brought me back to the old days when I would sit reading books in a corner of the lavish chambers where my father entertained dukes and earls.

My fingers brushed the strings with a surprising grace. I may not have been an excellent dancer, but I was a fair musician. The song was clear and strong and I felt proud of my choice.

"That was beautiful." The baron smiled. "Like the harpist it came from."

My face flushed a deep scarlet and burned like fire. Who did this old man think he was? He was not young and handsome like the men who came for Frances. Why couldn't I have been noticed by one of them?

All the ladies-in-waiting watched us. We were the entertainment for the moment. I slid away from Henry Carey and placed my harp on the ground next to the bench. I hoped they would look away.

He turned to me. "I shall come see you tomorrow afternoon?" He phrased it as a question, but I heard it as a certainty. Did I have no choice in the matter? I knew I had to please the queen. Margaret had once said that our duty was first and foremost to our country. If the queen was pleased, it was one less thing for Her Majesty to fret over. I had to at least pretend I accepted his affections.

I glanced over at Frances and Margaret. They were the only ones who seemed to be preoccupied with something besides my love affair. Margaret was staring into the courtyard; her eyes were focused on something out the window. Frances was occupied with some sewing that she hadn't the patience for a moment ago. I would receive no guidance from them.

I nodded hesitantly. "Yes."

He stood up from the bench and bowed low. Then Henry Carey strode out of the chambers as brazenly as he had come. The whole room sighed.

My heart felt as though it had been pierced with one of Frances's sewing needles. I had just told Henry Carey he could come and visit me again.

When Henry was safely out of earshot, my friends joined me on the bench. They sat on either side of me, a comfort in my time of need, and I forgave their lack of support for when Henry Carey had been at my side. Margaret sat on my left; she was my voice of reason. I valued her wisdom and her understanding of the inner workings of the court. Frances reflected my rebellious side, my desperate desire to escape the relationship that was being forced upon me.

"What should I do?" I cried as I buried my head in my hands. "I do not want his attention."

"Emilia," Margaret said softly, "you said it yourself—you have no money to marry. This might be the way for you to accomplish that."

"I was not expecting to be a mistress to a man thrice my age," I responded sharply. I recognized my error. It wasn't her fault I'd had the misfortune thrust upon me. I took a deep breath to steady my voice. "How can I make him lose interest in me?"

Frances shrugged her petite shoulders.

I looked back and forth between them, but neither seemed sure. Frances's face expressed the doubt she could not put into words. I took another breath. Could I do this? Could I really serve my queen in this way? It seemed wrong, and yet if the queen wanted it, it was right. Obeying her was like obeying God. My thoughts swirled through my head faster than the dancers on the floor at the ball.

True to his word, Henry Carey came the next day. I was the only lady who had stayed in the chambers. The rest opted to go for a walk around the nearby pond. Not even Margaret had stayed. I remained in the great room, pacing back and forth.

I bit my nails until they bled, hoping he had forgotten about me, about his promise. I silently pleaded with the clock in our chamber to never strike the hour when Henry was to come. I prayed that the strong, wooden doors would remain safely closed. I was almost sure my prayer was answered when afternoon passed and he still had not arrived. I was just starting to believe I was safe, however, when we heard a sharp knock. The handmaiden answered, and he entered. I grabbed my sewing and hid in a corner, hoping he would miss me. I wasn't so lucky.

"Lady Bassano," he exclaimed as he stepped through the door. His frame was larger than I had remembered.

"My lord." I smiled. I had to greet him with the utmost of civility.

He sat next to me, and I asked about his involvement in court and whether he was planning to visit his estates.

"I have no plans for travel," he said. "Winter has stayed far too long for my liking. I do not prefer riding in this type of weather."

"And Parliament?" I asked, because I couldn't think of what else to say. To me, Parliament was simply old men debating useless things.

"Tiring. Simply tiring. You, my dear, remain a sight for these exhausted eyes."

There was an uncomfortable silence as I tried to think of a response that would not offend him. Insults were all that came to me. "Will you play me another song, Lady Bassano?" He pointed to my prized harp.

I agreed, though beneath the pleasant mask I wore, I grimaced.

This time I sang a harvesting song. It was a tune I'd learned from the countess when I was first learning to play. My fingers danced along the strings. They knew the melody so well. It was simple; I didn't want him to think I was overly accomplished and admire me.

Once again his visit drew to a close, and once again he asked me if he was allowed to visit. I replied yes as before, but once again with regret in my heart. He gave me a smile and kissed my hand. His lips felt wet against my hand.

How nice it must be to be a man. They could go wherever they wished and do as they pleased, while we ladies had to suffer for it.

"A SIGHT FOR EXHAUSTED eyes. Can you imagine?" I said. The circle of ladies erupted in laughter. Distress was always laughable when it happened to someone else.

That night, as all the ladies sat together in the chambers, our nightgowns draping over our bare legs, Henry Carey and I suddenly became the prime subject of discussion. Up until this point I had not provided enough drama to be of any interest to the group. Before, the talk had always been about Lady Frances and her many admirers.

The darkness of the main room of our chambers did little to hide the giddiness on the faces of the ladies. The light from the single candle we had placed in the center of our circle cast a pale light on each girl's face. Our forms were cast as shadows on the wall.

"I pity you, Lady Bassano." Frances laughed, her voice a slight bit louder than it should have been. "He has always reminded me of an old toad."

"Lady Frances..." Margaret resumed the role of our guiding mother, her voice quieter than Frances's echoing tones. When she was away from the eyes and ears of the other ladies-in-waiting, Margaret could be as bad as Lady Frances, but when the ladies were gathered, she never engaged in gossip.

"What am I to do?" I asked the others. I wanted them to give me the answer I could not find easily in my heart. "I want to be loyal to the queen, and I do need the money he would provide, but..."

"He's a toad!" Frances exclaimed.

Margaret shook her head, but I agreed with Frances this time. He was far too old...and far from what I'd hoped. I could barely stand the thought of sitting next to him. How could I be his mistress?

But if I refused...what would the queen do? I could be banished from court, and I would have nowhere to go. I had no money or acquaintances to help me.

"There is only one thing you can do," a young woman named Bess answered. "You must accept him."

The whole circle stared at her, eyes wide. Lady Bess Throckmorton was a rather plain girl, but she made a pleasant enough impression. Her brown hair color was not remarkable, nor was the color of her eyes—her overall appearance was monotone. She was not married and had no prospects from what I'd heard, but she had been at court for some time and she was valuable to the queen...though not as valuable as Margaret.

"Why should she subject herself, Lady Throckmorton?" Frances demanded. "She is pretty enough. She just needs more time at court to establish herself among the younger courtiers."

"Yes, but none would be as wealthy as he," Bess answered. I

hated how calculating her voice sounded. "It is likely he would set her up with a well-positioned husband if she were to become with child. She can have the young, foolish poets all she wants, but none of them have the money to support her. We don't all have funds like you, Lady Sidney."

Frances looked away. It was a sharp movement, her face harsh and unfeeling. It was the first time I had seen Frances display anything but assurance of herself. I knew that Frances had been married very young to the older poet, Lord Sidney. He had died only a few months after the marriage, leaving his massive fortune to his adolescent widow.

"I cannot possibly," I said gently. I didn't want to offend anyone at court after I had been there such a short time. One of the first things the countess had advised me on was not to cause bad blood between members of court. She did not fail to remind me that the Boleyns and the Seymours had been enemies for centuries, all because of some argument at court. No one seemed to remember what it had been about, but their rivalry agitated for years until Jane Seymour bore Henry the Eighth a son and lost her life in the process.

"Then I'm afraid you will not find a good husband. You know that others make sacrifices," Lady Bess said. "Margaret never sees her husband for the sake of the queen and her many whims. Whenever Her Majesty needs her, she is expected to drop all things and run to the queen's side. You have little choice but to do the same."

With that, she stood up and walked over to her mattress in the next room and turned in for the night. The group was silent except for Margaret, who was humming softly under her breath. We remained this way until we heard Lady Bess's soft snoring a few minutes later.

"How would she know?" Frances scoffed, crossing her delicate arms over her chest. "She's not married."

"Perhaps that's why she encourages Emilia to be," Margaret said quietly. "This is an opportunity you should carefully consider, Emilia. I'm not saying you have to agree, but you should think about your future. The queen would be furious if you do not consent. If you refuse her cousin, she will never again see you in a favorable light. Let's say you agree..."

Frances almost interrupted her but was stopped when Lady Margaret put up her hand. Frances rolled her eyes, threw a knowing look at me, and let her continue.

"Let's say you agree and you become with child after a month. Then the baron will send you to be married to some other man, and you will be free."

"She won't be free. She will be married to someone the old toad thinks would make a good match," Frances insisted. She ignored Margaret's piercing look.

"Is that worse than turning him down and enduring the possibility of never getting married at all?"

Frances's face began to turn a light shade of red, disturbing her usually fair complexion. But somehow she looked even more beautiful. Even dressed in her nightgown and with her face the color of a ripe, red apple, she looked far more exquisite than I ever could. What a shame Henry Carey hadn't taken a fancy to her. She could have turned him down and not had a second thought about it.

"It is her life!" Frances cried. "She is the one who has to sleep with him." And she, too, huffed off to bed. I could hear her making sniffling noises under her covers.

Margaret gave a small chuckle. The room was quieter without Frances to object to everything. The soft light danced on the walls, and I fingered the hem of my nightgown.

"Frances was lucky to have Philip Sidney," Margaret said. "She is just upset that she didn't have more time to flirt with the courtiers before she was married."

I smiled halfheartedly. I was not so easily consoled. Although I understood Margaret's position, my mind and my heart could not agree with her advice.

"Don't worry, dear," Margaret said. For a moment, she reminded me of the Countess of Kent and how she had always called me her "dear." "There is still a chance he will tire of you or find someone else," Margaret continued. "Men are experts at that, and I have seen it many times in this court."

I gave a small laugh despite the circumstances. How lucky I was to have Margaret.

"Shall we go to bed?" she asked, standing up and addressing the other ladies. They yawned and stretched their arms above their heads before making their way to the pallets laid out on the wooden floor in their chamber. The tingling in my legs reminded me how long I had been sitting.

I gave Margaret a hug. She smelled of perfume and the soap we used to launder our clothes. I wanted to believe she knew the right decision for me to make, but I could not make the ache in my chest go away.

We separated, and I was once again alone with my thoughts. I crawled underneath my blankets and felt the softness and warmth envelop me.

Frances, after being married so young, was now free to marry a page if she wanted. But for this freedom, she had given a man she neither wanted nor loved her childhood, her youth, and her virginity.

Could I stand being Henry's mistress? Could I stand catering to his every whim like a dog on a leash or a falcon with clipped wings? Could I give myself to this old, married man? And what part of myself would I lose in the bargain? The thought sent shivers of dread down my spine.

Court was now my home. I had no estate to live in if I was banished. The Countess of Kent had been good to me, raising me like her own after my parents died, but I could not go back to her. She had conditioned me for life at court. The look that would be on her face if she found I'd thrown away all she'd taught me would be worse than the first night with the Baron of Hunsdon.

It was that moment that I realized I did not have a choice. I knew there was only one thing I could do. I decided if Henry Carey asked me to be his mistress, I must accept.

BESIDES TWELFTH NIGHT AND Christmas, Shrove Tuesday was the biggest celebration of the year. There was not so much dancing as there was at Twelfth Night, and that was disappointing for both me and Frances, but there was more wine, which heightened everyone's spirits. We primped and prodded each other in the chambers, readying ourselves for an exciting night. Skirts and clothing were thrown all about the main room as every girl tried to pick the right gown for the occasion.

Margaret refused to join us. She sat in her favorite high-backed chair and watched us warily.

"Aren't you coming with us?" I said to her as I brushed my hair behind me.

"I do not believe the queen could tolerate a maid of honor drinking as much as will be expected tonight."

"Oh, Margaret," Frances scoffed, "the queen would not care on Shrove Tuesday. *Everyone* drinks excessively."

"Trust me, Emilia," Margaret warned me, "things are said on Shrove Tuesday that should not. Do not listen to Frances and say something you will regret."

I assured her I wouldn't, and after a hesitant nod from her, Frances and I set out for the Great Hall, where the voices of the men already echoed between the solid walls.

The wine was fine and the night was young, but I was not in the mood to drink that night anyway. I knew Henry Carey might officially ask me to become his mistress, and Margaret's warning rang through my head like a steady bell. As we sat at the long table worn smooth through centuries of use, Frances passed me another glass, which I ignored, and poured a third for herself.

"Look at all the handsome men," she said, her voice higher and louder than anyone else's in the room. "You should think about having some fun before you agree to the old toad."

It felt like many hours later by the time Henry Carey came beside me. I couldn't help but fidget in my seat and scratch my elbow. He looked even older than I remembered, his face carved with deep wrinkles. He sat beside me, next to Frances and a couple of young men.

"You are beautiful tonight, Lady Bassano," he said. He reached for my hand, and I had to take his. "I've been meaning to give you this." He smiled. He took out a ring from his doublet and placed it in my other hand.

"Wear it, my love, won't you?"

The ring glinted in the candlelight. The gold band shone and winked like a flirtatious courtier. I hesitated before I took it, but Henry waited expectantly for me and I did not know what else to do. I slipped it on my finger.

Now it was official. I was his mistress. It took some time to force myself to do so, but I wrapped my arm around his. I glanced at his profile. His nose was quite prominent—a trait of his royal lineage.

I felt a hand on my shoulder, and the next thing I knew, Frances and I were being escorted back to our chambers by two maids. Margaret had apparently worried about us and sent them to keep us from making fools of ourselves. I can only imagine what she thought when she saw the state Frances was in. She smelled of wine and perfume, a disgusting combination of smells that repulsed me in my sober state, and her hair was disheveled from a frisky kiss with one of the courtiers. She hiccuped uncontrollably and laughed whenever one erupted.

"Go to bed," Margaret demanded. "Now."

I nodded and started to turn to go to my pallet. I should have been watching Frances more carefully rather than worrying about Henry Carey.

Frances crossed her arms across her chest. She refused to go to bed or to listen to Margaret.

"I was having fun." Her words were slurred.

"That's apparent," Margaret scolded. "The men can wassail all they wish, but we are ladies, and we shall act that way."

Frances agreed, but only because she was too wobbly to make her way back to the Great Hall. We both went to our mattresses, Frances swaying as she walked, with thoughts of wine and handsome men likely still on her mind.

THINGS AT COURT QUIETED down after the madness of Shrove Tuesday and Twelfth Night, and in the calm, rumors began to fly about the queen. Mostly they were rumors about war with Spain.

"They say the queen has broken his heart," Lady Bess whispered over her sewing one night at Greenwich Palace. She was referring to the king of Spain, Philip II. "She should not have refused his marriage proposal so many years ago. Spain waits with its armada. There's not a chance we could survive if they were to attack."

"Oh, do be quiet," Frances said. "I'm tired of hearing of such things." She did not sit with the other ladies and sew. Instead, she sat a bit away, near the window, so she could look out into the courtyard.

"I have not heard any of this," I insisted. I moved myself closer to Lady Bess.

"They are simply stories, Emilia," Margaret said from the other side of the room. She sat in her favorite chair with the roses embroidered on the arms.

When people have nothing to occupy their minds, they turn to things that will. The queen was the subject of other kinds of rumors too, ones involving Sir Walter Raleigh, the captain of our armada. I didn't know what to believe. I myself had never seen him enter her chambers or come close to her at important dinners, but others knew better than I. After all, I was a newcomer to the world the queen commanded.

I WORE HIS RING, but even two weeks after Shrove Tuesday, Henry Carey still hadn't called for me. He sent small gifts, mostly necklaces and rings, but I began to hope he would change his mind. Margaret wasn't so sure.

"He will call for you," she said. "It won't be long."

I hoped she was wrong, but I continued to receive his gifts. I pulled the ruby ring from Shrove Tuesday off and on again, over and over.

I learned some new songs to play on my harp, and that kept my mind at ease. Whenever I worried about Henry Carey, I would simply focus on making music and writing. The simple country melodies and my pen scratching across the parchment reminded me of less complicated times at the home of the Countess of Kent.

I thought of my parents and how they had done so little for me before their deaths. The only loving thing they had done was to send me to the home of the countess, where I could be raised as a lady. I might have always lived in a cottage and worried where my next meal would come from if they had not sent me away to be educated. But even if I hadn't come to court, I still would not have been free. I would still have been forced to marry. I still would not have had a choice.

I had just finished pinning up my hair for the night when I heard a knock on the door. Frances answered it and told the maid yes, I would come. The ladies-in-waiting rushed around me all at once. Margaret pushed them away to reach me. She instantly began unpinning my hard work.

"Tonight you shall go to him as you are. A young, beautiful virgin."

My hair fell to my waist. It was shiny and healthy. For once, I liked how dark I was. I looked mysterious. I had never looked so beautiful, and I hated that I had to waste it on this man.

I felt a tear run down my cheek. I hadn't known I was crying. I wished I could be in the countess's arms once again, back when I was a child, before she first told me what awaited me at court. I had never wanted this.

Life was not fair to the young. The old had it better. They could choose who they wanted. It was even better to be the queen. She had the power to choose her lovers, and to choose lovers for others. A simple lady like me had to do what others told her. I couldn't do anything but hug Margaret and Frances, wishing things could be different.

"Good luck," Margaret whispered in my ear.

I squeezed her hand in thanks. Frances ran a hand through my loose hair.

"What a shame," I heard her say quietly.

I followed the maid down the hall. The only light came from a maid's candle and from the brilliant moon, which shone through the stained-glass windows. Silver shields and weapons glinted off the walls. I felt as though I was doing something terribly wrong, even though I was doing my queen's will. She was sovereign. Appointed by God. If she commanded it, it was right. My soft footsteps sent tiny echoes through the empty halls.

We were all ants serving the great queen. We were doing her will for the good of our home, the good of England. Whether I wanted to bed Henry that night or not did not matter. If the queen thought it was the best, it was what I would do.

We stopped in front of a large wooden door. I knew Henry Carey would be waiting inside. For the first time in my life, I did not like Her Majesty.

THE NEXT MORNING, WHEN Henry Carey left me to watch the sunlight dancing on the chamber floor, I dressed, opened the well-built door, padded down the ornate hallways, and went to the bath. I passed by Frances, snoring and tossing. Margaret slept peacefully, and I tried not to awaken her as I made my way to the bath chamber adjoining our rooms.

I fetched my own water. It was no use calling the handmaidens at this hour, and I did not wish for anyone to know I was back yet. I was not ready for questions. I could do the task by myself. I stripped off my nightgown, dropped it onto the floor, and dipped a cloth into the basin where I had poured the water. I placed it on my skin. The warm water burned, and I felt clean. The previous night would never go away, but I tried to forget as the warmth from the cloth engulfed me.

I wiped down every inch of my skin, trying to rid myself of Henry Carey, but he was now a part of me. Men had it so lucky. They could have however many women they wanted and still feel free. I felt nothing but disdain for him, and I wished I had worked up the courage to refuse him. Was it such a terrible thing if I did not get married? It wasn't as though I were Frances or Margaret. I was a musician's daughter with no purse at all. Would it be such a crime if I didn't agree to matrimony?

I found myself twisting the ruby ring until it was entirely off my finger. What if I dropped it into the water and left it? When he asked where the ring was, I could say I gave it to a poet who visited our chambers that afternoon. That would keep Henry Carey away from me.

I ran my hand across my stomach. Could I be with child? If I became pregnant, I would be free of Henry. I thought of the other mistresses who had been assigned to older men at court. They had found freedom once they discovered they were expecting. I could raise the child with my husband, and we would be supported by the baron for the rest of our lives. He was rich enough to give us a handsome sum. There must be a child in my belly. There just had to be. If there was, I could leave the old man behind forever.

HENRY WAS A BUSY man. He had a wife at his estate, whom he visited often, and he was the queen's first cousin and one of her favorite companions. In addition to being a direct relative of Her Majesty, he was also an honored war hero. He sat near the queen at most events, and he sat in Parliament. We had not been together long when he received the honor of becoming Lord Chamberlain—a patron of the arts. His loyalty had won him the honor of overseeing all the entertainment that came to court.

We sat in his lavish chambers at times. My master liked to have me there when he worked. I did not often say anything and only spoke when addressed. I spent hours buried deep in his velvet-covered chairs. This day, however, I had brought a pen and a piece of parchment to write upon. As my scribbling added to his, Henry's head shot up.

"What are you doing, love?"

I hesitated before answering. "Only writing."

He stood up, and I shrank back. My father had done the same when I was but a child. I would write while hidden in the barn and in nooks and crannies of the house, away from sharp eyes, but he always found me. Even though my hands stung when he took the stick to them, the longing to write had not disappeared.

"Proper ladies do not write." Henry grabbed a corner of my page.

"The queen writes verses." I struggled to keep the paper in my hands, even though his hold on it was stronger.

He smiled. "Yes, but Her Majesty is our sovereign, my dear. She can do whatever it is that pleases her. You"—he glared at me, but somehow gently, like he did not really wish to say this—"are only a lady."

I dropped the paper and let him take it away from me. What use was it to fight the order of things? He locked my page in his desk with a firm *thud* then turned back to his work.

In the silence, I began to think of my father. I thought of the hours I had spent in the elegant homes of dukes and earls, traveling with his company in the bitter winters. The company was still active after his death, but I had heard they were limited on funds.

It was several hours before I found the courage to address Henry again.

"My lord?" I asked, my voice barely audible.

He looked up. "Yes?"

I laced my words with honey. "I have heard that you have been presented the honor of becoming Lord Chamberlain. I have an idea, if you are willing to hear me."

I had been thinking about this request since I'd heard the news but had only just built up the courage to ask. He stood up from his desk again. Making his way over to the matching chair, he nodded and motioned with his hand for me to continue.

"As you know, my father was a musician. After his death, his company decided to continue to perform around the countryside, but without the queen's favor—which my father had earned—they have not been invited back to court. Would you be willing to ask them to court?"

Henry stroked his chin. His foot tapped to an unheard melody. Would he reprimand me and scold, or would he consider my desire?

"I like the idea. I would be happy to support your father's company, my lady. We will do so in honor of your father, Baptista Bassano. Who knows? If it is successful, I might even think of investing in some kind of other amusement for Her Majesty. A theatre company, as well, perhaps? An excellent thought, my dear."

He kissed me on the forehead before dismissing me from his study. I couldn't help but smile as I navigated the halls of the palace. For the first time in weeks, I felt like I had done something good.

Henry Carey visited one afternoon in early February. He was wearing a fine doublet, so I knew he had been in session with Parliament. He brought news of the queen. Her cousin, the queen of Scotland, was said to have conjured a plan to have Elizabeth killed.

Margaret had run past our pallets in the middle of the night to Her Majesty's chambers. Her robes flew behind her while she rushed toward the sound of the loud cries. During the day she would have dark circles under her eyes—almost as black as the queen's.

They were accusing the Queen of Scots of treason, and Queen Elizabeth, by law, would have to sentence her cousin to death. Yet she was hesitant. We knew she was troubled. It was hard for any of us to sleep because of the noises from the queen's chambers, and we knew that for both political and personal reasons, she was having a difficult time deciding the fate of her kin.

And then, one afternoon, she chose.

"It is official," Henry said. "The Queen of Scots is to be executed."

We sat alone in the chambers; Margaret and Frances had let us be. Snow hit lightly against the windows as we talked, creating a steady rhythm.

"Mary was Elizabeth's heir," Henry said. "Now she will be forced to proclaim James, Mary's son, as the future king." He shook his head. "More Scottish blood vying for the English throne."

"Are there any other options?" I asked, biting my lower lip.

"A few." He shrugged his shoulders. "There are relatives, but there aren't as many as you might think. I myself am under consideration."

I stared at him. I couldn't imagine this man on the throne. He was a good baron and Lord Chamberlain, yes, but could he hold England together like his cousin had?

"Scotland won't be happy if it is refused the throne," I said.

Henry scoffed.

"They hardly deserve it. They are a bunch of barbarians. I hear they still worship the old gods with fires and obscene acts."

I ran my hands over the arms of the chair I sat in.

"Still," I argued, "Scotland would be a part of England and civilization if young James was to inherit them. That would be some improvement over what they are now."

Henry's face looked as if he was thinking over my argument. He smiled a little.

"My dear, you grow more and more like my aunt every day. She had a way of twisting things to make herself always seem right."

I did not want to be compared to Anne Boleyn anymore. I prayed often and shunned the Catholic pope. The only sin I committed was with Henry, but that had been my queen's wish, so it was not a sin. I was pure, but Anne Boleyn had been clouded with treason and adultery. I was doing the will of Her Majesty, while she had only thought of her own goals. I hated being considered similar to that witch.

The large clock in the chamber chimed.

"Is it two already?" Henry asked, pushing himself to his feet. "I'd best be getting back to Parliament."

Henry excused himself and left. I was once again alone. Silence was my companion as I thought over what he said. If there was no heir, the queen might be forced to take a husband, something she had refused since her coronation. If she were to bear a son, then her legacy would continue. If she didn't, she might have to give her throne to the Scots, and that was unthinkable.

THE NEXT DAY, FRANCES and I decided to take a walk in the freshly fallen snow. We bundled up in our furs and coats and went out against Margaret's insistence that our hems would become soaked if we journeyed into the cold. Snow covered the ground evenly, hiding the brown earth. I felt like a child, picking my way through. The queen's favorite oak tree was bent over from the weight of the snow.

"Have you heard that the Queen of Scots has proclaimed her innocence?" Frances loved gossip, and she smiled as she passed this on. "That's a death sentence for certain."

"Frances." She was right, of course, but it was nothing to laugh at.

"Maybe your old toad will take the throne after all," she said, her eyes bright. "He's been under Elizabeth's influence for a long time, and with him being the queen's brother—"

"Cousin," I reminded her.

Frances's eyes lit up. She was delighted to have another piece of gossip to tell me. "There are many who say he is actually King Henry the Eighth's son."

"How could that be possible?" I said. "I thought Henry's only mistress was Anne Boleyn."

Frances laughed.

"King Henry is as infamous for having as many mistresses as he had wives, if not more. Henry is the son of Mary Boleyn, Anne's sister. She was married to William Carey at the time, but she was the king's mistress first and foremost. Everyone knows she spent more time in his bed than her husband's."

"So Henry Carey is the king's son?"

She nodded and then rolled her eyes. The Countess of Kent had never been much for court gossip, so I hadn't known much about life at court until recently.

I wondered about my master. The queen's brother. No wonder he was in such a high position to take the throne.

But surely he wouldn't take the position. He was the kind of man who would only want the responsibilities he chose. I didn't think he would choose to become king.

Suddenly Frances let out a shriek.

"What's the matter?" I exclaimed.

"I have just thought of something amazing." She looked me in the eyes. "You could be the queen."

"What?" I stopped walking.

What could she be thinking? I was not related to the queen. I had only known her for a few weeks.

"Listen." She sighed. "Henry Carey's wife is getting old and could die at any time. If she died or is pushed aside, then you would be an obvious choice to replace her. Or if you could bear him a child, then your child would be in line for the throne. It would even be better if you bore him a son..." She trailed off.

"You mean to say my child could become a king?" I asked.

Frances began to dance in the snow, kicking some up on her dress. "If you would accept his hand in marriage...."

"I wouldn't," I stopped her.

Frances stopped dancing.

"What?" It was now her turn to look confounded. She stared at me with a mixture of confusion and disdain.

In the little time I had spent within Greenwich's walls, I had learned that perhaps being queen was not worth all the gold and fine jewels, if you had to execute your own relatives to retain them. I hadn't even been sure I wanted to be a lady. In some ways I wished I had stayed with the countess. I wouldn't have been forced to be mistress to a man forty-five years older. I could have continued to play my harp and sing and write. The queen had come from a long line of monarchs and had been taught how to do her job. I would have to learn. Besides, what kingdom would want a musician's daughter as their queen?

For the first time since coming to court, I had a choice. I was not destined for greatness of any kind, nor did I want to be. I did not want to be queen.

"I wouldn't accept," I explained. "Even if it was possible, I would not want to be a ruler."

Frances stepped away.

"But why?" We both knew she would have accepted immediately. I could almost imagine Frances as the queen of England. She would be good for the job.

"Some people are not meant for greatness, Frances," I said. "It would take a lot for me to become a queen, anyway. People would have to die; babies would have to be born. The queen would have to make changes. It's unlikely."

Frances shook her head and laughed. Her expression told me what she did not say. She would never understand why I would throw away something like this so easily.

"If I had the opportunity," she said as we turned back toward the palace, "I would want to be remembered for always."

THE DAY OF THE beheading came. We dressed warmly. The bitter February air would not be forgiving this day. Nothing would be forgiving this day.

I couldn't help but wonder what Elizabeth was thinking as we all made our way toward the Tower. I had never had a family, a real family, but I knew it would be difficult to get rid of your own cousin. Perhaps that's why she stayed hidden in her chambers that day. She couldn't live with seeing her cousin's head roll off the block. Some criticized her weakness, but I admired her. Her Majesty rarely displayed such humanity.

Bodies pushed against us as Frances and I made our way through the crowd. The square courtyard was packed with people, from simple farmers to dukes and earls and duchesses. Hostility was thick in the wind. It nipped at my hands and cheeks, and I pulled my scarf around my neck and over my exposed face. Boots thumped in impatience; people shivered from cold and anticipation. Everyone wanted to see the Queen of Scots punished. We were allowed closer to the front because we were recognizably ladies of the queen. The scaffold stood tall above us, a stage for the entertainment.

I rubbed my hands together, trying to warm them.

"I can't believe how crowded it is," I said.

Frances shivered and smiled at me knowingly. "Death is a popular show."

It was over an hour before we were allowed to see Mary. The cold was almost unbearable, and the crowd began to shout. When she was led out from the door to the Tower, there was a tremendous roar.

The Queen of Scots was a small lady with a tired expression. At first glance, she looked defeated; her hands were folded around each other. She wore a black mantle pulled tightly around her body, but her skin was as white as the snow on which she stepped. She pursed her lips as she made her way through the crowd with her loyal ladies-in-waiting behind her. There were more jeers from the crowd. Frances joined in, booing. I couldn't do it. It felt wrong to jeer someone in their final hour.

Despite all those against her, Mary's calm expression didn't change.

Before she stepped up to the scaffold, she handed her ladies-in-waiting the pearl necklace that hung around her neck. They carefully unlaced her outer robe and pulled it off slowly. Underneath, she wore a corset covered with red silk. She was wearing the color of the martyr. She believed she was dying for her country.

She walked up the scaffold steps, her feet crunching in the snow. The black and red were striking against the white. I saw her tremble, but she smiled at the executioner. She was braver than any warrior. To stand up there in front of hundreds, knowing they had all come to see her die…

My respect for her grew.

The executioner lowered himself to one knee. More gasps came from the throng of people. He bowed his head, and she put her hand on top. I couldn't hear what she said, but I was later to learn it was, "I forgive you, for you are about to end my troubles."

She was blindfolded and placed on the block. The crowd's jeers grew louder until the noise was deafening. Mary shook uncontrollably. The executioner raised the ax high, and then, suddenly, everything was quiet.

I heard the ax whistle through the air, and the next thing I knew, there was scarlet, like the color of her corset, everywhere. Blood flowed as a small river. The executioner raised his ax again; she hadn't been killed by the first blow. The whistle came once again. This time the damage was done.

The executioner held up her head by her brown hair. Blood dripped from the stub where her neck used to be. The expression on her face was serene. I went weak at the knees, and my stomach turned over. This woman had stood up to the crowd, to her cousin, to her executioner as no one else could, yet there she was, severed in two. This was what came of challenging Elizabeth. My fear of angering her grew.

"God save the queen!" the executioner bellowed.

"Come, let us go." Frances's face was ashen, and she took my elbow and steered me back toward the palace.

We returned to the palace to find Margaret waiting for us. Queen Elizabeth had been distraught until the deed was done. Now she lay on her bed asleep, exhausted.

"How was it?" Margaret asked when we had come back and sat down with some warm, spiced wine.

"It was like nothing I had ever seen," Frances said—and that was all that needed to be said.

AFTER THAT FIRST NIGHT, Henry didn't call for me for a few weeks, but I knew it was only a matter of time. I spent each night hoping he wouldn't call the next. I did not want to think about when he would. The memory of that first night grew worse and worse in my mind. I prayed he had forgotten about me and moved on to another young girl.

Margaret and Frances got into the habit of staying up with me in case he called. We chatted, mostly, or sometimes amused ourselves with games or sewing or reading. When it was past midnight we could rest peacefully; he would not call for me after that hour.

One night, though, I could not avoid it. He asked for me. As Margaret unpinned my hair, I began to bawl, the tears streaming from my eyes. My face was turning red and my eyes puffy. Frances handed me a kerchief. Her face showed concern, and that was very unlike Frances.

I came to him the same as I had before, my hair flowing, my nightgown clean and white. This time I made sure there would be someone waiting for me the morning after.

That one night, he called early. I came to prefer when he called late, because he was often tired and would fall asleep quickly. The nights he called early were the worst.

My throat throbbed from holding back tears. I couldn't stand the man. What was I doing lying with him every time he had a whim? I sat down on a stool.

"I can't do it any longer," I cried. "He must know how much I hate him."

Margaret sat beside me. The queen had long been in bed, so she was there to help me when I needed her. I handed Frances back her kerchief.

"That is the way men are," Margaret soothed. "They think of what will bring them pleasure. A woman is just a commodity to them."

Frances gave a soft grunt. "*I* don't see it that way. Men are a commodity to me."

Margaret sighed and shook her head at Frances. She looked at me seriously and stroked my hair. What was she thinking at that moment? How she was married and never allowed to visit her husband? How she could never find the pleasure she should be given?

"Oh, be quiet," I said to Frances. "You have no idea what it's like to have a really old man want to bed you. How much older was Philip Sidney? Fifteen years? Well, how about forty-five? He is forty-five years older than me."

I burst into another fit of tears. Margaret quieted me down by whispering softly, "Don't wake the other ladies."

"But why? Why did it have to be me? Why not Lady Bess?" I asked, searching her face.

Margaret closed her eyes and took a deep breath before she answered. Frances and I both waited, listening to the sounds of the other girls sleeping. They were so peaceful.

"Because," she started to answer. "The nights he is with you, he gets to pretend he is his father."

She looked me straight in the eyes.

"And you are his Anne Boleyn."

THE NEXT FEW DAYS were quiet. We all knew he would be back, but he wasn't a young man and I knew he could not deal with me every night. He was approaching his sixty-second year.

One evening, though, Margaret and I sat up to wait...but Frances didn't return to the chambers.

I had seen her with Thomas Campion, a young poet at court, earlier in the day. She had waved me back to the chambers while she kept eye contact with the handsome bard. She boldly inserted her arm into the crook of his and gave him a playful smile. Frances had a way of making the men think they were in control of her, when really she held the higher cards.

As we waited, Margaret paced back and forth, wearing a visible path on the queen's carpet. I pointed it out to her with a smile. She was always so worried.

"Frances will be fine," I assured her.

Margaret looked at me. She seemed so much older than even just a few minutes ago. Had I never noticed the wrinkles between her brows before? She worried more than a lady of her age should. First it was the queen, then me, and now Frances. How much would she go through before she herself would collapse under all of the pressure?

"The queen will be angry." She bit her lip harder.

"It is not your fault, Margaret," I said. "You can only do so much. Frances is just headstrong. You can't control her all the time. You can try, but she will always find a way to get what she wants."

"You don't realize what could happen to her if the queen found out. She could be banished, and she would have no place to go."

"The queen approves of my affair with Henry Carey. This is no different."

"You have her permission. More than that, she has encouraged this relationship for her cousin."

She was right. It made little sense that the queen would support one affair and forbid another, but Her Majesty always did seem more concerned with control than morality.

"Sit down," I ordered, patting the bed. "Frances can take care of herself."

"Frances cannot take care of herself." She breathed heavily.

I patted the bed again, and this time she submitted.

"Frances and I are the same age." I laughed. "Do you worry so much about me?"

Margaret shook her head. I put my hand on her back, feeling her uneven breaths.

"You are no longer a child. If there is one thing Henry Carey has done for you, it is that. Frances has no wisdom or reserve. She just does what she wants and does not think of those she might hurt."

She turned to face me. "Do you know who she could be with?"

I shrugged, though I did know. "There have been many who have come to see her, but I think she was with Thomas Campion, last I saw."

Margaret put a hand to her head.

"He was a friend of Philip Sidney's," she explained.

She straightened her legs, but she stood instead of pacing. Some of the color returned to her countenance, and I could tell she was a bit more poised. The way she worried about those other than herself was not healthy. She cared too much for those who could not be controlled.

Worrying about the queen was one thing, but Frances was another. Frances would always be high-spirited and willful. Anyone who thought otherwise was deluding themselves. My hands clenched. Had Philip Sidney done that to her? Or had she always been that way?

"Please," I said gently, "if Frances wishes to do this, well, that is her choice. She will have to face whatever happens." I finally encouraged Margaret to go to her pallet, but I was sure that it would be a long time before she felt sleep come to her. I sat up and began the long wait for Frances.

I sat up for hours. The large clock on the far side of the main chamber was my only companion and entertainment. Its face peered at me, almost like a person watching. The pendulum hanging like a long beard from its chin patiently swung back and forth. I pulled out my little book but thought of Henry's words when he had seen me writing, so I put it back in the pouch that hung from the belt

I wore. Instead, I thought of marriage, and I imagined my future husband's every feature.

He would be tall, taller than me. He would have a pleasant smile and kind hands that would hold mine. He would be a musician, and he would be happy with our one child, the child of Henry Carey. He did not have to be incredibly handsome, just so he was not wrinkled.

I thought of the house we would share. It wouldn't need to be expensive or filled with finely woven tapestries. I was a musician's daughter. I imagined a house in the country, where we could raise crops and take long walks through the forest. I pictured a simple life where I could visit court occasionally to see the rest of the ladies. It would be perfect.

When the sky began to lighten, I heard a soft knock on the door. Margaret had slept soundly throughout the night. Even now she was deep in sleep and the sound had not woken her.

I walked over to the door and opened it a crack. A clear blue eye met my gaze and I recognized Frances's smile.

"Emilia." She smiled. "Let me in."

I opened the door a little bit more so she could sneak inside. Turning to her sharply, I crossed my arms over my chest.

"Where were you?" I asked. I gave her a cold stare. "If the queen found out—"

Her smile fell. "You saw me leave with him…."

"I did, but Frances…," I began.

I was angry because of the state she had put Margaret in the night before. Frances thought of only herself, and it hurt me to see Margaret in that way. It was not right that Frances had fun while I had to suffer with Henry Carey, either.

"Then you should know." Her attitude suddenly became defensive. I wished not to make her upset, only for her to realize the distress she'd put upon one of her friends.

I looked her over. She stood with her hands on her hips. For a moment, I wondered what I could say in response.

"Frances, perhaps it is time you thought about someone other than yourself," I finished.

She laughed mockingly.

"Why should I? My father married me off when I was fourteen. He didn't care about me. My husband only wanted me to bear him children. My life has always been about pleasing others. You know what that is like. And someday, you will feel as I do. You will want to escape as I do."

I could not look at her. We stood there for some time. I was not as witty as she was, and I could not think of a response until it had been several minutes. She kept her hands on her hips while I looked down to the floor. The path Margaret had worn was still visible, the color now gone from that area of the carpet. At long last I spoke.

"Frances, we care about you."

She glared at me. It was as though she was scrutinizing me, like she did the first day we met. I felt as though she was again searching me to see if I was good enough to be her friend. She had no need to look through me like that. I meant every word I said.

She would not accept my sincerity. She turned on her heel and quietly huffed to her pallet without one word.

Our friendship seemed strong and also so fragile. But I knew at that moment that she and Margaret were my family and I was not about to let that go.

SUMMER WAS A GOOD time for mistresses. Wives waiting at home had to be visited, so husbands left court. Henry Carey prepared to journey to Hunsdon, and I can't say I was sad to see him go.

I saw him off. We met just outside the stables. The horses neighed behind us and the air smelled of horseflesh. I dressed in my dark green dress with the silver trim. I carefully avoided the mud that seemed determined to get on my hem. Henry kissed me quickly and swung onto his big bay horse.

He smiled. "Don't worry. I will be back in the autumn when the queen asks for me."

"Yes, my lord," I replied, lowering my eyes. I knew my duty as a mistress—and how to remain one.

"I shall send you a gift." He seemed to have believed my act.

"You are much too generous," I thanked him. "It would be most appreciated."

"Take care, my dear," he said, as he reined his horse in.

"You as well," I replied.

He gave me one last smile and then rode off. I watched until he was no longer visible, and then I ran inside the palace as fast as possible. My skirts swept out behind me. My face was triumphant. Henry Carey, gone for three months. I couldn't believe my luck.

My nights were free. I could do what I wanted and not have to worry about being called upon. I even returned to writing. My head was full of new ideas I had imagined while at court, and I shared them with that little book. It once again became a friend. I wrote late into the night, almost as late as I'd stayed up before. I was used to the hours and found I was most creative at night.

Frances caught me working on my verses one night. She had been out with a courtier again. The rooms were empty, as the other ladies had all elected to stay late in the banquet hall. It was the perfect time to work on the story that had been spinning in my mind all day. There was still decent-enough light that I only needed a single candle. It illuminated the empty mattresses around me. I settled in under my covers and began scratching words into the book.

When I heard the door to the chambers open and close, I tried to stuff the book under my mattress. Blankets flew and pillows fell as I tried to hide what I had been doing, but I wasn't fast enough.

"What are you doing?" Frances asked. She yawned, covering her small mouth with a hand.

"Nothing," I said, still trying to hide the little book from her prying eyes.

"Let me read it, Emilia. I've seen you writing. I want to see it."

"No." I shook my head. "My verses are nothing that would interest you."

I caught her eyes roaming toward my mattress before bed a few times in the coming weeks, but she never said anything about my writing again. I would not have been surprised if she pulled them out and read them while I was not in the chambers, but I never caught her.

WHEN THE FIRST LEAVES of autumn came, I started to dread my reunion with Henry Carey. I slept more than usual. I also refused to eat, which caused my thin frame to look even smaller. Margaret noticed a change in me, and she consulted the court physician. His diagnosis was low spirits. He bled me a few times and gave me some herbs to brew into a tea, but I did not feel much better afterward.

"Are you with child?" Margaret asked.

"No," I answered. "I bled last week."

She ran a hand over her hair, which was pulled back in her signature bun. I looked up at her from my bed. We were all alone. The other ladies had gone out to enjoy the beautiful day.

"You must perk up," she said. "Henry is coming back in less than two weeks. You do not want to lose his interest, do you?"

I was so melancholy that I was almost willing to. The thought of spending my nights waiting up for his command made me cringe. Was it really worth it? Maybe I could be like Lady Bess. She was not married, yet she served her queen and had a place to stay. She was content. I could imagine living here, serving the queen. I could even work my way up to a maid of honor position if I was loyal.

"Margaret, do you wish you had not married?" I asked. I sat up on my pallet. She stood above me, a motherly expression on her face.

"No," she spoke sharply. "I am happy. I am." She sighed, and I could tell that she was lying. "I just wish I had more time to spend with my husband. I have always hoped for children of my own. But being so close to my queen is the highest honor. Even if she has been closer to Sir Walter lately..."

"Sir Walter?" My eyes grew wide.

Sir Walter Raleigh. The queen's captain of the armada. I should have suspected.

"I should not have said that," she cried and covered her mouth.

"How long?" I asked. My mood was suddenly improved.

"I cannot say," Margaret refused. She covered her mouth again after she said it.

"Come on," I urged. A hand could not stop Margaret from sharing news. "You have already said it. I'm only going to assume the worst. Has he been seeing her every night? Is she with child?"

I said it as a joke, but Margaret became panicked.

"No, I have heard nothing of that, but you must promise not to mention this to Frances. It would escape like the wind if you let her know."

HENRY CAREY RETURNED TO court just as he said. I was there to see him off, so I was there to welcome him home.

The leaves were thick on the ground, and they crunched under his horse's hooves as the beast came up the path. I dressed in one of the new dresses Margaret and I had sewn over the quickly passing summer months. I was almost ready to receive my mother's dresses from so long ago—my inheritance—but I would have to wait until next year. They were meant for lighter weather. The dress I wore was a scarlet red; it was a nice contrast to my skin, which had become darker. I had spent time in the sun that summer, and my Italian heritage could not be mistaken.

Henry greeted me with a smile, and I could not help but notice how he seemed even older. In my memory he was younger-looking; he now looked even more like a toad. I forced a smile to my face and took his arm as we entered the palace. A groom led his horse away. He looked at it fondly.

"That horse carried me faster than any I have ever ridden before." He turned his gaze to me. "Maybe it knew how badly I wanted to get back and see my lady."

My stomach churned, but I kept a straight face as I had hundreds of times before. I was becoming as good as the actors in London. It was too bad they didn't take women into their troupes. I would have been one of the best.

"How are your children?" I smiled. He had many, if I remembered correctly.

He sighed. "They are busy with their own. It's a sad and humbling day when a man realizes that his grandchildren are nearly grown. It makes a man feel old."

I smiled sympathetically and patted him with my other hand.

"We have received several invitations to go hunting," I told him. "I would very much like to go."

He nodded slowly. "Yes, my love. But we shall not accept every one. I am getting too old to rove around."

It seemed it had never occurred to him that he might be too old for a mistress.

"It is wonderful to have you back, my lord." I let go of his arm and curtsied before I headed back to my chambers.

"You must come with me to London sometime," Henry said. "I've been looking into several theatre troupes there. They have some delightful shows written by a William Shakespeare that you would enjoy. And I will arrange for your father's troupe to return to court."

"I would very much like that," I said, this time in all sincerity. It would be nice to journey out of court for a while.

He reached for my hand and grasped it firmly before we parted. "I will call for you tonight."

CHRISTMAS WAS NOT AS merry as it had been the year before. Spain was still threatening war, and we were all anxious about what was happening with King Philip II. He had heard about the queen's idleness and her romance with Sir Walter Raleigh; he also knew that Mary, Queen of Scots, had been beheaded and that the queen had no heir. With this knowledge, Spain was poised to take over the throne.

We tried to make merry, even though we did not feel like it. We still performed the Christmas traditions that had been carried on for centuries, but there was little joy. We all tried to take our queen's mind off the threats Spain had sent her—but we would soon find that our attempts were useless.

The Great Hall smelled of holly. Cooked goose and puddings called to us from the table, while familiar carols beckoned us to dance. Henry and I sat at the long table, his hand resting comfortably on my knee. In the middle of our Christmas celebration, the doors of the Great Hall were thrown open and a man entered. His clothes were foreign, a black cape worn by Spaniards on special occasions. I could not remember seeing him at court before. The bright music stopped, and the dancers ceased their joyless prancing as we all watched him stride down the aisle towards the queen.

She did not raise an eyebrow. She did not seem surprised to

see the figure approaching her. Her golden throne, carved with unrivaled intricacy, made Her Majesty seem even more imposing than usual. The man handed her a single scroll tied with a ribbon. Her jeweled hand reached out and took it, slowly yet confidently. Elizabeth was not one to show fear. I could see her tightening her grip around the scroll before waving him away.

The man left without a word, his sword hitting against his hard leather boots, and the queen rose once the giant double doors closed behind him. She whispered in Sir Walter Raleigh's ear before picking up the hem of her dress and striding down the center of the Great Hall. She walked toward the heavy doors alone.

"Is she all right?" I said to Henry in a hushed tone as I watched her.

"Oh yes." He nodded. "Elizabeth always manages to take care of herself. It's probably more business with Spain."

"War?" I asked. His gaze said yes. "You would not be summoned, would you?"

He tightened his hand on my knee before shrugging his shoulders. "I have recently been appointed general in Her Majesty's army."

I should have been relieved, but I found I did not want Henry to go. If he were to perish at war, all my hopes for the future would die as well.

England, 1588
During the Reign of Queen Elizabeth I
Whitehall Court

As I feared, Henry left a few weeks later. He helped to lead the queen's army as they traveled to Essex while Elizabeth stayed at court.

The winter days were lonely. Whitehall Palace seemed empty, with most of the men gone. A few lingered on—either the very young or the very old. Henry Carey probably should have been among the latter, but being so close to Elizabeth made him a significant ally.

It was about this time that a new member of court arrived.

He was Robert Devereux, the Earl of Essex. The queen took an immediate interest in him. He was young while she was growing frail, but age was not an obstacle for the queen. They were often seen around the halls together. We did not know if they were talking of war or if they were speaking of things more personal.

One night at dinner, Frances turned from Thomas Campion, who was ceasing to interest her. The poet was one of the few men who remained at court; his skills did not include combat. He sat quietly, talking to me only if he felt the need to speak at all. Her clear blue eyes bore across the hall.

"Will you accompany me?" Frances asked. "I am going to introduce myself to him."

"The Earl of Essex?" I asked. I glanced over to where he sat. He was on the queen's right, in a chair next to her throne. Elizabeth had taken to walking around the Great Hall during the meal with some of her advisors, and I knew we didn't have much time before she would return and he would once again be at her side.

"I don't know if that's wise," I answered. "You know how the queen fancies him."

"It's only an introduction," she pleaded. "Besides, what harm could it possibly do?"

"I don't think so," I said. "Not now. It's not as though he's leaving soon—not the way the queen dotes on him. Perhaps when she is not present."

I turned back to Thomas. I could hear Frances sighing and huffing beside me. She was not used to being refused what she wanted.

After a few moments, she spoke to me. "Fine. If you won't do it, I will greet him myself."

She began to make her way around the other ladies walking about the room. She passed them with grace, almost as if she were dancing.

"Excuse me," I said to Thomas Campion, as I stood to follow her. I squeezed my way past clusters of skirts. Ladies peered at me curiously, but I had to reach Frances before she did something we would all regret.

"Frances," I said, catching up to her. She had already curtsied before him. Quickly, I did the same.

"This is my friend, the lady Bassano." Frances's voice dripped with false politeness.

The man looked up from his ale and nodded politely at us. "Charmed." He smiled. "A pleasure. Are you ladies-in-waiting?"

We nodded. He had a very sharp face, but it was still pleasant to look upon. His brown eyes mirrored his sly smile, while a full beard grew from his chin.

"How long are you planning to stay at court?" Frances asked. I noticed that her voice was slightly more hesitant than when she usually flirted with courtiers.

He shrugged his solid shoulders. "I am at Her Majesty's disposal."

"We look forward to your company." I looked to my left and noticed the queen returning. She was coming toward us rapidly, her political advisors surrounding her like bees. Her white dress trimmed in gold shone above all others like a beacon.

"You must come visit us in the chambers sometime," Frances insisted.

His eyes drifted to her small frame. "You can most certainly count on me."

I tugged on her skirt but knew it was too late. The queen had already seen Frances in conversation with her favorite. If we left now, it would seem we were ignoring Her Majesty's presence.

As the queen approached us, Frances and I curtsied deeply. I could see only the toes of her shoes poking out from beneath her dress.

"Your Majesty," we said.

"Lady Bassano, Lady Sidney." She emphasized Frances's married name. "Don't you think it's getting rather late? You'd best be getting back to the chambers."

"Yes, Your Majesty," I answered, keeping my eyes lowered. Frances and I turned to leave. I did not look behind me, but I could feel the queen's eyes on us until we were no longer in sight.

I WAS WALKING THE passageways to the banquet hall a few days later. I was going to meet Margaret, who had invited me to eat with her and some other maids of honor. I was dressed in one of my finest gowns, a dark blue satin. I fingered the silver chain around my neck. The halls were mostly abandoned. Some of the Christmas decorations remained, and I could still detect the scents of holly and pine. The sky was heavy and the air damp. A man fell into step next to me. His boots clunked at a steady rhythm, and I found myself walking in time to the noise. I peeked over my shoulder to see who it was. I recognized him as the playwright from Twelfth Night a year past.

He muttered softly. He did not seem to notice that I was there beside him. His brown eyes studied the floor as he walked.

"Excuse me," I asked, when I had finally built up enough courage to speak. "Are you talking to me?"

He stopped and looked up at me as if he was in a daze.

"Sorry?" His dark eyebrows lowered.

"Oh," I said. "I'm sorry. I thought you might be addressing me."

He smiled and shook his head.

"I was practicing lines." He grinned. "But I will address you now, if you like."

We began walking again. There was something about him that puzzled me. He looked the same as I remembered him, dressed simply but spotlessly. We began walking again and continued down the hall.

"That's all right; you don't have to," I said. "I rather dislike formalities, anyway."

It was quiet for a while. We passed some ladies headed back toward the chambers. They whispered and looked at me, and I thought I heard Henry Carey's name amongst their murmurs.

I looked over at the playwright to see if he had heard any of their conversation, but he appeared to be absorbed in his own thoughts again. My shoulders loosened.

"Have you been at court long?" I asked to break the silence.

"No," he said. "I come looking for support every now and then. I have a theatre company in London."

"You won't stay long, then?"

"Probably not," he replied.

His short answers frustrated me. Did this man have no manners? When I had found my way to the banquet hall, I was almost glad to excuse myself.

"It was nice to make your acquaintance, Master..."

"Shakespeare. Yours as well." He nodded his head. "Perhaps I will see you around court."

"Yes," I said. "Perhaps you will."

His eyes were vacant; he didn't seem to hear me.

"Parting is sorrowful," I said. I raised an eyebrow at him.

He looked at me, suddenly interested, and he nodded again. He turned and continued down the hallway, and I realized he hadn't even asked my name.

THE WORRIES OF WAR loomed closer, but the queen was distracted. The snow fell outside our window like bits of tiny lace from the gray sky. Frances, Margaret, and I sat in the main room of the chambers, wishing we could walk in the fine powder but hating the cold that kept us from it.

"She doesn't even care about our country anymore," Frances said. "England has given her full support and yet she seems to care not. All she seems to care about is that blasted Earl of Essex."

Margaret laughed. "Who could not? He is very handsome."

"You would think she would have more important things to think about," Frances insisted.

Margaret and I looked at each other.

"Frances?" My voice did not quite come out as strong as I would have liked. "Why do you keep mentioning the earl's name?"

"I do not," she said. She glared at me.

"Come, now. Be honest with us. You talk of no one else of late," Margaret scolded.

Frances sighed before she walked over to me. She looked at the floor and brushed off her skirts. Had I ever seen Frances so uncomfortable before?

"He is the first man who ever made me think of remarrying."

"Oh, Frances," Margaret exclaimed, going over to her and hugging her tightly. "What a terrible trap you have fallen into."

We pitied Frances. She had set her sights on an unreasonable goal. When the queen chose her favorites, she expected them to be devoted to her for the rest of their days. Sometimes the men she loved married anyway, but it only made the queen look upon them and their wives with spite. If the earl was to marry Frances, they would never again be in the queen's favor.

Frances's only option was to forget about the dashing fellow and focus on other things.

The war dragged on for months, but on July 12, 1588, the Spanish Armada finally approached England's shores. The queen moved to Essex, miles away from Whitehall Palace in London, with more men and soldiers. Court was empty. The only people who remained were the ladies. Elizabeth was to be a king and with her men. She was far from cowardly.

Queen Elizabeth readied the troops at Essex. It was said that she wore a silver breastplate over a white dress, the latter a symbol of her purity and virginity, as she gave a moving speech and rallied her army.

The Spanish Armada came down from the Netherlands; King Philip II allied with them and positioned his ships to sail from Spanish ports to Ireland and northern England. It was an ill-conceived plan. Anyone who had grown up in England knew that the tides there were unpredictable and unsafe. The Spanish did not know.

The Armada, the greatest naval company in the world, crashed into England's shores seventeen days later. Their ships were shattered and unable to fight. Without the Armada, Spain was lost.

England rejoiced. We had been saved. We were still at war, but we would win. Our queen was safe; not a single man had died in battle. There would be much feasting and merriment at court.

We all laughed and cried. The tension that had been present in our every interaction these past months was released, and we were able to relax. The queen would be home soon, riding triumphantly into Whitehall. Life at court would once again be as glorious as it once was.

I HADN'T EVEN BEEN born the day the queen was coroneted, but I know that it was a day of much celebration and happiness. Her subjects cheered the young queen and lined up along the streets to see her ride in on a litter trimmed with mink-and-ermine fur.

The thanksgiving feast that the queen put on to commemorate her Armada victory was even grander. It was said to be the biggest celebration England had ever seen. The queen made it very clear that this would be her finest hour. This victory would be her legacy.

Henry gave me a new dress and jewels for the occasion. Everyone seemed to be in a jubilant mood. I will always remember that victory celebration. There was so much dancing, and there was a parade and such a feast.... No expense was left unspent. We all knew that court would never be like this again.

Henry brought his wife to Whitehall for the celebration. She was an old woman. Fine clothing wrapped tightly around her rotund body, and the hair that sat on top of her head seemed to be a creature unto its own. Stray hair protruded from her wig, and the jewels she had placed in it looked like a pair of eyes. I now understood why he had given me the gifts—to make up for the awkward situation of having his wife at court. I felt strange about seeing her there, for I knew they were a much better match than my master and I. I was surprised that I felt guilty when looking at them. If she knew who I was, would she still be smiling and dancing with her husband?

Frances and I sat together, watching the dancers twirl and step in time to the music. Everyone was smiling as they paraded around the hall. Henry spun his wife around again, and her brilliant jewels caught the candlelight.

The bench I sat on was hard, and I could hear Frances sighing as she looked upon the queen and the attractive Robert Devereux.

"You have not danced this evening," I said to Frances. "And I cannot imagine your not being asked."

She shook her head, and her hair rippled along the back of her royal-blue gown.

"I don't want to tonight."

I looked over at Her Majesty. The Earl of Essex was at her side. She whispered something in his ear, and he laughed heartily.

Frances sighed again.

"I think I shall retire for the evening," she said suddenly. "I'm feeling tired."

She patted me on the shoulder before she crossed the Great Hall, her steps slow. I watched her until she disappeared into the hallway and I could no longer make out her blue dress. Only then did I look back to the throne at the far end of the room.

Elizabeth was seated on the high, raised chair. Covered in golden carvings, it had seated her father and her ancestors before her. She leaned out from her throne and kissed Essex. She traced a finger along the side of his neck, smiling suggestively at him and clearly marking him as hers.

No one could object. She was our sovereign and not to be disputed.

She was our beloved ruler, our gift from God, our virgin queen.

ENGLAND, 1589
DURING THE REIGN OF QUEEN ELIZABETH I
GREENWICH COURT

THE COURT WAS FULL of gossip and news in this time of peace.

Margaret hoped that maybe now the queen would let her go to her home in Cumberland to be with her husband. The queen had not asked him to court in many months. He waited at their estate, not knowing when Margaret would return home. We all wished it for her; she had a life that no one wanted to live forever.

When she was refused, she fell into a sadness that we hadn't seen her in before. We all knew that her greatest desire was to have her own children and her own home.

"Oh, Margaret." I hugged her ample waist.

"I am contented, Emilia," she said, smiling halfheartedly. "The queen needs me, and that is a great honor."

Even though we wished Margaret could return to Cumberland, there was no doubt that we needed her too.

One day I caught Frances alone in the chambers. It was a beautiful sunny day, and we had all agreed to pick strawberries in the court's garden. But I had forgotten to bring a hat. I could not risk getting burned—the sun turned my skin dark. Henry waited for me while I went back up to the chambers to fetch it.

I grabbed my pillbox hat decorated with a veil and a feather and was about to walk out when I heard a noise coming from the other side of the chamber. I followed the whimpers and whines to the corner of the room, where I found Frances huddled in a corner. Her face was buried in her skirts, and her shoulders shook in obvious distress. I had never seen her cry, and the sight frightened me.

"Frances…" I rushed over to her. "What is the matter?"

Her eyes were swollen and red, and it looked as if she had been crying the whole time the party had been out in the garden. I could barely recognize her. I only knew it was her by her golden hair and small frame.

"Do not come closer," she screeched and stood up with a start. "Get away from me."

Her eyes were wild and her voice harsh. She looked as if she had been locked up in the Tower for ten years and gone mad.

"Frances," I began in the calmest voice I could muster, though I could feel my hands beginning to shake.

"You always were Her Majesty's greatest supporter," Frances spat at me. "The one who always thought kindly of her. Is she so great now that you see what she has done to me? Is Her Highness thoughtful and loving towards her ladies?" She picked up something as she circled me. I did not know what it was. I tried to keep my eyes on her face.

"Frances, calm down." I chose my words carefully. "What happened?"

"You are weak, Emilia. You can't see how being so close to the queen, being so close to Margaret, can hurt you." Her words dripped with hatred. "Do you not understand? The queen does not care if you serve as Henry Carey's mistress till the end of time. She does not care if Margaret is lonely and wants to go home. All she cares about is—"

She threw the thing in her hand with such force that I had just enough time to step aside. I heard a crash behind me and cautiously turned. The jewelry box I had given her last Christmas lay smashed on the floor, her necklaces and rings spilled out onto the polished wood. Seeing it hurt me more than if she had hit me with it. I had sold some of my own necklaces to afford that box.

I felt tears well up in my eyes too, and I turned toward her. I couldn't believe that she would hurt me like this when I had done nothing to her.

She sank down to the ground and dropped her head in her hands.

My anger lessened when I saw how small she looked on the floor. I lowered myself to the ground and crawled over to her. It was harder than I thought it would be, but I made my way over to her without ripping anything. My hat was crumpled. I placed a hand on her back to let her know I was there. Her sobbing continued for several minutes. I thought of Henry, waiting for me…but Frances needed someone there for her. I had never seen her in such a state.

"He does not notice me," she choked out. "I have done everything."

I wrapped my arm around her small shoulders. Margaret would have known what to say.

"That's all you can do," I offered.

"You don't understand," she said, continuing to cry. "You have never had love that is not returned. How would you feel if every attempt you made was empty?"

Even still, I felt Frances was luckier than me. She had at least tasted what love was like, while I had never had that opportunity.

Frances gave a small chuckle. At least that lightened the mood a bit. "I don't understand," she finally said, looking at me for guidance. "How could he love her? He is far too handsome and she too old."

I shook my head. I had never understood why youthful men flocked to the queen. It was true that she had once been stunning, with her red hair and pale skin. She was intellectual and had a fiery personality, but her time for flirting with courtiers was long past.

I could not answer, but I held Frances and wiped away a few tears that had journeyed to her chin. The sobbing slowed, and the wild look in her eyes abated, simply leaving a sad girl whose love was unrequited. It must have been terrible, to have to compete with a queen.

Frances must really love him.

"He will want to marry," I continued. "He won't be at her beck and call until she dies."

"I hope not." Frances smiled halfheartedly.

I gave her hand a quick squeeze and then stood up. "Come. The strawberries look delicious," I said, reaching down and pulling her up. "And there are many men down there wondering where you are."

I WAS RIGHT. ESSEX wanted to marry. The queen had been supplying him with money for his gambling habit, but she had grown tired of his ever-growing need for more and now refused to grant him anything else. A reasonable dowry was incentive enough for him to try to find a bride.

He was very handsome, and once he started to distance himself from the queen's sight, many girls were interested. I, of course, was hoping he would forget Frances and her invitation to visit us in our rooms. Although I wanted her to be happy, I did not want the queen angry with her.

But he came to visit the chambers one day. Rain pattered on our windows, so none of us ventured outside, but we were all in good spirits despite the dark weather. I had taken out my harp and began to sing a song about Spain's defeat that one of the young poets had taught me. It was a lively tune, and soon the other ladies were singing along. Then we heard a knock on the door.

I stopped playing and we listened. At first I thought the noise was simply the thumping of our feet, for it was unlikely that any man would call at that hour. But we heard a knock again, and I placed my small harp on the ground.

"Lady Emilia, will you get that, please?" Margaret asked.

I nodded and made my way to the door. All eyes were on me and the solid, wooden door. I pleaded to God that it would not be Henry. He had been coming after lunch almost every day and asking for me almost every night. I did not want him coming at other hours too.

But when I opened the door, I found the Earl of Essex. He was as handsome as ever, wearing a crimson doublet and a large silver cross around his neck. Rings decorated his fingers, and his cape was made of the finest mink available. He looked past me into the room.

"Is the lady Sidney present?" he asked.

The last thing I wanted was for Frances to be connected to him, but the ladies-in-waiting were all watching me. I had no choice but to be truthful.

"Yes, my lord," I said. "I shall see if she would like to have you in."

I left him at the threshold and went to Frances. She sat on the ground with her sewing in her lap, her skirts ballooning about her. She kept her focus on her needle, which was flashing in and out of the fabric.

"The Earl of Essex wishes to speak to you." I looked down at her.

I expected her face to light up. Instead, her face was as blank as a canvas, and she kept her eyes on her hands and her mending.

"Good," she said. "Send him away."

The whole room had been watching the scene unfold, and I heard several ladies gasp as she spoke those words. I myself was taken aback. Why on earth would Frances send him away now? Was she serious? When she did not look at me, I moved back to the door. Perhaps she had changed her mind. Maybe she would avoid the danger the earl brought after all.

"The lady Sidney says she does not wish to see you," I spoke slowly.

The earl gave a surprised look and blinked once or twice before trying to look past me to see her.

"Did she say why?" he asked.

"No, my lord, just that she wishes for me to send you away," I replied.

He gave me a gruff look and shuffled his feet. He looked uncomfortable, as if he had been slapped in the face. I doubted that he had been refused before.

"Tell her I will come back tomorrow at this time," he said, and then he made his way down the hall.

I closed the door and took a long glance at Frances. She continued to work on her sewing, but with a smile on her face.

"DO YOU THINK THE Earl of Essex cares for Frances?" I asked Margaret. She had agreed to accompany me on my way to Henry

Carey's bedchambers so I wouldn't have to go on my own. Only a single candle lit our faces. Every now and then my eyes would catch a glimpse of the tapestries on the walls or the moon shining through a window. The halls of the palace were eerily dark, and our whispers were joined only by the sound of our quiet footsteps.

"I wish Frances's fate on no one," she said simply.

"I fear for her as well," I agreed. "But she is happy."

Margaret's face wore wisdom. It was easy to see every line of worry on her face in the flicker of the candlelight.

"The earl has been the queen's favorite for several months now," she explained. "When she finds that her favorite is looking for a bride and a substantial dowry, she won't be satisfied until she has made their lives miserable."

"Doesn't the queen have anything better to do than to ruin courtiers' marriages?" I asked.

Margaret smiled. "You were once so devoted to her...." I heard the strain in her voice.

"I still am," I replied. "But I don't see why she needs to be so possessive about the men at court. They still admire her; they think she's a righteous queen. What more should she ask for?"

Margaret sighed. "The queen is in love with Essex."

At first I thought she was jesting. The queen did not fall in love with courtiers. The only person she had been in love with before was Robert Dudley, long ago. The Earl of Essex was just a pastime.

"She is?" I whispered.

Margaret sighed again.

"How do you know?" I asked.

"She speaks of nothing but him. Even the lowest maids of

honor know. It's only time before the news reaches the other ladies. And she has noticed that he has been preoccupied lately."

"What would she...do?" I asked. My eyes were open. Was Frances in danger?

"I don't know, but whatever she would choose would not be good for Frances." Margaret shook her head. "Frances cannot be involved in this. We must talk to her, for you know he's only after her fortune. If the earl were to propose..." She trailed off.

We reached Henry's large oak door.

"Of course," I said. I would need to make sure that Frances was safe.

She smiled and gave me a soft kiss on the cheek like a mother might and then sent me on my way to Henry Carey's bed.

THAT SUMMER, HENRY BROUGHT my father's troupe to court to entertain the queen. War with Spain had delayed any artistic endeavors, but now in this time of peace, Elizabeth had agreed. We looked forward to them with eager anticipation.

I had been given a seat of honor in the Great Hall, for it was my suggestion that Henry support them. The troupe played on the far side of the room where everyone could see them. They stood with their lyres and flutes; the whole room swayed to the music.

Wine and food had been laid out for us. The sun peeked through the stained-glass windows, warming everyone at court. The queen was much entertained and pleased. Her eyes looked favorably upon her cousin that day, and, in turn, Henry's eyes looked favorably upon me. The queen invited the troupe to stay for the rest of the summer season. They played several songs—one of which I knew was the queen's favorite, since she had requested it at Twelfth Night. Some young ladies-in-waiting even convinced some courtiers to dance.

I rejoined Margaret and Frances after the performance. They had both enjoyed the music and noticed one thing in particular: the harpist.

"Do you know who that is?" Margaret asked.

I took a closer look at the dark young man, who was talking to the other musicians.

"He seems familiar," I said.

"He quite resembles you." She narrowed her eyes. "My, he is handsome, isn't he?"

He was. His angular face was tanned very dark from traveling in the sun.

"You must introduce him to us," Margaret encouraged.

I agreed. I wanted to find out who this was. The other two ladies followed me as we made our way over to the musicians, who were packing away their precious instruments. The young man had his back to us, and I felt it would be rude to touch him when I did not even know him. I waited until he turned around.

I recognized him as soon as he turned to face us. He looked like my mirror image. There were a few differences; I had inherited my mother's frame, and my eyes were darker, almost black. His were more of a deep brown.

"You're Alfonso Lanier?" I asked. He was my cousin. I had known he was a member of the troupe, but I hadn't seen him in years.

"Indeed," he replied. "And you would be...?"

"Emilia Bassano."

Once I said my name, he nodded like he remembered who I was. I needn't curtsy for him; I was in a higher position than he. He gave a quick bow.

"It's been many years," he said stiffly. "Was it not at the Countess of Kent's that I last saw you?"

"Yes," I replied. I noticed that his eyes traveled to my bodice as I spoke. "These are my friends, the lady Sidney and the lady Russell."

He bowed to each one of them.

"You play beautifully," Margaret said. "It must run in the family."

"Yes, my lady. Lady Bassano's family and mine have been musicians since the beginning of time," he said.

"The queen seemed to be delighted by your performance," Frances added.

He looked to her, but he did not run his eyes up and down her figure or eye the expensive rings around her fingers. Most men were infatuated with Frances from the moment they laid eyes on her.

"It is an honor to play for Her Grace. It could not have been possible without the help of our patron, Baron Henry Carey." His eyes connected with mine. He knew that I was mistress to his supporter. Did everyone know?

"We look forward to hearing your music for the rest of the season," I added quickly. This conversation was growing more and more uncomfortable.

"And hopefully much longer," he said. He bowed one more time and then turned his back to us.

As we walked away, I heard whistles and calls from the men in the troupe. The queen had let in a group of animals.

THE QUEEN COULD NOT miss the signs of Frances's affair much longer.

Margaret and I knew it was time to talk to her. I didn't want to risk Frances's anger, but I feared the queen's wrath more than my friend's. We took her out of the palace for the day and went around to different shops to pick up the things we would need for the coming season. Frances picked out pearls and satins I could only dream of wearing. I knew she wanted to look her best for Robert Devereux.

As we headed home, the carriage rattling, Margaret cleared her throat, signaling that now was the time. We were going to make this as easy as we could. We hoped to suggest that Frances was making a mistake and that she would come to her senses on her own.

"Frances, how does the Earl of Essex fare?" she asked.

"Oh, excellent. He's offered to take me to plays in London."

"London?" I said.

I glanced over at Margaret. She nodded her head, encouraging me to continue.

"Do you think that's wise?" I asked.

Frances laughed.

"I fail to see why I would *want* to refuse, Emilia. The earl and I get along very well."

The carriage bumped along the cobblestone streets. It was beginning to get stuffy inside. I fidgeted on the velvet seat and looked through the window to the people on the street. Some carried baskets of food or clothes to launder. They moved out of the way of the carriage.

"Is it you he gets along with so well, or is it your purse?" I said.

Frances clenched her teeth and immediately looked out the window on the other side of the carriage. She tugged on her glove. Perhaps I should have approached the topic more compassionately, but she needed to hear the truth.

Margaret glared at me. "Frances…," she began.

Frances raised a hand.

"I do not want to hear any more of it."

The only sound for the rest of the journey was the wheels of the carriage creaking and the horses' hooves pounding on the stone. I had spoken my part, and now it was up to Frances to make her choice.

AUTUMN WAS IN THE air. The leaves fell and time seemed to slow. The crisp leaves crunched under our feet as we walked the palace grounds, and we enjoyed our nights drinking spiced wine in the chambers with the crackling fire sounding throughout the room.

Henry called me into his room one day so I might help address the invitations for a hunt he was organizing.

"Of course we shall invite the Earl of Essex, and probably Sir Walter Raleigh," he said as he signed his name on one of the invitations. Henry had used his finest paper, complete with his official seal printed on the bottom. "What of your cousin, Alfonso?"

"What of him?" I asked.

"Do you think we should invite him?"

I rolled up a piece of paper that he had signed and tied a ribbon around it.

"He is a musician," I said. "Does he know how to ride?"

"I would assume so," Henry replied. "It is difficult not to know, when you are a man."

I was quiet for a while. We must invite him. We both knew that. But we also knew that was not what he was really asking. He wanted to see what I thought of my cousin—and whether or not my cousin had grabbed my attention with his handsome face.

"Very well, then," I said quickly, avoiding the old man's knowing gaze.

"You do not like him?" he asked.

I contemplated my response. I did admire his visage. He was such a change from Henry that I couldn't help but be curious. I could lie to Henry, but I always felt guilty after I did. If I told him the truth, however, he might not want to continue supporting the troupe, which would be a shame. Even if I did not approve of the men who were in it, I felt they were my only connection to my deceased father.

"I do not mind him." I chose my answer carefully.

Henry smiled and then put his pen back to paper. "Invite him, then."

A FEW DAYS BEFORE the hunt, Henry called me to his chambers. He handed me a letter from the queen. I slid my finger under the already-opened seal. She would not attend. I sighed and skimmed over the words on the page. The perfectly spaced lettering did not match the signature on the bottom of the page, and I could imagine Her Majesty sitting by the fire, dictating what she wished to say while someone transcribed it for her. I rolled up the piece of parchment before handing it back to Henry.

The day of the hunt dawned clear. Both Margaret's husband, Lord Russell, and the Earl of Essex would be there, but neither Margaret nor Frances was invited.

Margaret and Frances helped me into my riding habit. I had personally chosen the fabric for it. This was to be my day. I would ride at Henry's side. My new riding cap sat nicely on my head, and my dress fit perfectly.

"You look lovely, Emilia," Frances praised. "Look how the black piping complements her hair and her eyes so."

Margaret smoothed the back of my dress. The train was like an emerald-green puddle on the floor behind me. I checked to see that the row of buttons along the bodice was properly fastened.

"She looks like a queen." She smiled at me proudly. "Not a man will be able to keep his eyes off her."

I thanked them and went to join Henry at the stables a few minutes before we were to set off. I found Alfonso with him. He stared at me with a coy smile. I ignored his eyes as I walked to Henry's side.

"Ah, my darling." Henry smiled. "Tell me, Alfonso, is she not the most beautiful lady in court?"

"She is like a flower. A rose," he said without smiling.

"A musician and a poet." Henry laughed, though it was a bit forced. "What a talented family."

We made our way to the horses. Henry went to inspect his bay, and while his back was turned, Alfonso grabbed my arm. His fingers dug into me.

"You are a flower today, cousin." His dark eyes looked into mine.

"No rose is without a thorn," I replied, struggling to get my arm away. "Be careful, or you shall bleed." My cousin might have been attractive, but he was also a boor.

He dropped my arm. His face was hard as I ran over to Henry. I would have to stay close to him that day. For once I was glad of the old man's presence.

When everyone gathered, we all mounted. I was eager to get on with the hunt, as Henry and I would ride at the front as the host and hostess while Alfonso had to stay to the back.

We set off at a quick pace. I adjusted my seat in the saddle. The leather creaked beneath me. The men wore sturdy, protective vests and carried bows on their backs so they could remain a safe distance from the stag's sharp antlers. Dogs trotted around our horses' feet, ready to get along with the chase.

I was a fair rider, and I started to relax as the hunt went on. Some of the men caught sight of a stag and chased after it, whipping their mounts into a fast canter. The hounds bayed, and I watched as Henry and the others followed. I urged my mare on. We got thicker into the forest, and it was more difficult to see. I had to follow the sounds of the dogs and the horses' hooves. The men pulled farther ahead.

I saw an open meadow and slowed my horse. I would stop and rest and find them again when they came out of the woods. The grass was much easier to ride through than the forest. Wildflowers dotted the field like the stars on a clear night.

I heard the pounding of hooves behind me—someone had been following me. My hands shook. I said a silent prayer that it would be Henry.

I heard sticks breaking, and I tightened my grip on the reins. Turning my head, I saw a shape coming through the brush. Alfonso appeared through the thicket, slowing his horse until it stopped next to mine.

"Lost, my lady?"

"I could say the same to you. It is one thing for a lady to be lost; she has little or no experience of hunting. It is another for a man."

"I am not lost," he said. "In fact, I think I quite found what I was hunting."

He had no manners at all. He knew I was Henry's mistress and yet he approached me with these advances. Any curiosity I had harbored about him vanished.

I kicked my mare into a fast gait. I needed to find Henry quickly. I heard crashing through the trees, and I thought I saw a glimpse of Henry as he chased after the bloody stag. I rode hard and was glad when I found the party stopped. The deer had escaped and was running toward the top of the next hill.

"Blast," Henry exclaimed. "I thought we had that one." He turned to look at me. I am sure I looked none my best. I had rips from thicket thorns along my sleeves, and I felt mud seeping into my dress.

"My dear, were we going too fast for you?" Henry asked. His eyes followed the stag.

I nodded, trying to catch my breath. Alfonso appeared not long after me, his horse galloping at a rough pace.

Henry dismounted and strode over to my horse before softly touching me on the knee. He did not look at me; his head was turned in the direction the stag had escaped.

"Would you like someone to take you back to the palace?" he asked.

Did he offer because he really cared about my affairs? Or was it only because I was slowing the party?

"Thank you," I replied.

"Very well," Henry said. "Alfonso, will you please escort Lady Bassano back to Greenwich?"

"No, my lord," I said. "I would prefer that you escort me yourself."

The men laughed, and I felt like a small child clinging to its mother.

"I cannot very well leave the hunt." Henry laughed along with them.

I looked at him with pleading eyes, but he seemed not to see it. He thought too highly of Alfonso to expect that I would be in any danger.

"Well then," I huffed, "I suppose I will escort myself." I turned my horse around and headed down the path. I heard the ensemble laughing behind me, but Alfonso did not follow. At that moment I could not help but think how foolish men were and how glad I was that my horse was a mare.

WHEN I RETURNED TO Greenwich, I found it mostly deserted. I handed my horse's reins to a stableman and made sure that the mare was given oats for her hard work. I went up the stairs to the chambers with my dress torn and my riding cap on one side of my head.

Frances greeted me as I entered. She was hopping around and wearing the biggest smile I had ever seen. She took my hands like she had the day she realized that I had a chance to become a queen.

"What is wrong with her?" I asked Margaret, who stood watching us.

"She wanted to wait until you got here," she explained. "What happened to you?"

"It's a long story," I replied. I brushed a strand of hair away from my face.

Frances looked at me. "I didn't even notice. Look at your cap—and you are so muddy. Something's wrong."

"Come, tell us what happened." Margaret crossed her arms, and I knew there was no way of getting out of it.

"Must I wait to tell her my news?" Frances asked, her voice thick with impatience.

"Frances can say what she needs to," I replied. She usually did anyway.

Frances's eyes glowed and her cheeks were red as she took a deep breath. Her smile shone like the sun.

"All right," she said. "Robert Devereux asked me to marry him."

We both glanced at her. She looked so small, so innocent, so unlike the Frances we knew.

I said a prayer in my head. Then I took one of her hands in mine and regarded her. "You cannot agree to marry him," I said.

"You have to refuse," Margaret continued.

I expected Frances to be angry with us. Instead, she simply kneaded her hands together. Her face was pale.

"No, no, no…," she muttered softly.

"Frances?" I asked.

"Frances," Margaret spoke as quietly as Frances had, "you must say that you cannot marry him. Even if by some miracle the queen were to give her permission, she wouldn't look upon you with favor."

It was the queen's duty to match her ladies with husbands. She would never agree to this marriage. And if the queen did not approve and they married anyway, they would be guilty of treason.

"Remember what sort of wrath the queen shows those she does not like," Margaret said.

Frances pulled her hand away, and her eyes glossed over. Her expression was more frightening than anything I had ever seen. The only time I remembered seeing a face that eerily subdued was when the Queen of Scots had known that the ax was about to meet her neck.

Would Frances be beheaded too? Would the queen be that cruel? All she had done was fall in love, like all girls are bound to do. My hands grew sweaty and my breath short.

The silence in the room frightened me as we waited for Frances to speak. It was as if time had stopped.

"I can't turn him down." Frances finally unleashed her words. She stood in place, her hands kneaded together. She was astonishingly calm. It was as if she had seen a ghost. "I can't do that. I love him."

"But the queen, Frances," Margaret urged.

"I can't," Frances said. Her eyes flashed something that I recognized. "Because I have already accepted."

"Frances…," I said. Didn't she understand?

"No!" she exclaimed. "All my life I have done what Her Majesty wanted, what everyone thought she approved of. I had to marry Philip Sidney, a man I did not love. I had to be her lady-in-waiting, and I have had to make sure that I don't offend her. I cannot lose the only man I have ever loved to the queen. I would rather face the block."

Margaret gasped. Frances was prone to dramatics, but there was something in her tone that made me think she was speaking the truth. What would life at court be like without Frances? Would it really be worth it to marry Robert Devereux?

"You know what this means, Frances," I said. "It's—dangerous to—"

"To associate with me?" she finished for me.

I looked over at Margaret before nodding.

Frances reared her head back as though she had been slapped. Margaret and I had always been there for her, but now it was clear that we would not be by her side. We would be her friends, but we would not follow her to the executioner's block.

She gazed at each one of us. First at Margaret, her only friend before I had come to court. Margaret simply shook her head. Frances's eyes darted towards mine. I saw in them both indignation and distress. Something in her face made me wish I could change things between us, but it was too late. Frances had used me and pushed me. When she was upset, I had to give her my full attention; when she was angry, I had to humor her. I was sorry that all she could think of was her own self and that she was so lonely, so angry at the world and at the queen—but I was not that way.

I looked at the ground. I heard stomping as Frances made her way across the chamber, her hurt echoing on the floorboards.

"You are both invited to my wedding," Frances said coolly from across the room. "But after that, I never want to speak to you again."

ENGLAND, 1590
DURING THE REIGN OF QUEEN ELIZABETH I
WHITEHALL COURT

IT WAS A BEAUTIFUL wedding. The chapel at Essex had been decorated with lovely white roses and fine lace. Delicate roses hung from the sides of the pews. Rose petals dotted the floor, while sunshine shone through the windows and onto the smooth stone.

The Earl was dressed in a white doublet. The queen sat on her throne, brought from court. Her lips were a small, fine line that did not move during the duration of the ceremony, and her eyes were hawkish. Her hands clutched the arms of her throne, and every so often she glanced at the empty seat next to her.

I will never forget the image of Frances walking down the aisle. She spent a great deal of money on her dress, and I had never seen one its equal. She was covered in the most expensive lace possible, with a long train following several feet behind her. Pearls hung from her ears and draped around her neck. She left her hair long and fastened white roses in it with pins. She looked like an angel sent from heaven, and at that moment I desperately wished that I had been able to be her friend in her darkest hour. I wanted to stop her halfway down the aisle and tell her how I was sorry. But she did not look at me or Margaret. Her eyes were on Robert Devereux, her husband-to-be. Looking back now, I can see that losing Frances was both a misfortune and a blessing. I know I would not be the same person that I am today if she had not cast us out. I would have had a much easier life if I had had Frances there to fight my battles for me. Maybe God knew that this was for the best and that I would be a stronger person if Frances was not there. She had been the sister I'd never had, and I knew I would never have that again.

After the ceremony, we journeyed to the large banquet hall in Essex's manor. It had been decorated with obvious care. Tapestries hung proudly, the room was littered with hundreds of roses, and the tables displayed roasted swan as the bride and groom's meal of choice.

When Margaret, her husband, the Count of Cumberland, Henry, and I went to wish Frances luck in her new life, she greeted us as strangers. She was sweet—overtly so. She treated us as if we were not once her closest confidants, her best companions.

"Congratulations," I said, handing her my wedding gift. It was a length of fine blue velvet, Frances's favorite.

"Thank you," she said with ice tingeing her words. She looked beautiful in her wedding gown, her veil pulled back from her luminous face. Her cheeks wore circles of natural blush, and curls, so perfectly placed before the ceremony, escaped from her crown.

Margaret handed her a gift before letting Lady Bess pass us. Frances welcomed Bess with open arms, giving her a warm hug and a kiss on the cheek. I wondered if Lady Bess knew that she was being used as a pawn in Frances's game.

That night there was a great celebration. The new bride and groom were full of spirits, and the rest of the company followed suit.

The queen was not among them. She had already begun her travel back to her palace. She had refused to go through the receiving line and to even acknowledge the bride and the groom. The game Frances was playing had only just begun.

LATER THAT SUMMER HENRY called me to his chambers to meet someone new to court. He told me to dress finely, and so I wore my scarlet gown because it complemented my skin tone. Margaret helped me brush my hair smooth and bind it into a bun. I wore a necklace that Henry had given me and the ruby ring from when he'd first asked me to be his mistress.

I trudged to Henry's chamber with a melancholy feeling. I couldn't help but think of Frances. Daily, I had been checking the correspondence that came to the chambers for a letter from her.

I entered Henry's chamber with a placid smile. I found him with his back turned toward the door; he was focused on something on his desk. Another man stood beside him, pointing at the object. I leaned forward. It was a piece of paper.

"Excellent, excellent," Henry proclaimed. "This is first-class."

I made a small noise in my throat and both men turned around.

The first things I noticed were his eyes. They had such a soul, a beauty that could not be described with words. I saw a thousand dreams, a thousand ideas, and a thousand new experiences. They were unlike anything I had ever seen. How could I not have noticed, when we'd met before?

"Ah, there you are," Henry said.

I could barely hear him. I was still hypnotized by those *eyes*. All I wanted was to stare into in them.

It was only when I felt Henry's arm around my waist that I remembered who I was. It was as if I had awakened from sleep and only wished to fall back into my dream.

"This is the lady Bassano, the jewel of the musician family," Henry said. "She advises me in all my duties as Lord Chamberlain. This, my dear, is William Shakespeare, the playwright."

He bowed his head, a small smile still on his face. I noticed the hoop earring he wore like a gypsy and his simple style of dressing. He wore a plain doublet and worn leather boots.

"We've met. Have you been well since I saw you last?" His voice sounded like Alfonso's harp. He looked out of place in Henry's exquisite quarters, with its fine curtains and dark oak desk. Still, he did not seem to be uncomfortable.

I didn't know if I could speak. This man had captured me in a way that I had never felt before. I felt nervous, excited, scared, beautiful, and unworthy all at once. It was almost too much.

"Very well, thank you," I forced myself to say. "How long do you plan to stay at court, Master Shakespeare?"

He laughed a musical tone. "Please, William is the name I prefer, Lady Bassano."

"It is not every day one meets a man so humble."

"That is where you are wrong," he said. "For humility is said to be the virtue I most lack."

"William has such a way with words, darling." Henry unwrapped himself from my side. "He has written several plays and acted in them as well. He is part of the theatre troupe I am now financing. William, that was by my lady's urging, mind you."

William laughed once again. "Yes, but I am a poor actor in

comparison to many. I only do it because I imagine my characters after myself. They take on my mannerisms. After I've written about them so much, I can't imagine anyone but myself playing that part."

Henry appeared to be delighted, a smile decorating his face.

"I hear you are friends with the harpist, Alfonso Lanier. Lady Bassano is his cousin."

"Yes, I have known Alfonso for some time now." His eyes then returned to me. "It's odd, but I see no resemblance between them whatsoever."

I gave him a half smile. "You must be saying this in jest. I have always heard that we look exactly alike."

"Oh no." He shook his head and clicked his tongue. "You see, my lady, you may find this strange, but I do not much rely on appearances. I often find them false. You are as unlike your cousin as the dark side of the moon is the fair side."

"I find it hardly strange at all," I replied. "I believe we would all benefit from your ideas."

He displayed that small smile, and I felt a strange stirring in my stomach. It was like the feeling I had at the Queen of Scots' beheading. It was curiosity but also nervousness. I did not know what to think.

"The queen has invited me to stay at court for the rest of the fall season and perform one of my plays. She is a great patron of the arts and, I hear, a poet herself."

"She is thrilled to have you here." Henry strode over to his desk and picked up the piece of paper. "This is a great work. The queen will be pleased."

I did not ask to have it, even though my hands burned to take it out of his and read it for myself. I hated that a lady had to show manners at all times. I made sure that I kept my hands folded in front of me.

"Thank you for coming, my dear." Henry smiled. "I know how these matters weary you. You may go back to your chambers now."

My shoulders tensed. It sounded as if I were a child. I gave a curt nod and turned to leave. My heart still fluttered faster than I thought possible. How on earth could I feel this way? I had barely met the man, and I felt as though I were an entirely different person. Hesitating, I balled my hand into a fist and tightened it. I had to force my feet to move; they remained firmly in place. How could I leave now, just when I had discovered who this Shakespeare really was? Eventually, I was able to make my way to the door.

I should have been ashamed for the thoughts that were running through my mind. I knew nothing of him, and yet it felt as if I knew everything. When his eyes met mine I encountered an emotion that I could not control. I felt so feeble. Instead of going straight to the chambers, I made my way to the palace chapel. Kneeling in front of the cross, I prayed and confessed. The desires I felt were unhealthy.

After I finished my confession I did not get up. My knees were so sore that I could barely stand it, but I stayed there. I couldn't stop thinking about his eyes. The sky darkened. I knew I had to go back to the chambers when no more light shone through the stained-glass windows. Margaret would be wondering where I was, and I needed to return in case Henry called for me. A pain shot through my legs when I stood up. I yelped and rested on my knees. Eventually I was able to limp back to the large wooden door of the chambers.

I knocked on it, expecting to see Margaret's worried face on the other side. No one answered, however, and I had to pull it open myself. All the ladies had gone to their beds. No one waited up for me. I took a glance at the great clock that stood in the corner before I also went to my bed. It was well past midnight that his eyes lingered.

I SAT UP FROM my pallet the next morning and walked stiffly over to where Margaret sat with a handful of fabric in one hand and a needle in the other. The room was neatly arranged—the handmaidens had probably just come and gone. The ladies were not on their pallets. I assumed they had already gone to break their fast. Birds chirped outside, greeting the morning with joy.

Margaret looked exhausted, and she held a hand to her head to steady herself. She did not know that I was watching her.

"Good morning," I said. I fell into a nearby chair, afraid my knees would give out. The pain was strong.

"Good morning." She smiled. She glanced at me with a tired expression, her eyes glazed over. "You were out late."

I sighed. It was no use hiding where I had been.

"I was in the chapel."

"Oh?" She was surprised. "That must have been an immense sin."

"I was also praying," I added.

She bit off the thread from the mended bodice. It was one that she had worn more than once or twice.

"For a child?" she asked. She stood up and placed the garment on a nearby chair. Her hair was down; it was one of the few times I had seen it loose.

"Yes," I said. It was partially true.

"You're young." She strained to smile, as though she were so fatigued that it was all she could do. "You will soon get what you have asked for."

She was unusually pale, and her stomach looked as though it were going to burst from the corset that enclosed it.

Now I understood—Margaret was with child. No wonder she always looked so tired. She had to carry this baby and look after the queen and watch over the new ladies.

"Margaret?" I asked and pointed to her belly. "Have you been given what you asked for?"

She sighed. She placed a hand on her round stomach and nodded.

"I must ask the queen for her permission to leave court," she said.

"Have you?" I asked.

She sat down with difficulty, and though an intense pain shot up my legs when I stood, I went to her side and steadied her. Margaret was with child. What wonderful and terrible news all at once. If the queen knew, there was no telling what she would say or think. Elizabeth had control over all the ladies' coming and goings.

"No," she replied. Margaret always seemed so much older than me, but she was only thirty. She seemed more wan now that she was carrying another life around with her.

"You need to. Lady Bess and I will take care of the fresh group of ladies. You need to go home and rest. When will it come?" I carried a footstool over to her and made her place her legs upon it.

"In about five months," she said. "You can see why I didn't tell you. Frances left, and then the queen did not want me to go. I couldn't tell her that I was with child, Emilia, I just couldn't."

Fat tears began to roll down her face, and I wrapped my arms around her neck. I worried over her. Here I was, infatuated with a man I'd just met and confessing for hours while Margaret needed me.

"We need this baby," she said. "George and I, well, we are no longer as young as we used to be and the child..." She swallowed. "The child would help. I have miscarried once before this, and the other boy died in infancy."

"Oh, Margaret," I cried, tears coming to my own eyes. "You should have told me. I would have helped. It was dangerous to be carrying it without anyone knowing."

Margaret smiled and a tear rolled down one side of her mouth. She looked so ragged. How could I not have seen it? Curses on Frances. She always attracted all the attention. It was easy to overlook Margaret, even when she was obviously with child, because of Frances.

"We must tell the queen," I said.

"We cannot." She took my hand with force. "She will be furious that I did not come to her when I first knew."

"You have no need to be ashamed," I said. "You were busy with all the other things that the queen insisted you do."

Margaret intertwined her fingers.

"Emilia?" she asked. "Would you mind?"

I knew what I needed to do. I would have to go to the queen myself and insist that Margaret be sent home. "I will go to her. You are my friend and deserve to go home and raise the child. At the most you will be gone a couple of months, and then you can return. Lady Bess is fully equipped to take over for you while you are gone."

I did not know if the last statement was true, but I worried that if Margaret stayed any longer she would be too far along to move.

I fetched a cup of water and made sure that she drank it all. If she minded my mothering, she didn't mention it.

"You are so good to me, Emilia," she sighed. "When will you go to the queen?"

"I will get dressed and talk to Henry. He might be able to set an audience with her sooner," I responded. Perhaps William Shakespeare would be in the chamber again. I tried not to look as though I wanted to go.

"Very well. Let's hope the queen is in a forgiving humor."

I HAD TO WAIT only a day to see the queen. I was fortunate that Henry was so close to Elizabeth. I wore my Easter dress with the embroidered flowers dotted along the skirt and bodice. It was late summer and autumn was just around the corner, but this was my finest dress.

I waited outside the throne room for an hour, my hands shaking. I took large breaths, but they didn't seem to help. I needed to do this for Margaret, but I wouldn't have done it for anyone else. I didn't know if this would jeopardize the queen's opinion of me, but I did know that this was necessary for Margaret's health. I fingered the silver chain around my neck and found myself scratching my forearm even though it did not itch.

I was let in just as the clock struck noon. I had been in the throne room, where she met with her subjects, only once before. I was suddenly transported back to the day I had arrived at court, my first audience with the queen. I was so naïve about the world and the people in it. Had I changed? Or was I still naive, thinking that the queen cared what I had to say? I walked the length of the room with my hands folded tightly in front of me. I kept my eyes down as I had those four years ago.

The room was long, with solid wooden floors and a red carpet leading up to the queen's throne. The floors had been freshly stained, and I could smell the substance they had used to make them shine so impressively. Stained-glass windows cast colors onto the boards, and every now and then my silk slippers would pass into the light it cast.

"The lady Bassano."

Once again I curtsied and once again I felt her eyes upon me, judging every breath I took, every time I blinked. It was all I could do to keep from turning around and running back out of the room.

"Rise." The queen's powerful voice echoed throughout the room.

I rose from my curtsy, my sore knees shaking. I wondered how many men and women had felt as I did in front of that throne.

"I hear that you wish to speak to me," she said.

I finally mustered up the courage to look to her face. She looked younger than she did from a distance. There was not a wrinkle on her face, which wore a harsh countenance. Her eyes were the only thing that gave her away. They were soft. They had not been that way at Frances's wedding, nor when I had seen her at holidays. She looked upon me with favor still. I did not know if that would change after I made my request, but I prayed it wouldn't.

"Yes, Your Majesty," I said. I was afraid that my voice would come out frail, but it was stronger than I thought it would be. I couldn't help but feel a little proud of myself. "The lady Russell, Countess of Cumberland, is with child."

The queen's face didn't falter. Her eyes remained the same. She acted as though she hadn't heard. She fingered a ring on her right hand.

"And?" she asked.

I was taken aback. I thought that she would at least seem upset or surprised, but she was neither. She was as calm as a summer's day. It took me a moment to think of what to say next. I'd had it perfectly rehearsed in my head before I came, yet now the words seemed to fly from my mind.

"As her companion, I think it would be best that she return to Cumberland with her husband for a few months," I said softly.

"So be it. Tell her I will call her back when I need her," the queen replied.

I curtsied and was about to turn and leave when the queen addressed me.

"You remind me so much of my mother. I was only three when she died, but I still remember her. A child does not forget those who are kind to her."

"Thank you, Your Majesty." I took it as a high compliment, even though I was fearful of associating my reputation with Anne Boleyn's.

"Take care, Lady Bassano. We must all remember where our allegiances lie and how best to serve them."

She seemed to be thinking aloud more than talking to me, but I took her advice to heart. It was easy for her to say. She could choose her lovers and friends and had unlimited funds...but there was wisdom there.

"Thank you, Your Grace."

Retreating quietly, I left the queen alone with her thoughts and memories. She continued to finger her ring and stare out the large stained-glass window. She did not even seem to notice that I was leaving. Her mind was far, far away.

I rushed back to the chambers. I could only imagine Margaret's face when I told her of the queen's lenience. Her greatest wishes, to have children and to be with her husband, were about to come true. Now we all had to learn to live without her.

MARGARET LEFT THE NEXT day in a litter. I went down to the courtyard to see her off. She looked relieved. I told her to write as soon as the baby was born and to keep in good health. The queen would need her as soon as she got back to court, and she needed her time to rest.

It was strange to wake up each day and not find her there. She had been such an influential part of my recent life. I no longer had anyone to talk to, and I felt alone. I waited up nights for Henry by myself, wondering how Margaret was doing at her home. Was she sewing baby clothes and singing lullabies? Was she enjoying motherhood? I imagined her sitting in a rocking chair, waiting for the baby to come.

Lady Bess and I began to spend more time together while Margaret was gone. I kept my thoughts off Margaret and Frances during the day by helping Lady Bess with the younger ladies. There was a peace between us now that Frances had left.

Autumn was breathed alive, and we all waited for the day when William Shakespeare was to present his play to the members of court.

I often saw the troupe walking to and from the Great Hall where they rehearsed, though I never saw him. Every now and then I would go to a window that looked over the path that led to their quarters, pull aside the scratchy drape that hung in front of the window, and watch them pass. I made sure to pull it across again if someone looked my way.

One day as I was heading back to my chambers, I passed the Great Hall. I heard his voice echoing throughout the room, his instructions to the players loud and concise.

I peered through the door for only a moment, just to see if he was how I remembered. My hand went to the silver cross I wore around my neck. He stood in front of the naked stage.

"No," he said, waving a hand. "That is not the way I wrote it, and that is not the way you will perform it."

My heart pounded. It seemed as though I was intruding on some secret meeting. The tables had been pushed to the sides of the large room to make space for the stage. People sat on the floors, watching the other actors perform their parts. The actors on the stage looked as if they were trying to act out a scene of court life but bumbled and ran into each other instead.

Shakespeare raised his hands in frustration, and before I could escape, he turned around. His eyes went straight to mine, and I thought I detected a hint of a smile on his face. I could feel a blush creep from my neck to the crown of my head. I took one last look at Shakespeare and then darted away. I hurried my return to the chambers, my heart beating to the steady tempo of my hurried footsteps.

HENRY REFUSED ALMOST EVERY invitation for the autumn hunts. That fall, he focused mostly on the different troupes he supported and the financial duties of the Lord Chamberlain. Henry Carey's days of pretending he was a young man were over.

The court was excited for Accession Day—the day the play was to be performed. It was a holiday we celebrated every year to honor Elizabeth's ascension to the English throne. It would be the first feast that we had celebrated in quite some time, and I wanted to enjoy myself. It was so much easier to forget my absent companions' faces with wine and merriment.

Henry and I entered the Great Hall that night wearing royal blue; he admired the color.

I helped him as he limped into the room. We took our seats. Roast pheasant was placed before us, posed as though it were still alive. Spiced wine was poured all around, and wine glasses and beer tankards were knocked together in cheers. The chandelier above our heads, made of strong iron, lit the room brightly. Henry smiled at me every now and then.

We all clapped when William Shakespeare stood before us, the queen included. She nodded at Henry. Shakespeare introduced his troupe, his voice echoing clearly through the Great Hall. It was an actor's voice. A beautiful voice.

Several men hauled out a wooden set. After all the time the troupe had spent rehearsing and planning, I'd thought the stage would be grander. The background was crudely painted to depict the throne room of a palace. I looked about me. Everyone else's expressions seemed as confused as my own.

The costumes were also poorly put together. The woven linen frayed at the end of their shirts, and their sleeves were different lengths.

It seemed that the men who wore them were also the ones who had sewn them. They were supposed to represent kings and queens of old, but they looked more like peasants. We all turned to the queen. Her face had suddenly changed; she wore the hard line I had seen at Frances's wedding. She gave a weak wave for them to start.

A man in one of the cheap costumes spoke.

"Open your ears; for which of you will stop the vent of hearing when loud Rumor speaks?"

It was that moment when the world around me seemed to disappear. The Great Hall faded, and I could only see what was on the stage. I forgot what I had first seen and focused on the actors, the expressions, the lines. They spoke so eloquently, so rhythmically, in a way that every person in that room could understand. We could all imagine ourselves as king or lord. I felt as though I knew Prince Hal and that his journey of becoming king became my own. The stage disappeared. It was no longer a play; it was a life. It was real, living and breathing.

Henry turned to me as the actors left the stage after the first act. "Are you enjoying this?" He smiled.

All I could do was nod.

I hadn't even realized that I was crying until it was over. Only when all the actors had taken their bows did I feel the wetness on my cheek. Music was one thing—it opened the soul. But this play was a soul of its own.

Henry ambled over to William Shakespeare after it was over. I could not walk to him so boldly. I stood a ways from them, fingering my cross. The feast had been cleared away, but a few men who had decided to stay and drink the night away remained. A crowd stood around Shakespeare. They slapped his back and smiled their congratulations. Only when Henry motioned me over did I return to his side.

William looked overwhelmed as people introduced themselves and praised his work. His eyes fogged over. As we drew near, he recognized us and his small smile appeared.

"That was brilliant." Henry smiled and shook his hand. "The queen looked as if she enjoyed it."

William Shakespeare gave a chuckle.

"I knew the costumes would attract some attention, but I hoped the lines might change Her Majesty's first impressions."

He turned to me, and at once I felt that sickness in my stomach. "Did you enjoy it, Lady Bassano?" he asked.

"It was beautiful," I replied. "I have never seen anything like it."

"Is it your first time to a play?" he inquired.

Once I nodded, he gave a small start.

"My lady, you offend and honor me. I am happy to know that you have been introduced to the theatre by my humble little play, but if you were to be introduced, it should not have been by my humble little play."

I gave a laugh. For someone who wrote such serious drama, he had a sense of humor.

"Well, William Shakespeare, I would not know a good play from a poor one, so you are saved from my critical eye."

He in turn laughed at my words and faced Henry again.

"Since it is the lady's first time to the theatre, I would be happy to show her around, if it is by your permission."

"Of course." Henry yawned. "Though I think I shall retire to bed. Old men were not meant for such amusement."

I was going to object, but I couldn't manage to speak. All I could think about was being alone with the playwright. My fingers scratched at my dress.

William Shakespeare and I watched as Henry walked out of the hall. Once we could no longer make out his frame, the playwright led me over to the set where the backdrop hung. It looked even more drab up close. He placed a hand on it and stroked the canvas.

"I'm sure you know what this is," he said.

I nodded and put my hand on it too.

"This is the set," I said, though I wondered if it was fair to call it that. I was almost afraid to touch it in case it fell to pieces. I felt a halfway-hammered nail under my palm.

"Not so, my lady." He smiled. "This is the sea."

I noticed a piece of wood on the floor crudely cut to look like a sword. I picked it up and held it out to him.

"And this is not a prop." I smiled back. "It's a sword."

"Not so, my lady." He laughed like he had in Henry's chambers. "This is the king's sword. It was crafted in Verona and laid with gold in the hand. The king paid thirty-five pounds for it."

He took it from my hands; I could almost see what he described as he fingered it.

"That was quite a lot a hundred years ago," he added. He took my hand and I felt shivers run up it. It felt like stepping outside on the first freezing winter's day. I felt a child's wonder again. I admired how his fingers seemed so strong but yet so gentle around mine.

We were on the stage now, looking out unto an expanse of empty chairs and tables. The queen's throne was on the far end of the room, and it was raised so she had the best seat. The men who had been drinking were now gone, leaving empty tankards—and us—to the quiet. It was only William Shakespeare and me.

"And this..." He stopped and glanced at me mischievously. "Well, what do you think it is?"

I looked around me. I was beginning to understand that in his world, nothing was ever quite what it seemed. After some time I answered.

"It is the king's throne room, where he looks out unto the sea. The floor of this room is made of stones found along the English countryside, and the throne has been passed down from his father. The carpet is the finest fabric that he could import, perhaps from China or the Indies."

"It's Persian," he said and laughed. "But otherwise you are right."

His eyes turned to me, and I felt as if I had been blind to the world all along. Was anything what it seemed anymore? Why did I have the urge to touch his arm? I wanted to kiss him, but I had to force myself not to. What would be said of me if I was found kissing Henry's playwright?

I let go of his hand. I wanted to feel his fingers wrap around mine once again, but I thanked the Lord that my better sense had gotten hold of me. I gave Shakespeare a smile to let him know that he had done nothing wrong. All he had offered to do was show me his set and his stage, and now here I was, acting like a lovesick girl.

He smiled back but then looked to the other side of the room, away from my gaze. I hated to see him feel that way, but I did not know what else I could do. I couldn't have these feelings toward him. It was impure, wrong.

I thought about what I would say to him. How could I convey

that it was not he whom I was upset with? "Thank you for showing me your stage, Master Shakespeare."

"William, please," he corrected me for the second time.

"Well, thank you," I said. "I hope I will continue to see you around court."

He nodded and followed me down the steps to where I exited the stage. His eyes didn't shine as brightly. I was guilty of making them dull.

I gave him one last glance before I departed. My heart wanted more, but my mind was telling me what was correct. I clenched my right hand, and I left the hall with neither a clear conscience nor a satisfied heart.

WHAT HAD I DONE? What if he came to Henry and told him about my behavior? What would I say to defend myself? That I had an intense attraction to him and worried what might happen?

I was getting ahead of myself. Even if I had felt something toward this man, that didn't mean he felt the same way about me. He had met me only a few times; he hardly knew me, and I hardly knew him. He must be married. A brilliant man who could bring the sea indoors must have children. It was a sin to think of him as I did. It wasn't just that I felt physically drawn to him; yes, there was much of that, but I also admired how his mind focused on the smallest details. The words he wrote outshone anything I had ever read or heard before. He was brilliant. That much was clear.

The next morning, I decided to dress and go talk to Henry. If

William Shakespeare had complained to Henry about my actions the night before, I would have to explain myself. I washed my face and put on a simple dress. I did not bother to place my hair in a nice bun, merely braiding it into a long tail that hung down my back. I looked nothing more than a milkmaid. I appeared innocent.

When I reached Henry's door, I stood outside, listening for movement in the chamber. I heard his voice along with another's. I pressed my ear to the door to see if I could identify who he was talking to.

It was William Shakespeare.

He must have come there to talk of the night before. I could turn away. I could apologize to Henry later. But I did not know how long it would be before they would be done, and I had duties concerning the new ladies. Today was their first day meeting the queen, and they were frightened. I hated the thought of putting it off any longer. And as much as I hated myself for it, I wanted to see Shakespeare.

I knocked on the door, pausing each time my knuckles met the hard, solid wood. I heard shuffling inside and footsteps as someone came to answer it. I filled my lungs with air before the door swung open.

William Shakespeare stood on the other side. He wore a simple doublet. I couldn't help but smile when he grinned in return. It danced before me, its meaning as mysterious as he was.

"My lady," he spoke. He said it slowly, almost with too much kindness.

I curtsied and walked past him into the room. Henry stood with his arms open, and I walked to him. He gave me a hug and an approving kiss on the cheek. Would William Shakespeare think I preferred this man over him?

"My dear, you came just in time. William is about to leave for London."

It was as if a knife had torn open my chest. I had spent all that worrying about how I would go on with him so close, and now he was leaving.

"The baron has graciously offered to help me establish my troupe in a real theatre." Shakespeare laughed. "No more canvas sets."

I laughed, too, to hide my disappointment. So he was to go; he would take part of me with him. What was I to do? I could never sleep with Henry Carey again after this. I had felt more excitement holding William Shakespeare's hand once than in all my years of being a mistress to the baron.

"You must come and visit." William spoke to Henry. "You too, my lady."

"Of course we shall," Henry added, but the way he answered made me realize that he would be the only one to see London. "I can see you inspired a new passion in my mistress."

Indeed he had. The expression on Henry's face was undeniable. William was now a threat. He wrapped an arm around my waist protectively, shook William's hand again, and congratulated him on the success of the night before. William thanked him for his patronage and grinned at me.

"Thank you, my lady," he said.

"I have done nothing." I smiled back. He had forgiven me for my actions and hadn't mentioned it to Henry. I should have been thanking him.

"You have done more than you know," he said. He gave a final brisk bow to each of us, and then, like a player on a great stage, he made his exit.

England, 1591
During the Reign of Queen Elizabeth I
Greenwich Court

Christmas came and went and I tried to forget William Shakespeare.

It was not long after Christmas that I received a lengthy letter from Margaret. I had been sitting with the young ladies-in-waiting in the chambers. We all huddled around the large hearth like moths to a lamp. The cold English air chilled our bones through, and I could hear the wind moaning outside our window. Empty cups and trays littered the room, while the kettle we placed over the fire began to steam. I opened the letter with haste, for I was sure that it was the child's birth she wrote about. I brought the letter over to the small desk the ladies shared, for I knew as soon as I finished reading the letter I would want to correspond.

Dear Emilia,

The child is born. She is a girl, a beautiful baby girl with a face like George's. She seems healthy, not sickly like the little boy we lost years ago. I have named her Anne. She wails in the night like you would not believe, but I am glad to hear it. I would rather have a screaming baby who is strong than one who does not make a sound.

George and I have been experiencing some difficult times. He is upset that the only child I have given him is a girl. We were once so in love, but you can see how love does not guarantee a happy matrimony. I do not believe I can conceive another child, Emilia, nor do I want to. This little girl is all that I have ever wanted, but I worry what George will say when I am not able to bear him more children.

I do not know if you have heard from Frances yet, but I hear she is also with child and won't be attending court. I feel as though I took away your friendship with her, and for that I am sorry. These days away from court have been days of thought and meditation.

There is nothing like having a child for your own, Emilia, and I wish it for you. I want to let you know that from the second you agreed to be Henry Carey's mistress, I have prayed as fervently as you have that you would be with child and free from that man. He has been kind to you, I know, but there is something about being in love, whether it turns out for the good or for the bad, that every woman should experience. I know it does not make sense, especially after I have written about my own situation with my husband, but I now know these things and you must believe me.

Do not give up hope. Our God works in mysterious ways. If you are not meant to have a child now, you will sooner or later. He hears you, my dear, just as He hears all of us and understands.

In blessing,
Margaret

I had missed Margaret before, but now I could hear her voice as I read the letter. Once I was finished with it, I read it again, this time savoring the message at the end. I wrapped the shawl tighter around my shoulders, shivering from the brutal cold that penetrated the walls of the palace.

I wanted to tell her that I did not know whether I had fallen in love. I wanted to ask her whether I could have fallen in love so quickly, or if time mattered. I wanted to know if she saw the same things in George's eyes as I did in William Shakespeare's.

I picked up a pen to write back and tried to think of what to say. I did not wish for words on a written page. I wanted her voice to tell me what I should be feeling and what I should do. Hesitantly, I put my pen to paper.

Dear Margaret,

I am overjoyed to hear the news of the addition to your family. I was concerned about your health, with you traveling when you were so far along, but now I see that it brought no harm. I have always loved the name Anne. I am sure it fits her personality and her face. I can't wait to hold her in my own arms and play the part of the loving older sister or aunt.

Court has been quiet since you have been away. Henry is growing years older every day, it seems. He still remains in Parliament and continues to stand by the queen's side. William Shakespeare, the playwright who had arrived just before you left, performed his play for us. I have never seen anything like it. I hear he is opening a new theatre in London.

Lady Bess and I have kept an eye on the new ladies who have come up. They remind me so of when I was young. They will definitely learn much in the next few months, and hopefully it won't all be during Shrove Tuesday. Lady Bess and I have worked together often and are starting to enjoy each other's company.

As for Frances, I wish her only the best. I congratulate her if she is with child, and I wish any hard feelings mended. I can only hope that with time, she can see that both you and I only wanted her happiness and safety. And I am concerned that Robert Devereux might return to the queen's side when he comes back to court.

I cannot wait to see you and hear your voice. I shall tell you of all that went on while you were gone, and perhaps we can sit around at nights together again, watching the baby Anne and waiting for Henry as we always have done.

Your friend,

Emilia

JUST AFTER SHROVE TUESDAY, Henry and I decided to meet in his chambers and organize a picnic for the spring. I sat in my usual velvet chair, sinking deeply into the seat and enjoying the opportunity to raise my feet after a long day of watching the new ladies-in-waiting. Henry sat at his desk, ruffling papers, calculating expenses, and looking over at me every so often.

"What do you think, my dear? Would early spring be a good

time? There should be enough sun, and the blossoms will be full in bloom. Shall we make it a joust as well, to satisfy the men?"

I agreed. What better place for young lovers to meet than a joust?

"Only if you promise not to participate yourself," I said.

"I am not as old as you think I am," he said with his hands on his hips—which made him look very much as I imagined his father, King Henry the Eighth. "I keep you satisfied, do I not?"

I did not have the heart to tell him that he did not. The king's son he may have been; a young man he was not.

"Of course, my lord, but the greatest men know when they must submit to time. Only foolish ones continue to play the games of the young."

He seemed to be content with my answer and did not badger me anymore.

"Very well. A joust it will be, then."

"It sounds lovely," I sighed, running a hand on the familiar chair's arm. "We must be sure that it will not conflict with the Easter festivities, but I think if we schedule it a bit later, everyone would be at liberty to come."

"Excellent." He folded a sheet of parchment and dropped some sealing wax on it. Then he pressed the ring he wore on his finger into the hot wax. "Should we invite the queen? Perhaps your friend Margaret?"

I turned in my seat so he could see my gratitude.

"Thank you. She might not be able to come, for she has just had a child, but she will appreciate the invitation anyway."

"Is there anyone else we should include?"

"What would you say to inviting William Shakespeare?" I said.

"As I recall, Her Majesty much enjoyed his plays and his troupe. They could provide some entertainment."

One long glance from Henry told me that he had seen through my plan like one looks through a clear pool of water. He cocked his thin lips to the side of his mouth and his eyebrows rose.

"The bard is awfully busy in London," he said. "He's putting on a play at the Rose Theatre during that time. I sincerely doubt that he would be able to come."

I lowered my eyes to the rug, both from shame and disappointment. I had given myself away, and now Henry would do anything to keep me away from Shakespeare. I sighed quietly so he wouldn't hear. It would have been better to say nothing at all.

I suggested several less imposing names, including the poet Thomas Campion and a few dukes not too far from court, and then I asked to be excused. Henry kissed my cheek and smiled farewell and let me go. I walked down the crowded halls, bumping into many different colors of skirts. I knew I needed to forget William Shakespeare, for if I didn't, others would try to make me.

Spring always made me content, with its blooming flowers and greenery. I was given a new dress and a new pearl necklace for the joust. It contrasted nicely with my skin and made me feel elegant. I had Lady Bess tighten my corset while I held tightly to a four-poster bed. I hated the feeling of a corset, but it did make my waist appear smaller and give me a womanly figure that I did not seem to have naturally. I made sure my ruby ring was securely fastened on my finger and that my hair was smoothed back from my face. I wanted to look as elegant as possible for this event. Then it was time to go down. I straightened my gown and hurried out the door. I hoped I had done the job of a mistress well to such an important man as Henry Carey.

The field by the palace was decorated with banners and music. I was gladdened by how it turned out. The green grass sparkled under a layer of dew, while the sun shone brightly, casting everyone in a healthy, anticipative glow. Horses were led by amiable young stable hands. Men in armor paraded by in gallant reds and blues and handed kerchiefs to ladies, who grasped them tightly in their hands. It had taken more out of Henry's purse to put this event together than both he and I would have liked to admit, but only the queen could have done better.

I was a little late in coming down to the field, and Henry had already settled himself in the middle of the benches used for seating. We had invited the queen and were surprised that she had accepted. When she was younger, she had attended all sorts of celebrations, but now that she was getting older, it was harder for her to run a country and pretend to be merry at all times. I feared she would watch my every move.

I joined Henry, who presided over the field as though he owned it. He looked as though he had spent a considerable amount of time hiding his age with lavish clothes and jewelry. Fine rings tried to distract from his swollen knuckles, and his belt was cinched tightly around his waist, but when the sun hit him, I could see that his skin was old, almost translucent, and his head balding.

"You are late, my dear," he said as he gave the signal for the jousting to start.

"I am sorry," I replied. "But I had to make sure that I looked as nice as possible, for I have never seen a joust as jubilant as this one."

He smiled, took my left hand, and kissed it.

"You look as beautiful as this spring day."

I pulled my hand away, but not so quickly as to offend him. "Who is up to joust?" I asked.

"Sir Walter Raleigh is up soon. He and the Earl of Essex want to have a bout." He laughed.

"The Earl of Essex is back to court?" I asked. I could hardly believe it. Frances would still be with child...or maybe have just given birth. The Earl should be at her side, not here at court.

"Does the queen know?"

Henry shrugged.

"Is she here yet?" I looked around the field for the earl and the queen.

"I have not seen her." He peered across the expanse of horses and riders. "Ah, wait. Here she comes."

Elizabeth came toward us in her full majesty. Her skirts were twice as large as mine and decorated in the finest satin and lace. The large collar she had taken to wearing was edged in pearls, and her hair was twisted high upon her head in several complicated knots. She wore no crown, but the elaborate golden net covering her head could have served as one.

When she had come close enough to address us, she nodded her head. Henry and I both stood and bowed at her presence.

"Dear cousin; Lady Bassano. I don't believe I have ever seen a joust as gallant as this one." She spoke in a smooth, even voice.

"Thank you, Your Highness. My lady and I are beyond honored to have you here with us," Henry said.

"Your lady is lovely today," she said.

I could feel the color rise to my cheeks, and I gave a smile to the ground.

Henry moved so she could occupy the highest seat of the stands. He chose the next available one, the one to her right. I, in turn, sat to his right. I could not help but think how fortunate I was to have been paid such a high compliment.

"Isn't that your cousin?" Henry said to me, pointing at an approaching horse and rider.

I swore under my breath, but not loud enough for the queen to hear. He was right. Alfonso was coming towards us. His dark eyes burned into mine, and I felt the same as I had when he followed me during the hunt. I did not need any distractions at the moment.

"Lady Bassano." His voice was full of insincere civility.

"Yes?" I asked. My eyes went to the queen. Could he not see that I was in Her Majesty's presence?

He held out a purple handkerchief. "I ask that you carry this with you, by your heart."

Henry and I looked at each other. It was the last thing I would have expected of Alfonso, but it did not repair the distress I felt when near him. I worried for my honor, but now was not the time. I wanted to refuse him, but no one was looking toward us at the moment and I wanted to keep him quiet.

Henry grunted and looked away, crossing his arms over his chest as he did, though I was sure he was watching me out of the corners of his eyes. Although it was a common practice for handkerchiefs to be given to whichever lady the jouster wished, jealousies and rivalries often erupted from the simple gesture. However, if I refused, I would not be showing my full support of my father's troupe, and it might bring shame upon my name.

"Very well," I sighed. I took it from him and stuffed it down my bodice. His eyes followed my action, and I instantly regretted it. He nodded his head at Henry and kicked his horse into a trot.

"I did not know that your cousin thought of you in that way," Henry said, jealousy evident on his face. His lip quivered in anger.

"I assure you he does not," I spoke harshly. "Think nothing of it, my lord."

As soon as Alfonso left, Essex approached. He galloped up on a muscular bay and bowed, still on horseback, with a flourish. His armor was somehow brighter than anyone else's on the field, and his eyes traveled to the seating area to meet Her Majesty's gaze.

"My queen," he said, his smile framed by his full beard. "Permit me to offer you this token of my admiration."

I looked over to the queen to see what her reaction would be. Surely she would not take the handkerchief, knowing Essex was married. Then again, this would be just the kind of thing Elizabeth would delight in. Frances's pain would taste awfully sweet to the queen.

She reached out a pale hand to take the wine-colored cloth. Then she stood and waved it in front of the rest of us, so all knew the name of her favorite.

The earl gave a closed-lipped smile. It was an all-knowing smile, as though he had the queen hanging on his every action. I wondered if he really believed that, or if he understood that the queen was always the one in control.

Essex saluted her and then urged his horse onward as the trumpets sounded for the joust to begin. I peeked to see what the queen was doing. The handkerchief was folded perfectly underneath her right hand.

Henry would not speak to me. He seemed indifferent to what was going on around him. It was a beautiful day and everyone loved the tournament that he had put on, so I did not know why he was upset.

"What is the matter?" I asked him.

"My dear, you seem to find all the men on the field more interesting than myself," he replied.

He was a silly old man. I laughed and wrapped my arm around his, but the sad reality was that he had spoken the truth. I was glad I had not been around William Shakespeare more. I could only imagine his jealousy if I had been caught with his esteemed protégé.

"My lord, some men may be fairer of face, but none could have been kinder to me."

SPRING SLOWLY SLIPPED INTO sleepy summer days. Henry was off to visit his wife once again, and I was free from his constraints. The days never felt so liberated or so wonderful. I spent most of my time out in the sun, and my skin turned the darkest color it had ever been. I was often the jest among the younger ladies who so painstakingly covered themselves so that they would not even turn even the slightest color of red.

Lady Bess approached me one day. I had been writing on a bench in the courtyard, the soft air brushing my face. Birds chirped around me, swooping over my head and threatening to land on my hat. The stone bench was hard, but it was the best place to sit down with a pen and my little book.

Lady Bess suddenly sat down beside me, peering at what I was doing. I moved over to make space for her and tried to hide my book on the other side on my skirts.

"Emilia? Do you have time to talk with me?" she asked, gazing at me a bit suspiciously.

"Of course," I replied. I wanted to distract her from my forbidden activity. "What do you wish to speak of?"

Bess was always so curious about others' doings. She smoothed her peach-colored dress and adjusted her gold necklace. Bess had always been a plain girl, but in the summer sun she looked as lovely as I had ever seen her. She smiled as though she felt pity for me before continuing.

"There is word going around that you accepted your cousin Alfonso's handkerchief at the joust you and Henry Carey put on."

I groaned. Of course rumors would have sprung from the simple action.

"Yes," I replied, "I did. But it was only to get him to leave me alone. I was with the queen at the time."

Lady Bess nodded as though she understood. She pursed her lips and smoothed her dress once again.

"I would be careful if I were you," she advised. "Everyone is saying that you are secret lovers. If you can, I would avoid him, if you don't want these rumors to continue."

"You need not worry. I hardly enjoy his presence."

"Good," she replied. She ran a hand over the bench. "Would you take a walk with me? This summer air is so wonderful. Seems a shame to waste it."

I agreed and slipped my little book into the pouch I wore tied to my belt. I looked over to see if she had noticed, but she was preoccupied with her own skirts. I gladly walked the length of the courtyard with her, surprised and grateful that she had warned me of the rumors crowding the palace.

MARGARET SENT A LETTER to me in late June to say that she was journeying back to court at the end of July, by order of the queen. I hadn't been able to respond since I had taken the younger ladies out for a ride. That evening, I sat down at the small desk all the ladies in the chambers shared and began the letter back to her. It was late, around eight o'clock. The other ladies congregated by the pallets and gossiped. The night outside devoured the courtyard, and I couldn't see anything out the dirtied window. I had to admit that ever since Lady Bess and I had been watching the new ladies, the chambers had become increasingly messy. Shoes and hats were strewn around the floor while petticoats covered chairs, making them look ghostly. They looked even more haunting in the dark.

I had just put my pen to paper when I saw Lady Bess out of the corners of my eyes. She sneaked around the back of the room and headed for the door. I was not sure if she had seen me yet. She did not want me to know that she was leaving the chambers. Keeping my eyes focused downward on the forgotten pages, I addressed her.

"Are you going somewhere?" I turned to meet her, twisting my body in my hard, solid chair.

She turned around quickly, her robes swishing about her. She seemed surprised to see me. Her knuckles were white as she clutched her silk robe. She looked exactly as I did when I was about to go to Henry Carey's bed.

"Emilia," she cried. "You startled me."

"Did you forget something in the Great Hall, Lady Bess?" I knew fully well where she was going, I just didn't know to whom.

The smile that she had been wearing replaced itself with a frown. "No..."

"Lose something in the garden?"

"No..."

The image of Frances that one time when she had come back from Thomas Campion's bed flashed through my mind. She and Bess had exactly the same expression on their faces. Bess knew it was wrong.

I sighed. She had become my friend in the past few months. She would never replace Frances; I don't think she even suspected she might. I did not want to make the same mistake as I had before, even if she wasn't as dear to me.

"I won't tell anyone. I give you my word that this will be our secret," I spoke slowly and truthfully. Bess's relationship had not been sanctioned by the queen, making it unacceptable. "But I want to warn you, this is the path Frances chose to take, and now her beloved Essex is once again at the queen's side."

Lady Bess nodded. The world paused for a moment while she decided. Her eyes were first on the ground, then at the clock, and then at the door. She opened the door and walked through the opening. Her face was the only thing visible as she looked back.

"Thank you," she said.

Then, she was gone.

LATER THAT SUMMER, ABOUT the time Margaret came back to court with her baby, it was discovered that Lady Bess was pregnant. One of the younger ladies had seen her vomiting in the privy chamber and ran to me, crying.

"Lady Bess needs you," she spoke hurriedly, taking my hand and dragging me to her side.

Bess lay in a disturbing heap. Her skirts were in disarray and pushed far back behind her to keep them from getting dirtied. She could barely look up at me in her shame.

"I know what I did was wrong, Emilia. But now I don't know if even Sir Walter can save me."

Her worry was well deserved.

Lady Bess was sent away from court when the queen found out that her lady-in-waiting was secretly married to her paramour. She was locked in the Tower of London along with her husband, their fates uncertain.

I remember watching her from an upstairs window as the rain danced on the top of the carriage she left in. She maneuvered through the cramped carriage door, looking up at court for the last time. I closed the window, the cold air ceasing its journey into the room.

I later heard she'd miscarried that cursed child in the Tower, but by that time, it was too late for Lady Bess.

England, 1592
During the Reign of Queen Elizabeth I
Hampton Court

We were all happy when Margaret returned to court with her baby. She seemed happier than I had ever seen her, and we all rejoiced in having her to guide us once again. But it was a hard time to be a mistress. Margaret was so exhausted from her days that I waited up for Henry's word by myself. The clock became both my ally and my enemy. After midnight it was my saving grace; before, there was danger in it.

One afternoon I was washing clothes, wringing them out in the convenience room adjoining the chambers, water dripping on my apron, when suddenly I felt ill. I searched for something to hold onto. I grasped the edge of the large tub of steaming water and waited for the feeling to pass. I took deep breaths, steadying myself enough that I could return to work. After a few moments, I tried to move and began to hang clothes again. It was nothing. It would pass. The water from the clothes soaked my dry sleeves.

Then, I felt it coming on again. I glanced around, searching for something I could vomit into. I ran around the tiny room before I couldn't hold it in my stomach any longer. I placed a hand over my mouth, but it was useless. Bile covered the freshly cleaned stomacher in front of me.

I bit my lip before I could curse. It would have to be scrubbed again.

I placed the bodice back in a tub of soapy water and sighed, starting over again. I thought about what might have caused my upset stomach. I had eaten that day—and not too much, either. I was tired, but I felt no other symptoms of sickness.

I sat down on an upside-down washing tub. My thoughts danced with possible reasons—sour milk, spoiled ale—but none of them seemed to make sense to me. I ran a wet cloth over my face, trying to calm myself. I touched my stomach.

Then, it dawned on me. This could only mean one thing.

I quickly forgot the wash and ran to Henry's chambers. People in the passageway watched me as I whisked past them along the familiar path to his rooms. I heard voices inside. I wrung my hands impatiently. I would have to wait. They were probably some members of Parliament and such, but no state matter could be as important as this.

I paced outside his chamber door, eager to tell him the news. He would be the first to know. I tapped my foot. My heart was racing, and my face wore a smile. I was to be married, my dream since I had been in the Countess of Kent's care. To think that I had almost given it up. Now it was as clear as day, a beacon of light where there once was dark. The excitement overwhelmed me. There were so many things I could do now.

When the men finally left Henry's chambers, I practically ran into the room. Henry sat at his desk, as he had so many times before. His smile was wide. He was happy to see me. He stood and gave me a kiss on the cheek.

"Darling," he said. "What is this news that you came to tell me in the middle of the afternoon?"

All I could do was beam. What would he do when I told him?

"I'm with child."

I loved the words as they came out of my mouth. Such words, such brilliant words. For as long as I could remember, I'd dreamed of those magical words of freedom. I had been under the control of others for so long. I had even given up any hope of having the life I wanted, and now here it was, staring me square in the face. I was free.

I did not care if Henry kissed me or slapped me. I would no longer have to come when he called me at nights. I would no longer have to sit with him at state dinners or host hunts or jousts or anything of the sort. Most of all, I would no longer have to lie with him.

He had been good to me; there was no doubt about it. He treated me fairly, as a mistress should be treated, and he helped me gain the favor of the queen. I had given myself to him, and I would be rewarded for it. He would pay me a sum every month and set me to marry a fine gentleman.

A flash of hope went through my body. What if I were to marry William Shakespeare? Could that happen? I thought of the feeling of his hand holding mine, and shivers went up my spine.

"Are you certain?" Henry's smile faded, and his drooping eyes searched mine.

I nodded. "Yes, my lord. I have missed my cycle this month and had a sickness in my stomach." When I first noticed that my bleeding hadn't come, I thought it was from the disturbing instance of Lady Bess's ordeal and thought nothing more of it. Now I understood.

He nodded. He sighed and tapped his fingers on the desk a few times. His eyes followed my every movement. He was losing me, and it was as sudden as a whim. I had been his mistress for six years.

Henry tottered back over to his desk and moaned. He put a hand to his head as he sat down. He was taking it worse than I thought he would. Of course he would not feel the same way I would, but I did not care that he was upset. I had been upset for all these years.

"You have been a faithful mistress to me. I will look into only the best husband for you. How much would you like a year?" His voice quavered.

He struggled to find some parchment to write the sum on. He clenched his hands before tightly grasping a quill pen. He bent his head over the paper so I could not see his face.

I thought carefully before I answered. If I requested more money, then the quality of the husband would probably diminish. A better husband would be able to pay for new gowns and things that he didn't need to consider before he married.

"Whatever my lord is willing to give," I replied, hoping I said the right thing.

"All right," he said. "How is forty pounds a year? That should buy you the necessities that ladies insist upon."

I agreed. He was being more than fair.

He shook his head and gave a small chuckle. He looked older than ever, and it was hard to believe that he had caused this spark of life inside of me. Yet there it was.

"I have had a few mistresses," he said, trying to hold back the tears gathered at the corners of his eyes. "But none, Lady Bassano, have been as kind or as beautiful as you. This is a loss."

I smiled softly. I appreciated how he cared. He had been my protector, and for a moment I had a twinge of guilt for not being more saddened by our parting. For that's what it was. I was leaving Henry that day. I would see him around court, and he would speak to me until we found a husband, but this was my official farewell.

He continued.

"I will miss you, as will the ladies of court. But you will promise me that you will come back?"

I nodded again. I could not help but feel how the Countess of Kent must have when she promised me that she would visit me at court. She never had...and I didn't know whether I wanted to return.

"Thank you," he finished. I could see the water in his eyes, and a single tear escaped. It would be a greater loss to him than it would be to me.

"You may go."

IMMEDIATELY AFTER THE AUDIENCE with Henry, I went to Margaret. She held me tightly, as if I was a little girl.

News travels fast around court. Everyone knew in matter of days. It was the best news we'd heard recently. The pregnancy of a musician's daughter was nothing of the gossip that Lady Bess and Frances had generated, but many were still as surprised as I that it had finally happened.

When the blossoms of early summer began to appear, court seemed to wake up. We all were more joyful and hopeful. The queen's mood must have improved also, for she released Sir Walter Raleigh from the Tower. He would never come back to court with the freedom that he had before, and he would have to go to his estate with Lady Bess at his side.

I heard that William Shakespeare was coming back to court. The queen called him to perform for her again, and he left his new theatre in London for Her Majesty. I waited expectantly for him to come.

On one of my daily walks outside the palace, I heard some rumbling from down the long road that led to the castle.

I walked toward the noise, into the sunlight. My skirts skated along the green grass. I squinted, blocking the sun. I wished I had brought my hat—or at least a fan to shade my face. The sky's blue was unrivaled by any other color I had seen in my life. It expanded above my head like the giant dome of a church, painted with birds and clouds softer than any fabric.

Some people were coming toward me on horseback, pulling a cart loaded with large objects. As they came closer, I could make out wooden beams protruding toward the sky.

"Excuse me." I stopped them as they were about to pass me. I recognized an object on the wagon. "Is this the set to the play going to be performed here? Are you members of the Lord Chamberlain's troupe?"

A man with a round, dirtied face turned his horse around to talk to me. The gloves on his hands were worn, and his hair was disheveled from travel.

"We are, my lady. We are the actors, at your service." He gave a theatrical bow.

"Do you know if William Shakespeare is here?" I asked.

"Will? He had some business to finish in London, but he'll be along soon. Just finishing up some writing, I think. Right, Richard?"

A man in more distinguished clothing, black with silver lining, nodded.

"He'd better be. If I don't get those pages to deliver to Wriothesley soon..." He turned back to his cart. "We better get this stage into the palace. Her Majesty will have a royal fit if we aren't ready to perform when she demands."

The man with the round face laughed. "All right, then. Good day, my lady."

I thanked him, my heart dancing la volta inside my chest. He was coming back to court. I was to see him again.

I hurried inside, breathing hard. I leaned my back against a cool stone wall, feeling it relieve the heat from the sun on my shoulders. My chest rose up and down. I was breathing hard for more reasons than one. I might have stopped running, but my thoughts were still racing in my mind.

HENRY DID NOT KEEP in contact with me as he had. This was to be expected, but I wished that he would give me more news of prospective husbands. I hoped to be married before the year ended. I did not know if I would have the baby before then, but it would be nice to have a house to give birth in. The traditions of court birth were horrendous. A woman would be locked in a room a month or two before the birthing, sometimes earlier if a miscarriage was possible. Maids would place hangings over the windows, blocking all the light. She would be in the dark for all those months, lying on her back. I was frightened of the idea. A home was much more comfortable and practical.

I started to notice changes in my figure. I had once been very thin; Margaret had been trying to put more weight on me ever since I had come to court. I now wore curves and needed to expand my dresses. I spent a lot of time in front of the mirror, running my hand over my budding belly.

"Have you heard from Henry?" Margaret asked me.

"No." I shook my head. "I was hoping to soon. Are there any more prospects?"

"Not that I have heard."

"We'd better hurry," I said. "It won't be long before this baby is born."

"It's hard to find the right match. He must be wealthy enough that he can take care of you and your child, but poor enough that your dowry tempts him," Margaret spoke wisely. "Are there any courtiers that have caught your fancy?"

At first I thought I might actually tell her about my feelings for William Shakespeare. However, I thought better of it and once again shook my head. I did not want to know what she would say.

Margaret picked up a petticoat I had carelessly thrown on a chair and placed it in her laundry basket. She had been burdened with even more things to do since I had become with child. I helped the best I could, but there were special precautions a woman must obey when she was pregnant. That was probably the reason Lady Bess had lost her child in the Tower. It would be almost impossible to follow those rules while locked in prison.

I could not bend over often, nor could I eat too much. The more I ate, the harder the birth would be. I drank tea made of rose hips to soothe my stomach and to ease the pains. I had not become any more beautiful while the child had grown, but it was a fact of life. I might never have the same figure that I had before, and the skin on my stomach might permanently wear scars. It was all worth it. The life I would live would be worth it all.

"No," I said. "People keep mentioning the poet Thomas Campion. But I don't think he could support me."

Margaret nodded. Her eyes were on my belly as well.

"He is but an unknown poet," she agreed. "I will keep asking around. Henry, of course, would know better than all of us."

"He does not pay attention to me anymore."

"I will go to him if I must," she said firmly. "This is important." She turned. "By the way, it is said that the playwright"—she cocked her head—"what's his name again?"

I pretended not to know. "Smith?" I offered.

"Shakespeare, I think. He wishes to speak to you."

My heart leaped to my throat.

"Me? Why?" I asked.

Margaret picked up another article of clothing and shrugged, giving me a sidelong glance. Did Margaret know?

The thought of seeing William Shakespeare was almost more than I could handle. My breath quickened, and my heart thumped in my chest. I wondered if Margaret could hear it. What would he think of me now that I was with child and growing larger? Would I be able to face him?

"What time does he wish to come?" I sighed, as if it was the last thing I wished to do.

Margaret raised an eyebrow. "What time do you want him?"

I SAT AT THE seat in the window. I wished to wear my finest gown, but I was afraid to put it on in case Margaret might suspect. I wore a simple, clean gown instead. It stretched over my belly tightly. It wouldn't be long before I would have to loosen it, as I had all the others. I pulled my hair back in a bun. I was no longer a young girl, and I must keep some dignity.

It had been a year since I'd seen him last. An eternity and a moment. With all that had gone on with Lady Bess and Sir Walter, time had gone by quickly; with being a lover and being lonely, time dragged on. But now he was here. He was here.

The knock on the door sounded like trumpets. I motioned a maid to let him in. My hand went to my hair before I could stop it. I made sure it stayed in place.

And then there he was. He stood with his head cocked to the side, as if he were observing some rare plant or animal. He was observing me. His eyes shone, and his hands hung at his side. What was he doing? What was he thinking? Was he noticing my growing figure? No, he was looking at my face.

"Master Shakespeare," I said. I pointed to the seat I'd set up for him across from me. It was the chair Margaret had sunk into when she'd told me she was with child. It was the chair Frances had sat in when we waited up nights for Henry Carey.

He walked over. He did not stride like many men. He walked with a proud actor's grace. Was he playing a part? Or was that the way he had come to walk after all of those years on stage?

William Shakespeare came to talk business. He was even more handsome than I remembered; his eyes were more brilliant than I had ever seen them. He was nothing like all the other men at court who cared only for love and money. Here was a man who cared about something more. He brought words, marvelous words, into this world. They were beautiful, and so was he.

"What reason do I have the pleasure of your company today?" I asked.

"You see, my lady..." He smiled a small smile. "The baron has been very generous toward me and my troupe. I wish to give him a surprise. A performance."

"Master Shakespeare...," I started.

"William, please."

"I am not sure I can help you," I said.

"Of course you can," he said. His fingers traced the pattern on the chair's fabric. I recalled what it felt like when that hand had touched my own.

"You know what plays he likes and admires. I want to write him one. What takes his interest?"

I wanted to say that he liked to bring young girls to his bed, but I caught myself. Henry had been good to me for many years, and I needn't be judging him now. I thought before I answered.

"He is dreadfully fascinated with kings and queens and great people. What was that one you performed while you were here?"

"*Henry the Fourth*," he spoke without hesitation. Did he remember that day as I did?

"Yes, he enjoyed it. Do you have another one like it?"

"Several." He smiled sheepishly, as though he should be ashamed that he was writing so much. "They are mostly about France or Denmark."

"Henry would want something about England," I replied. I watched to see if his face would change, but it did not.

"I don't have anything of that sort," he said. "But I could write one in a few months, I suppose."

I nodded, even though I did not really care a bit what kind of play Henry Carey received.

"What if you wrote more about Henry the Fourth or some other king?" I asked.

"I could do that. Would he like that?"

"He would love it." I smiled. I expected him to rise and leave, but he did not. His eyes bore into my own. They were so intense that I almost had to turn away.

"About that day when I was showing you my set..." He chuckled. "If I offended you, my lady, I did not mean to."

"Well"—I smiled and played with the ring on my finger—"I do become offended at kindness. It's a terrible fault of mine."

He laughed. Still, he showed no sign of leaving; I wanted to grab him and force him to stay.

"How long do you plan to be at court?" I asked.

If he could sense my intentions, he did not let on.

"Through the summer season," he said.

I silently rejoiced. If he had a family, he would return to them this summer, for he had been at the theatre the whole past year. It was strange that a man like him hadn't been married for at least a few years, but I suppose that he traveled so often....

"Well, we are glad to have your company," I said.

At that he stood up.

"Thank you very much, my lady. You assistance has been most helpful."

"It was no trouble at all," I replied, trying to hide my disappointment.

He grinned and nodded in parting. I sighed after I heard his footsteps disappear and heard the door close behind him. He hadn't given any indication that he thought of me as I thought of him.

I was just about to turn back to my sewing when I heard the clunking of his boots once more.

"I'm sorry," he said as he appeared again. "I quite forgot something."

He bent over and kissed my hand, and I caught my breath once again. The touch of his lips on the back of my hand lingered long after he left the room. I knew who I wanted to marry. I had only known him a short time, but he had known me forever. I could imagine us in a small house in London, next to the theatre. We could walk to it and watch his plays being performed. The baby inside me would become an actor and convey his father's beautiful words to an audience. I could almost hear the crowds gathered and see the colors. Finally, my life was becoming what I wanted it to be.

A FEW DAYS AFTER I met with Shakespeare, Margaret and I went shopping for new fabric. I could no longer fit into many of my gowns, and I had decided to pick out some red satin for a dress that would cover my belly. The shop bustled with activity, ladies eyeing new shipments of silks and velvets. The milliner had raised the prices to a ridiculous amount, hoping to fool the unsuspecting ladies.

"I would have never believed we would have such trouble finding a suitor for you," Margaret said, running her fingers along another length of satin.

"Neither would I," I replied, hoping my disappointment didn't show in my voice. "You would think someone would be poor enough to want my dowry."

"You know, I had thought of someone that might have been a good match for you, before I went to the queen," Margaret said. "I thought of that playwright, Shakespeare."

I turned away from some Spanish lace I had been admiring.

"You did?" I asked.

She nodded. "I found out he's married, though. With several children, I believe."

I breathed in quickly. It only made sense. Why wouldn't he be happily married? I hid my disappointment by disliking every choice of fabric that the milliner offered me, even at reasonable prices.

A MONTH LATER, I was called to visit the queen. For the first time, I was eager to see her. My nicest dress had been loosened considerably and my hair brushed back into a tight bun. I wore the ring that Henry had given me so long ago as a symbol of my loyalty to her family.

The throne room at Hampton Palace was smaller than either Whitehall or Greenwich, but it was impressive nonetheless. I walked briskly but without forgetting my place. I kept my eyes down, trying not to stare at the splendor around me. Carvings adorned the room, decorating the surrounding windows. Hampton was altogether lighter in appearance than Greenwich, but then again, everything seemed brighter in my life at that moment. The queen's seal was everywhere. The Tudor rose decorated the banners that hung on the walls and was carved deeply into the walls themselves. A hearth, unused in this hot weather, stood at the far end of the room next to the queen.

The queen sat as regally as ever. She was wearing a dress draped in pearls, her favorite accessory. I entered, knowing that it might be the final time I met with Her Majesty. If I were to be married and sent off, I would be away from court—at least for a while. And even if I were to return, I would live in chambers with my husband, not among her ladies.

It was the first time the queen had ever smiled at me. It would also be the final time. I curtsied before her and waited for her to speak. "Rise, Lady Bassano. I hear and see that you are with child." She said it coldly, but not as coldly as previous times.

"Yes, Your Majesty," I said.

"In that case," she continued, her voice powerful and yet feminine, "a husband is in order. My cousin, the Baron of Hunsdon, has mentioned that a particular man has caught your fancy."

I blushed more than I thought could be possible. How could anyone know about William Shakespeare? I had not told anyone, not even Margaret. Had Margaret been mistaken about him being married? How could the queen have known I admired him?

"I approve of the match," she added. "I wish you nothing but happiness."

I dared to look up at her. She had been tolerant toward me, something not all ladies could say. She had been my idol, and now she was acting like a friend.

I had her permission to marry. I could not contain my pleasure, and a smile escaped from my lips as well. We stood there, two women, smiling. I forgot for a moment that she was a queen and I was a musician's daughter. We were one and the same for that instant.

"Alfonso Lanier is the most handsome of men. You have done well, Lady Bassano."

I could not breathe. I felt my heart descend to my feet.

Alfonso? She thought I wished to marry Alfonso? Suddenly I remembered the joust, when I had taken his handkerchief. My hands immediately went to the cross around my neck. I tried to keep from swaying from surprise in front of Her Majesty. I could not speak back to the queen, however. I couldn't even go to Henry. I had no say in this matter now that it had been decided. My eyes welled up with tears and my hands started shaking. What could I do? What could I do?

I tried to smile as the queen nodded her head. It was finished. I was excused.

As soon as I left the throne room, I ran and ran, tripping over my skirts, almost falling. Courtiers and ladies watched as I made my way through the halls. I must have looked very strange, a pregnant woman running throughout the halls crying. I did not care. Finally, I made my way outside and collapsed on a stone bench. What was I to do? What was I to do?

I don't know how long I stayed like that. It must have been at least an hour, and I'm sure many a passerby saw me with my head pressed on the bench, my skirts on the ground about me. I was to marry Alfonso. I remembered what he had said that day in the clearing. I would be his.

Henry had decided among his favorites, and Alfonso had no doubt expressed an interest in me. What was I to do?

I thought of all my possible choices. Running away seemed foolish, and I could not do it with a child in my belly. If I refused Alfonso, all the funds that Henry was giving me would be cut off, and I would be as penniless as a beggar on the street.

I had thought Henry Carey was bad. He was no competition for Alfonso. Henry had manners. Alfonso had nothing, no regard for a lady at all. I could only imagine what he would do to me. I was scared. I had entered the meeting with all the hope in the world, and it had all been tossed away.

My legs started to go numb. I'd sat there for a long time. My eyes were sore from crying, and the pain in my chest grew stronger. I just stared ahead for several minutes into the roses, thinking.

I thought of Margaret. I thought of Frances. I thought of the countess. None of us had a choice. Margaret had married a man she loved, but she had lost his love because of her duties for the queen. Frances had been forced to marry a man she didn't love and then, when she found love, lost everything else. The Countess of Kent had married the count purely out of family duty.

Then I thought of the queen. She had never married. She had been denied the greatest love of her life; she had done that for her country. She had done it for the peasant and for the earl. She had done it for us.

These were the women who defined who I was and how I felt. Why had I thought it would be any different for me? Why had I believed happiness was something I was owed? I did not want to be like Lady Bess. I could not defy the queen. If the queen wanted me to marry Alfonso Lanier, I would have to. I did not do it for myself. I did it for her.

PART TWO

I love to hear her speak, yet well I know
That music hath a far more pleasing sound;
I grant I never saw a goddess go;
My mistress, when she walks, treads on the ground.

—Sonnet CXXX

England, 1593
During the Reign of Queen Elizabeth I
London

I was married that autumn. I walked down the aisle with my head held high, but my heart was far away. Henry spared no expense.

The chapel where we wed was not as large as the church where Frances's wedding took place, but it had been decorated with equal care. My dress was made of inexpensive muslin, my veil composed of Spanish lace. Over my dress I wore a velvet cloak, which was heavy on my shoulders. I also held a bouquet of white roses, my favorite flower.

The queen did not come. I did not merit her attention. I had given myself up to this man so she would be happy, but she wasn't there to congratulate me. Several others did come. Lady Bess and Sir Walter came, and Margaret and George. Frances and Robert Devereux had also come. I tried to catch her eye before the wedding began, but she ignored me. I was not forgiven. She was there only out of duty.

My husband-to-be stood triumphantly at the end of the aisle of the church. He was handsome, much more handsome than William Shakespeare, but it meant nothing to me. I would have taken William Shakespeare's eyes over Alfonso's pretty face.

The only good thing about my marriage was that I knew that

my husband would not be home for much of the year. He would travel, just like my father had. If the child I bore was a girl, then she would stay with me. If he was a boy, then when he was old enough, he would go with Alfonso and learn the trade of the musician. The Bassano name had died with this union, but the family business was thriving, mostly because of Henry's generous funds.

I did not know when I would return to court. I had not wanted to come back at first, but now I considered it. Our small house in London would not be far from a few of the palaces, and I could come if the queen wanted me.

Each step down the aisle felt as if I were walking to my death. The high church ceilings, colorful stained glass, and exultant bells, which normally made me feel joyful, now signaled the worst hour of my life. Ladies in brightly colored dresses smiled and sighed at me as I walked past. The large altar loomed closer and closer and had a golden cross standing proudly on top. I saw Henry in the front pew wearing a white doublet. He gave me a melancholy nod as our eyes met. He knew as well as I that this was our duty. I smiled at him, a thank you.

I saw Margaret near the front of the church, her eyes filled with tears. I couldn't tell if it was from happiness or disappointment.

Even then I found myself searching for Shakespeare, like so many times before. I did not see him. It was probably better that I did not.

There was a small reception after the wedding. I thanked each guest for coming and let them place a hand on my belly and smile longingly at my handsome husband. I would have gladly given Alfonso away to any of the ladies who found him so attractive, but I could not alter my fate now.

When Frances and Robert Devereux came up to me, I was at a loss for words. What could I tell her? That I missed her? That I waited for her letters and her smiles?

She said she was happy for me. Her face was tired and worn. Alfonso shook Robert Devereux's hand. Then they were gone. She had gotten what she wanted and hadn't cared who she had hurt in process. If only she had known.

Music continued to play in the background, provided by Alfonso's troupe, and young people danced joyfully, letting out squeals of youth. We had set out a table so they could eat and drink all night. Though I could not join them, I remembered the many dances I had shared with Henry, and I wondered how he was enjoying the merriment. I looked for him, but he seemed to have disappeared, leaving me alone with my new husband and my new life.

Lady Bess was full of smiles. She lost her child in the Tower, but there would be others, as we all knew. She glanced at my stomach fondly. Sir Walter mimicked his wife and smiled at me pleasantly. Bess had been my friend when she needed me, but she had not contacted me since she had been safe in Sir Walter's arms.

The hardest part of the day was saying good-bye to Margaret. As Alfonso and I prepared to leave, she hurried over to me, her arms outstretched like a bird's wings before it takes flight. I wrapped my arms around her supple waist, memorizing her smell and her touch.

"You must come visit me in Cumberland," she said. "Or let me see you. I will bring baby Anne."

"I would love that." I prayed she would keep her promise. "And I will come back to court when the queen asks for me."

She embraced me tightly, my unborn baby between us, and

kissed me on the cheek before she departed. I watched her until I could no longer make out her blue satin gown.

I felt as though I was saying good-bye to the life I once had. I was marrying Alfonso Lanier and starting a new life. It wasn't the life I wished for, but I was sure that being a lonely queen wasn't the life Elizabeth had had in mind either. I had given my dreams up for her, and she had done the same for her country. The least I could do was be grateful.

THE DARKNESS OF NIGHT swallowed us as we made our way to the house Henry had bought for us. Alfonso opened the door with his shoulder and hoisted my trunk, light with belongings, into the house. I waited a moment before I walked inside.

I could see no furniture save a wooden table in the cramped kitchen area and an old, musty chair. The walls and floor appeared to be the same washed-out gray; aside from the hearth in the far corner, where the chair sat, there did not seem to be any other color.

Alfonso grunted in the larger bedroom, and I heard the sound of my trunk hitting the floor. I thanked God that he could not touch me tonight. He wouldn't dare.

But I was wrong. As soon as I changed into my nightgown, he looked at me greedily, the way he had looked at the pile of gold Henry had given him to purchase the house.

"Do not," I said as he took hold of my shoulders. "It will hurt the baby." I said it firmly, like I was scolding a small boy.

"What is the baby to me?" he asked, gripping me tighter. He

kissed me hard. I hated it. He tasted like wine. I strained away from his grasp.

"The child is still a part of me," I said. "If you injure it in any way, I could miscarry."

His lips snarled and he walked away angry, but I had held him off. I heard some grunting in the next room, where he was making himself comfortable in the one chair we owned. He would sleep there that night, and I could only imagine what his mood would be in the morning.

I sighed with relief. Once I was sure that he would not bother me, I crawled into the bed and pulled the covers snugly around me. I blew out the candle that stood precariously on the slanted floor. Once it was completely dark, I wrapped my arms around myself. I felt worthless. I was nothing.

I had been raised a lady. I had been treated like a lady so that when I was married I would know how to act and be a good wife. But I was married to someone no greater than a simple musician. Maybe I deserved it. Perhaps this was penance for wanting William Shakespeare so badly. He was married, and still I wanted him. The thoughts that ran through my mind were not holy. They were disgraceful and sinful.

Before I could stop myself, tears were falling on my pillow. I tried to cry as silently as possible, for I did not want Alfonso to hear me. I would seem weak, and I had to be stronger than he. I had found his weakness. He could be scolded and pushed away. I would put him off for as long as possible. Eventually he would tire of it, but for now it was my saving grace, at least until the child came.

The house was not what I imagined—the spouse either. This wasn't the life I wanted, but it was the life I had.

The boy was born on January 15. The pain was unbearable. The midwife who came placed a cloth in my mouth and had an assistant hold my hand. The poor girl yelped when I squeezed. After that I held the sheets on the bed.

He was a strong, healthy baby. He had Henry's hands, but he had my darker skin and face. He almost could have passed as Alfonso's child, and I was sure that Alfonso would present it that way if needed.

I named him Henry, in honor of his real father and in spite of Alfonso. It had been a difficult choice and I thought several days on the matter, going through names while he nursed. I won't say that the name of William did not pass my mind, for it did. I considered it hard before I decided against it. There was no use in naming the child after someone I had only wished for. I would be reminded of that every time I called for the boy.

But Henry's name came back to me over and over as I looked upon the infant's face. He was so beautiful. I could not believe that his body had once been in mine. His tiny fingers looked like a doll's, and his face was straight from heaven, soft and bright. He was a quiet baby. He never cried out just to cry. There was always a reason for his complaints.

One day not long after Henry was born, I held him in our bed, smiling at him with more joy than I could contain. The room was filthy. Alfonso's clothes lay on the floor, and his boots lay strewn next to the door. Since the baby had come, I had not had the time to clean up after him. There were no windows in the room, so I had left the door open to bring in some light from other rooms in the house. I held little Henry close, feeling the beat of his heart against me like a hummingbird's wings.

Alfonso burst in, tripped over his boots, and looked at me.

"Are you going to pick those up?" He pointed to his clothes before tugging his boots on.

"They will be taken care of when you get back." I looked up from Henry to meet Alfonso's eyes.

He nodded. I suppose I had given him the proper response. He ruffled his hair and ignored the child resting in my arms. He glanced at Henry as if he were nothing more than an insect. The boy was not his. Why should he care?

I brought Henry closer to my chest. Someone needed to care for him, and it obviously was not going to be my husband.

"Will you have dinner on the table when I get back?" he asked.

"I would if we had something to cook."

He glared at me, and I realized that I had to be careful with my replies. His eyes held a warning.

"I will be back late," he sneered. "That should give you plenty of time to think of something."

He strode out the door. After I was sure he was gone, I got out of bed, my baby still in my arms. I walked as briskly as I could over to the dirty window that looked out into the street. Alfonso was walking down the street with several men from his troupe. They punched him on the shoulder and laughed. I wondered if he was going to work or if they were headed to the local tavern.

He often spent money on drink and entertainment, and I worried how long it would be before he took the funds that I received from Henry Carey each month. How could he be a father to this baby when he was a child himself?

It was around this time that I began writing again. I composed simple poems, nothing like what I had aspired to write when I was younger. They were poems for Baby Henry. I wrote of fairies and spirits, things I thought would make good bedtime stories for him when he was older. I created characters that resembled people from my own life. The fairy queen was most certainly Elizabeth, with her regal air and need for control over everyone. The character Hermia was Frances, refusing to follow what others told her to do in order to satisfy her own heart. I knew these characters as I knew the people in my own life.

Henry grew faster than I thought he would. I was surprised by how much he changed in such a short time. I had been told that children grow before our very eyes, but I had never believed that. It was true. In a month his eyes were wide, not sleepy like a newborn's. His curly dark hair and his smile made me jump inside every time I saw it.

Eventually there came a time when I had to submit and let Alfonso have his way with me. He had been bothering me each night since the baby had been born, and I was beginning to grow more and more afraid of what he would do if I kept refusing him. At first he just stormed into the other room and slept on the chair. Then he started throwing things. I had been given a new set of dishes from Lady Bess, and I heard him smash one each night I told him that I was not yet ready.

I worried for both my safety and Henry's, so one night when he stormed in after having too much to drink, I figured I must not aggravate him. I waited up for him. Henry had been put to bed, away from harm, and it was very late. I was in my nightgown, my hair down. My body had developed more fully since the baby had been born, and I was no longer the vision of a pretty young virgin. I appeared older and wiser—sadder. Time was not a friend to some.

He strode in. I watched as he disposed of some letters, throwing them into the burning fire one by one. I waited until he was done and did not bother him. In truth, it was a way to postpone the inevitable. Once his hands were empty, he turned and faced me. He gave me the expression that I had seen him wear when we were at the hunt. But now he was my husband; he could stare at me as longingly as he wanted to. However, that didn't make it any less awful.

"Am I finally allowed to have you tonight?" he asked. Perhaps he wasn't as drunk as I'd thought he was.

"You are my husband," I said, my arms crossed over my chest. "I suppose so."

"You do not want me." He spoke gruffly. He placed his hands on his hips and looked away from me. He clenched his jaw and breathed in deeply through his nose.

Was he actually hurt? His jaw grew tighter and tighter.

"What would it matter to you? I am your wife. Now I am at your disposal."

He nodded and smiled cynically.

"Finally," he said.

I WAS GLAD WHEN the queen called him back to court a few months later. I would not go with him because of the baby, but I didn't mind. I was starting to enjoy the small house. We purchased another table to put in the kitchen and some more dishes.

Alfonso sometimes came home for a few days at a time. He would be distant. He would hide in the bedroom during the day and expect only one thing at night. He only came out of the room for meals and when he was going out with his troupe. Daily actions seemed strained when he was there. I always felt like he was watching me, even when he was in another room and couldn't see me.

One day he emerged from the back room at an unusual time. His hair was disheveled, and a beard was beginning to grow on his chin. He looked like a drunk or a beggar on the street. I wondered if the ladies at court would think him so handsome now.

"Where are you going?" I asked as I put another stitch into Henry's new diaper. He was growing quickly.

"Why would you care?" He wiped a hand across his nose.

"You haven't been out since yesterday," I said.

He huffed. "It is business. Women should not ask their husbands about business." He looked disgusted, as if I were a disease that he could contract. "I'm going to the playwright, Shakespeare. He has need for some musicians for his plays. May I go now?"

I tried to ignore the feeling in my stomach.

"Yes."

He stormed out without bothering to comb his hair. He slammed the door, causing Henry to break out in a bout of tears. I went over to comfort him, my heart beating against my ribs.

William Shakespeare? I was married and yet I found I still had feelings for him. How could this be? I had thought that once I was married, these thoughts would disappear. I thought the playwright would be a distant memory. I held Henry close, rocking him back and forth before settling him into a comforting slumber.

I collapsed into a chair. He was married. I was married. I did not know him. He did not know me.

Could I really be in love?

Once again I pushed it to the back of my mind. There were things to be done. It was just an impulsive thought that had crossed my mind. I was no longer a young girl.

Henry awoke a few hours later and I made supper for one. I did not know when Alfonso would be back, but I did not want to wait for him. I began to wonder what could have kept him.

It was late when I heard a *bang* on the door. Alfonso usually just barged in, so I was surprised to see that it was indeed Alfonso, and he was with William Shakespeare. I realized that my heart had only been fluttering before. Now it was crashing inside of me. They walked inside the house. Alfonso ignored me while Shakespeare gave me a small nod.

"Lady Lanier." He smiled as if we were old friends.

"William." I nodded back at him. William Shakespeare was in my house. He was exactly the same. His eyes were so brilliant—I felt guilty looking at them.

"Ah, yes, you know my wife." Alfonso waved me on.

"I do." William Shakespeare's eyes remained on mine.

Alfonso went over to the table, sat down, and placed his feet upon it. Dirt crumbled off his boots, and I noticed a ring of sweat around the neckline of his shirt. He put his hands behind his head.

"Emilia, pour me and Will some ale and then go. We're going to talk about business."

I obediently went to the cupboard and took out a cheap cask of ale, sadly, our finest. I uncorked it as quietly as possible as I tried to hear the words that were being exchanged. They talked of business for some time, including when the bard's next play, *Titus Andronicus,* would open at the Rose.

"Will you need me there to play for you?" Alfonso asked. "I will do it for the same price."

"If you are not working somewhere else this next week, yes. Your troupe is most certainly the best I've worked with."

"All right, then," Alfonso agreed. He flicked a speck of dirt off his vest. "The queen wishes me back at court later this year," he said. He was bragging, but his behavior was still more pleasant than it would be if Shakespeare wasn't here.

"She has said that she wants me back next Twelfth Night," Shakespeare said.

"Yes, she likes your plays." Alfonso shuffled in his seat. "And I am her favorite musician. How lucky are we?"

I served the ale as Shakespeare laughed. Alfonso took a swig of his and then motioned me to our bedroom. They talked long into the night. I changed into my nightgown, kissed Henry, and crawled into bed. What were they talking about? Were they talking about me? That idea both delighted and horrified me. I only heard laughter and the clinking of glasses followed by muffled, incomprehensible words.

I heard a *bang* in the kitchen as Alfonso got out another bottle of wine. Whatever they were talking of must have been serious. I began to memorize every crack in the ceiling. There was one over on the right that looked like the river Thames...and some smaller ones coming from there that I made into streets in my mind. It was a map of London on my ceiling. It wasn't at all accurate, but it distracted me for a while and I wasn't so worried about what they were saying in the next room.

It must have been early in the morning when Shakespeare left. I heard the front door open and close, and Alfonso was now coming to bed. He entered the room, took off his pants, and slipped under the covers. He rolled over on his side, away from me. The only sound for some time was our breathing. His chest would rise when mine would fall. It was only after I was sure that he was calm that I asked him the question burning my tongue.

"Why am I not returning to the palace with you?"

I wondered if Shakespeare would be there.

He sucked in his breath.

"I do not think court is the best place for you."

"The queen has not wanted me to come back?" I asked.

My husband did not say anything.

I had wondered why she hadn't wanted me to return. I had done everything possible to fulfill her wishes. It seemed odd that after all I had agreed to, she did not wish for me to rejoin them.

"Please," I said, my voice more pleading than I would have liked, "tell me the truth."

When he did not respond, I understood. The queen *had* wanted me. I thought of the letters he burned. Had the request been in one of those invitations?

"She wished me back, didn't she?"

He grunted. I felt like slapping him. Because of his jealous nature and selfishness, I would not be able to see Margaret until the queen remembered to think of me again. It could be months or even years before I crossed her mind. My heart longed for my dearest friend. I missed her greatly.

"I have your best interests at heart." He was sneering, I could tell, even if I didn't see his face.

"If that were true, you would have let me go to court." I climbed out of bed. "Then you would be able to watch my every move."

He turned to face me. "What, and have you there with the Earl of Essex or that poet, Thomas Campion?"

"I do not care for them." My voice rose. So that's what this was all about. Jealousy.

He took my wrist and began forcing me to lie back down.

"Enough," he ordered. "Be quiet."

I had taken much from Alfonso without complaint, but the feeling of his rough hand squeezing tightly around my wrist made me want to burst into tears and lash out at him.

"I do not care for them, but I would rather be in their beds than yours," I yelled.

I felt a hard slap on my cheek, and I fell to the floor. My elbows and knees hit the wooden floor, and my side smacked into the bedside table. The room was dark, but I could make out the outline of his body. He loomed above me on the bed. My face stung in some places and I couldn't feel it in others. He hit me. He hurt me.

There were rumors of unhappy marriages at court, but I had never heard of a lady being struck. We were all ladies and had been expected to marry gentlemen. This man—no, this boy—before me was not a gentleman. He was nothing but an animal that had learned how to play the harp.

He got out of bed and picked up his pants that were still on the floor. He pulled them on, cursing. I did not know where he was going and I did not care. I hoped he would leave me. I hoped he would leave me and little Henry alone for the rest of our lives. He stomped out of the room, slamming the door.

Henry awoke, crying. I got up from the floor and held him in my arms. What were we to do? I had worried before that Alfonso might hurt me, but now it was apparent. Would he hurt Henry? I held the baby closer. I could not let that happen. Where was I to go? I couldn't go back to court without an invitation from the queen, nor could I journey back to Kent. I did not even know if the countess was still alive. A million scenarios raced through my mind, but none of them seemed like good options. Once again I had no choice. The tears erupted as I realized that my only option was to stay with Alfonso.

What use was the queen's favor now? I might have married to receive it, but now it did not matter. I could not leave, nor could I stay. I must try to be obedient or I would be risking my own skin, not to mention my son's. Henry mattered most, and I knew that I would have to bend to Alfonso's will in order to keep Henry safe.

Alfonso did not come back for the rest of the day. He was so angry when he left that I figured he wouldn't come back until his time at court was over. Months. Several months. In the next few hours, my eye grew swollen, and I went out into our small plot to pick some herbs to reduce the swelling. I poked my finger on a few thorns, drawing a shade of scarlet from my fingers. The red-and-green reminded me of the Christmas balls at court.

Henry and I spent a quiet day at the house, even though I needed to buy food from the market. I was afraid to go out. I was afraid of people's stares and glances. They would know that I had been beaten like a common housewife. It was hard to believe that not long ago I had been a lady at court, a mistress to the cousin of the queen. Alfonso came home only once before leaving for court, to gather his things. I hid in the kitchen and heard crashes coming from the bedroom as he stuffed his clothes and other belongings into a trunk. I heard the clomping of his large boots across the floor.

"Where's my harp?" he yelled.

I did not answer. I was too frightened.

There were more bangs and bumps. I wondered how he could have lost something like a harp. After a moment, he walked out of the bedroom with it in his hand and his trunk under his other arm.

He did not even say good-bye before he left. He simply stared at me, his eyebrows lowered and his lips tight. He repositioned his trunk under his arm and left without a word. I heard the door slam with a mighty crash before I let out my breath. For the time being, I was free from Alfonso.

One evening, I heard five knocks on my door. I had just finished bathing Henry in the basin in our kitchen and wrapping him in a clean rag. Once I heard the knocks on the door, I placed Henry on my hip, for he was now old enough to sit up on his own. I walked over to the door to let the stranger in.

He looked like a ghost. He was dressed in what was once a bright, white shirt and a dark leather vest. At first I thought him a spirit of a lord or duke come to haunt me, but then I realized the man was just covered in some chalky white powder. He was smiling, and he looked rather embarrassed as he brushed off the front of his doublet. William Shakespeare laughed softly when he saw my face.

"Hello, Lady Lanier."

"Master Shakespeare..."

"William."

"Very well," I agreed. "Then to you I am Emilia."

He laughed again. "All right, Emilia. I am afraid I must ask a favor of you. May I come in?"

I stepped aside and let him through. Even underneath the chalk odor I could still smell his scent, a mixture of paint and sweat. "What is it that you need?" I asked. I shifted Henry to my other side and closed the door.

"Well," he began, "I believe you can see my predicament."

"Really?" I joked. "I did not notice."

He looked at me, his eyes intense yet light and joyful. I wished they didn't amuse me so. I wished that I could just forget them and be happy with the life I had. There was a freedom in his eyes.

"There was an accident at the theatre," he explained. "It was just a small explosion."

"Forgive me for asking," I said, "but what were you...exploding?"

"I can't tell you." He smiled once again. "It is a surprise."

"For me?"

"For everyone."

I felt my cheeks burn like fire. Was I so quick to give away what I thought of him?

"What do you need?" I asked again, trying to cover the expression on my face.

"Just a wet rag to wipe my face and some of your husband's clothes."

I nodded and left him standing near the front door as I made my way into the bedroom. Alfonso's clothes were in our armoire, and I had to dig around before I found a doublet and a pair of pants that would be suitable. I put Henry in his bed and delivered the garments into William's hands.

"Thank you," He smiled. "Can I change into them here?"

"Yes," I said, motioning him to the back bedroom. "But you live in London. Why don't you go to your own home to change into your clothes and clean up?"

He paused, his smile hanging there like a crooked picture frame. I knew that there was more to that smile than he was saying. He shuffled his feet before answering.

"You live closer to the theatre, and I must be back soon."

He looked at the floor, as though he were ashamed.

I didn't question his reply, and I couldn't tell whether or not it was true. What was going on in William Shakespeare's mind? It was a task to decipher it, and I was not quite sure I was up to it. It could take me years. How many layers would I have to go through before I found the real man, the man underneath the ideas and fantasies?

He went into the bedroom while I went to the kitchen and pulled out a bottle of wine. William Shakespeare was here. Alone. With me.

I poured some wine into a wooden cup. I could hear his movements in the next room. I tried to focus on the taste in my mouth. My mind wandered to the bedroom, and the thought of him dressing made me almost swallow wrong.

The wine tasted cheap, and I wanted to spit it out, but I forced myself to swallow. Before I could stop myself, I was creeping over to the bedroom door, the cup of wine still in my hand.

I pressed an ear to the coarse wood. I could hear him muttering inside, his voice traveling out from under the door. I tried to make out words, but they were muffled. I hurried back into the kitchen, but then I heard his steps behind me.

I turned to see him holding my black, leather-covered book of writings to Henry.

"I didn't know you were a writer."

"I am not."

He leafed through the pages, stroking them softly as though they were his own.

"This looks like writing to me," he said.

"You haven't even read it," I protested. "How would you know if it is?"

His eyes returned to the little book, and they remained there for several minutes. He turned the page every so often. All of him focused on my simple story. I was so nervous I downed my glass of wine right in front of him. It was frightening to stay, but I couldn't leave. I would just have to wait until he finished.

Once he had read through it, he closed the book with a *thud*. His eyes returned to mine. I could not read their meaning, just as I never could. I never knew what he thought or felt.

"This is very good." He grinned. "Have you ever thought of publishing something? I could ask that the theater company print a quarto of this."

I laughed. "I hope you are jesting."

"No, I only jest when I am on the stage playing a part," he jested.

"It's a simple child's tale," I explained. "I wrote it for Henry."

"The simplest stories are sometimes the best," he said.

"I am a woman," I continued. "Women do not write."

He shrugged and set the book on the kitchen table. His earring caught the light from the sun coming through the window.

"They rule countries, sometimes fairly well."

I laughed louder. "Alfonso seems to have the opposite opinion. He thinks a woman is nothing but a slave. I'm sure he would have the queen off and married if he had his way."

I could not believe that I confessed my husband's ills to this man. What was I thinking? I had not even told Margaret what I thought of my husband, and now here I was confessing my deepest thoughts to this man. What must he think?

Despite what I revealed to him, his face remained the same, his brow smooth, as if he already knew. He probably did, I realized once I thought about it. Alfonso wasn't necessarily known for his kindness.

"He is your husband, not your God," he said. Suddenly his face turned very red, as if he had said too much as well.

We did nothing but look at each other. I could feel my face growing as red as his, but I could not look away. We stood there almost frozen.

Then Henry cried out, and I bustled from the room. He held out his pudgy arms to be picked up. I wrapped his blanket around him and placed him on my hip once again.

When I came back to the kitchen, William Shakespeare was at the door. He looked uncomfortable now, as if he had been exposed in some way.

"I should go back to the..." He stopped, as if he had forgotten why he was there in the first place.

"Theatre?" I finished.

He nodded quickly, and I opened the door for him. He kissed my free hand and left in a hurry. His boots slapped on the cobblestone streets of London. He left in such hurry that we had barely time to say good-bye.

He was different from anyone I had ever met. Henry Carey was so old, while Alfonso treated me badly, even if he was my husband.

When I went back into the house I thought about what Shakespeare had said. Could I write? I had always dreamed of it. Even now I still clung to that dream, hoping it could help me escape from the life I found myself in. I looked at my little notebook. He had said my story was good. Was that the truth? Either way, what could it hurt? I would write when Alfonso was gone, which was most of the time. Before, this had been simply a child's poem, but William Shakespeare encouraged me to make it into something more, and I vowed that was what I would do. I would do it for him.

AND THAT'S WHAT I did. I wrote and I wrote and I wrote until my hand cramped up, and then I wrote more. My mind filled with lovers and fairies. I was in a daze. The scratching of my quill brought back memories, and the ink smelled like an old friend. I ran my hands over the parchment, writing as small and as straight as I could so the words would look legitimate on the page. It felt good; the words flowed from my pen like water from a pitcher. I did not know if I was doing it correctly, but I did not stop to make sure. I moved Henry's cradle right next to my chair, so if he needed me I could be right there for him. He was quiet most of the time and only cried when he was hungry or lonely. Most of the time he was more my companion than my child. He would smile at me when I glanced down to make sure he was doing all right. He was six months old now, and he was beginning to outgrow his bed. I would have to ask Alfonso to build him a new one when he got back.

After I finished writing late at night, the characters and scenes still danced inside my mind. It felt so real; I lived in that world. I would pick up Henry and put him in my bed and hold him in my arms as his tiny breaths faded into sleep. My eyes stared wide open at the cracked ceiling. But my mind would be in the forest with my fairies and lovers. I did not want to leave.

I RECEIVED A LETTER from Margaret.

Emilia,

We miss you at court. Without you or Lady Bess, life here has been slow and lonely. I have Anne, but there is no one I can talk to or confide in.

I see Alfonso every now and then, his brow furrowed, going to and from the queen's chambers. She is very demanding of him and requests that he play for her and whichever courtier has taken her fancy whenever she commands.

I wish you back, and I wonder how you fare as a

married woman. Please write back soon. Your companionship is missed.

Love,

Margaret

I WAS INTERRUPTED ANOTHER day, a few months later, by five knocks on the door. William Shakespeare was back. I dressed quickly. All I had done that day was write, and I had gotten stuck at one part in my story. Henry laughed as I tripped over my skirts. Did he know about my absurd attraction? Was he laughing at my folly?

I attached the back of my dress nimbly, while he knocked his signature greeting again. I fumbled toward the door and then realized that my hair was loose around my shoulders. I opened it anyway.

"Lady Lanier." He smiled and grabbed my hand, pulling me over the threshold. The feeling of his hand in mine was familiar and just as wonderful as before, but still I could not hide my astonishment.

"What is going on?" I cried as he started to lead me down the street.

"The surprise," he said plainly. I remembered him mentioning it at our last meeting.

I quickened my step to keep up with him.

"Where are we going?" I asked.

"The theatre."

"Wait." I stopped. "Henry."

Shakespeare swore and turned around quickly. We rushed back to the house. I had left the door open, and Henry was still in his cradle, laughing. I had been so caught up in William Shakespeare holding my hand that I had completely forgotten about my own child. I placed Henry in my arms and made sure the door was firmly closed behind me before we set out once again.

"Could the child stay with someone?" Shakespeare asked. "The theatre is crowded this time of day, and I wouldn't want anything to happen to him."

He was asking me to choose between Henry and this so-called surprise. Or did he want me to decide between Henry and himself? I looked down into my son's face. I hesitated. Henry smiled naively. I bit my lip.

Finally I agreed, knowing that he was right; Henry would be overwhelmed. We went to the house next door, where I had talked to the mistress of the home over the fence. She was hanging out her laundry. I had left Henry with her before, for short periods of time, when I went to the market to buy food, fabric, or parchment and ink. She seemed pleasant. She was an older woman whose husband had passed away, and I figured there was no better person to watch Henry than she.

We knocked on her door; William's fingers played on his coat, nudging the decorative buttons and toying with the worn leather.

The elderly woman opened the door. She did not seem surprised to see me.

"Excuse me," I asked. "Do you mind watching my son?"

"For how long?" her voice croaked.

I turned to William, who stared impatiently down the street towards the theatre.

"Two, perhaps three hours," he replied, but his mind was clearly somewhere else.

"How much?" she asked, grinning. She was missing a tooth. I told her a number, and she smacked her lips and reached for the child.

Once Henry was safe in the lady's arms, she looked at Shakespeare quizzically. She must have been certain that he was not my husband. William took my hand once again and began to lead me to the theatre.

The streets were crowded, and we had to jostle our way through the throng of people headed to the Rose. I had never been this way through the city. I had only gone to the market since moving to London, and I was beginning to find the city a fascinating place. Most of the people here were peasants, and Shakespeare seemed to be right at home, navigating his way through the crowds and dodging the horses and carts. I held tightly to his hand and let him drag me, as if we were a horse and cart among the many others.

He squeezed my hand every time we came across a puddle or a horse that he needed to steer us around. I felt as if I were young again.

We passed through a narrow alley. The buildings crowded together like birds on a sill. I could hear the shouts of London as we came closer to the main street that led to the theatre. The smell of sweat and dirt and manure pervaded the air.

There were so many people. I had never seen a congregation like this, except perhaps at the Easter holiday or the Queen of Scots's beheading. This was different, however; people weren't coming here to see violence or God or the queen. They were coming to see Shakespeare.

When we finally reached the theatre, Shakespeare pulled me along toward the back. There weren't as many people there, and I was glad for the ability to stop and rest, for we hadn't slowed since we left my house. Shakespeare let go of my hand, and I missed the feeling of his fingers laced with mine. We entered through a lonely door, and when we stepped inside, I was amazed to find that we were in a dark room with a wooden ceiling above us. Light from above escaped through the slats.

"We are under the stage," William whispered. His voice caressed my ear, and I smelled his distinctive scent.

There were clunks and thuds above us as the actors and musicians walked. The scent of spiced food wafted throughout the air, and my stomach groaned. I hadn't eaten, since I had been writing all morning. I did not care. I was too engrossed in what was going on.

We reached a flight of stairs, and I followed William up them. The wooden boards creaked beneath our feet, and then we stepped out into an auditorium. The light hit my face, blinding me. I held my hand over my eyes, shielding them from the bright light until I could make out the silhouettes of objects and people. There were several hundred here. A sea of faces. They had all come to see this man's work.

The expansive stage took up most of the area; it stretched lazily out, like a dock into the ocean. High beams supported the upper level, where the elite sat. I felt as though I were in the middle of a rainbow, surrounded by the bright colors from the audience's clothes. I felt important, as if I was a duke's escort. I took a peek behind me to see the set. It was much improved, with real flowers and a vibrantly painted sun.

"Come," he said, leading me across the stage. I heard a few whistles from the pit, where the less fortunate spectators stood. I had forgotten that I had kept my hair hanging about my shoulders instead of putting it in a cap. I pulled it back with my hands and tried to make something of it, but I had nothing to tie it with. It would have to hang there, as if I were a silly virgin.

I hoped no one I knew was present, for what would happen if someone caught me like this with William Shakespeare? They could only assume the worst.

We climbed a set of wooden stairs toward the balcony, where the wealthier members of society sat. Several men recognized Shakespeare and shook his hand, congratulating him for a play that had not even started. He smiled confidently and thanked each one of them, as I was sure he had done a hundred times before. The ladies were dressed in fine silks, and I felt foolish in my simple muslin dress. I wished I had had time to prepare myself a bit more.

"Performing today, Master Shakespeare?" a man asked. He wore a thin beard and rings on his fingers. I recognized the stones that sat on top of each ring as rubies and sapphires. His blood-red doublet was trimmed in silver lining, and it matched the belt he wore around his slender waist.

"No." Shakespeare smiled. "I let Kempe have this one today."

The man turned to me. He must have thought ill, for I looked nothing like the woman next to him. She was pale, and her hair was pulled back under a cap, which only heightened her beautiful features and made them more admirable. No doubt, underneath her cap was a trail of golden hair. "Who is this lady?" the man said as he kissed my hand. "She is lovely. What is your name, dear?"

"Emilia," Shakespeare answered quickly before I could. I noticed he had hurried to hide that I was married and a Lanier.

We sat down in the seats he'd saved. I felt his elbow touch mine.

I prayed he would not move it away, and he did not. It was a whole feeling, like when you were hungry and you had your fill. It was like wanting wine and finding that the bottle you chose tasted better than you expected.

He stared straight ahead, oblivious to the feelings rushing inside me. It was easy to pretend that they weren't there; it was much harder to admit to myself that they were. The loud voices quieted when a man in costume, decorated in a page's hat and leather boots, stepped out onto the stage with a scroll in his hand. He unfurled it slowly.

"*Henry the Fourth, Part One*," he announced, his voice loud and clear as it traveled the theatre.

It was the play I had requested that Shakespeare write for Henry Carey—the precursor to the play he'd performed for us in court. I turned in my seat to see if my old master was there, but I could not see him. I looked to see if William was watching my reaction, but his eyes were focused on the sets and the actors now on the stage. He had brought me here to see it, but it was clear his mind was on his creation.

The play began in London with the ailing king and his advisor. The costumes, once so drab and shabby, were now neat and true to the time period. The painted scenes showed what Greenwich might have looked like at that time—darker, with less ornate furniture. The actors moved about, speaking their parts and creating a whole world. It seemed so real—the actual stage and theatre brought the scenes to life better than a simple canvas set had. I was soon lost in the story.

Partway through the play, I felt a set of eyes on me. I turned to meet the gaze of Shakespeare himself.

"What do you think?" he said softly.

What could I say? The first time I had seen Shakespeare's work in the queen's court, Henry Carey had asked me the same question. I began to speak but closed my mouth promptly. There were no words that could express how I felt here, watching his art, being with him.

His fingers wrapped around mine once again, and this time it wasn't because he was showing me something or leading me somewhere. He did this because he wanted to. Our breathing matched, our chests rising and falling to the same rhythm, and I could feel us drawing together.

We watched the players on the stage, but it was as if our own lives were entangled in it. I could not find where the stage started and where it ended. Who were the actors and who were the spectators? Where did William end and I begin? The lines were becoming blurred, and I was no longer certain of anything.

AFTER THE PLAY WAS over, William and I went down to the stage. Everyone who hadn't congratulated him before the play did so now, and we were swarmed with people from every class. Shakespeare treated them all with kindness. He was modest about his plays; there was always a bit of doubt in his voice when he thanked the spectators. They would tell him it was excellent, and he would nod hesitantly, as if deciding whether they were right.

"Excellent, Master Shakespeare." A man in garb nearly as fine as Essex's patted him on the back. "You must put on another soon."

"I will if I can actually get it written," William joked.

I hid farther away, nearer the edge of the stage. I did not want anyone to assume that I was more than an acquaintance. William looked back at me a few times, but I could not walk over. I let him enjoy his moment.

Some people asked who I was—mostly the dwellers of the upper classes—and he replied the same every time. I was simply Emilia. I was not a former mistress to one of the most influential men in England, not the daughter of the king's musician. I was not married to the queen's favorite harpist. I was just Emilia. It was insulting and liberating at the same time.

I froze when I thought I saw Henry Carey with his wife shuffling toward the door. I turned away. If he saw me here, I was sure to die of shame. I hid my face from the crowd trailing toward the exit. After a few moments, I peeked under my hand to see a broad back facing me. He was leading a robust woman wearing fine lace through the door. I did not know if it was Henry, but I could not have been more relieved that he did not recognize me if indeed it were he.

Once the theatre cleared out, it was just him and me—William and Emilia. We looked out onto the now-empty seats and pit where crowds had stood. The once-busy building was now quiet. I stood next to the cannon, the one that had caused William's appearance that day at my house.

"So." He smiled mischievously. He pointed to an intricately carved piece of wood. "What is this?"

I recognized the game we had played at court. It seemed so long ago. Back then, this piece of wood would have been a simple stick. Henry Carey's money had served them well.

"The scepter of England," I replied after some time. "It has been shipped from Rome by the pope for the king's coronation—a gift, if you will. The handle"—I picked up the prop—"is solid gold, and the cross on the top was a pendant on a necklace His Holiness wore around his neck. His alliance is supposed to be with France, but he would like to see the young country—and its young king—succeed."

I waited for a response from William, but I received none. He was looking at me, and just me. Usually I saw many things in his eyes, but at that moment, I saw nothing but my own reflection smiling back at me. He took a step toward me...and then a step back. Was he unsure about what he thought of me?

We waited there. What was holding him back? It was as if he were deciding whether I was worth it. Something I had done had changed his mind. What could it have been?

He shuffled his feet and looked away from me, around the theatre. He'd made his decision. I felt my heart drop as I realized that I had been expecting more, something that showed that he thought of me the same way I did him. But there was no such revelation. He smiled, but it looked painful. His eyes were once again filled with ideas and stories, and I was just a passing thought.

I tried to hide my disappointment, but I wondered how clearly he could see it. I looked at the floor of the stage, at the boards perfectly aligned.

"We must get back to Henry," I said, now that I was sure of how he felt. "He is probably lonely." I hadn't thought of my son in hours.

Shakespeare nodded and plastered a smile on his face. He took my hand once again, but this time without the warmth that I had experienced earlier. After all, I was just a friend. Not even that—the wife of a friend.

The streets weren't nearly as crowded as they had been before, and we were able to make our way home quickly. Every now and then I would look at his face, hoping to see something that would support his earlier actions, but I could find none.

When we reached my neighbor's house, he knocked on the door. Just two quick knocks, not five consistent ones. When she came to answer the door, she had Henry asleep in her arms. He looked as if he'd weathered the experience of being in someone else's care fairly well. I thanked her and offered to pay, and she held out a hand as she eyed Shakespeare suspiciously. William pulled out a coin and handed it to her. After that, he didn't seem so suspicious in her eyes.

William escorted me to my own door. I held my child close. I felt bad for leaving Henry so suddenly, but it had been a day that I would not forget. I hadn't remembered how good the sun felt on my cheeks. It was refreshing to hear applause and laughter and praise, and I loved the smells and sounds of the theater. I opened the door.

"Well." Shakespeare sighed. "Thank you for going with me to the theatre. It wouldn't have felt right without you."

I nodded in thanks. "I should be thanking you. It was magnificent."

"Beauty breeds beauty," he added simply. "It was your idea."

I felt my cheeks flush. Did he think me beautiful?

"Thank you again," I said before I entirely lost my wits.

"You are welcome, my lady," he said. He kissed my hand and began his way down the steps. My eyes followed him as he walked farther and farther away. He only looked back once.

He waved. I waved. I watched him until he was gone, but he was still in my heart long after he left.

England, 1594
During the Reign of Queen Elizabeth I
London

Alfonso returned home just before Twelfth Night. It had been a busy season for him, first at the queen's court and then, during the Christmas holiday, traveling throughout the country. Noblemen invited him to play at their homes for a few days or a week, before he packed up and left for the next estate. It had been a good year for him financially, and his stock of beer and wine increased.

It was strange, living with him again. We were tedious at first, living like those newly married. We tried not to make mistakes in front of each other and never spoke out of turn, but he still didn't apologize for hitting me, and I wondered what I should do if he did it again. It would only be a few more years before Henry would be old enough to go with him and learn his craft, and I worried about the boy's safety.

After a few days, things returned to normal and Alfonso hid in the bedroom once again, only coming out if he was meeting the troupe for a trip to the pub. I did not want to know where else he went, nor did I ask him.

William Shakespeare did not return to see me while Alfonso was in town. After the play, William had not come to see me at all. I often waited to hear his knocks on the door, but they never came.

I wondered what I had done that day to discourage him from visiting me. I spent nights sewing and mending and thinking about that wonderful and terrible day. Remembering it was like rehearsing a play inside my head. If I had done something differently, would the outcome have changed? He no longer came to the door to see me—only my husband, his business partner. I would rarely see him. They would leave together before I was able to say hello.

Days ran together while Alfonso was home, and there was no escape through writing. Alfonso would not allow it while he was there, so I did not even try. I felt as if I was letting myself and William down. The only thing that changed from day to day was Henry; he grew from a baby to a walking, talking toddler. He remained my greatest companion and joy.

"I'm going to the pub," Alfonso called on his way out one night. It was his third night in a row away from me and the baby.

I placed a spoonful of mashed peas in Henry's mouth; he was eating solid foods now.

"When will you be back?" I asked.

"Does it matter?" he grunted. He was just about to the door.

I thought for a moment. I had been thinking about asking whether I could return to court in the summer with him. He was in a relatively good mood, so I decided to make my proposition.

"No," I said. I put another spoonful in Henry's waiting mouth.

"Good." He began to walk away.

"I want to go to court this season," I said quickly, curtly.

He stared at me. It felt like it was minutes, but I'm sure it was only seconds before he spoke. His face was hard and stiff, and it appeared as unbreakable as marble.

"No," he answered. He strode away.

I heard the door close. I dropped Henry's spoon on the table and placed a hand on my forehead. I had no freedom at all. Was I to be shut away like a criminal?

The thought of spending more months alone made me cringe. Henry, my child, was my closest friend. It was both a beautiful and a desperate thing. I knew everything about him, from his smiles to his frowns to his cries of laughter to his groans of sorrow, and I loved that I knew him so well.

But I wished for Margaret and Anne. I wished for Margaret's hugs and her motherly love. I wished for Anne's laughter, and I wanted to introduce her to Henry. They would be good companions for each other. I wished for things to be the way they had been before.

I decided I would do whatever I could to return to court.

I WROTE TO MARGARET the next day.

Dear Margaret,

I find myself longing for you and Anne more than I can stand. The only people in this world who would understand me are you and my son, Henry. I wanted so badly to be happy in this new life, yet I find no joy at all. Alfonso is nothing but a spoiled child. We knew that long ago, didn't we? We knew he used others for his own benefit. I worry about you and George. I worry about Lady Bess and

Frances. I even worry about Her Majesty, though she is old enough and wise enough to take of herself.

I miss you. My friends here are Henry and the playwright, William Shakespeare. William has come over a few times when Alfonso was gone, and he treats me kindly. His kindness is a welcome relief. I find myself waiting for him. It is silly, I know. But you would understand, I think.

Perhaps the real reason I write is that Alfonso has forbidden me to go back to court this next season, even if the queen has requested my presence. I'm afraid I will never see you or Anne again. I do not think I could live with that. I will try to convince Alfonso to let me go, but I must ask that you write to me as soon as you hear of the ladies who are invited and write to me if I am one of them.

Take care, Margaret, and please write back soon. I will be waiting for your words of wisdom and your gentle manner of suggestion. If anyone can make this better for me, it is you.

Emilia

It would be days or even weeks before I heard from her, but the possibility of receiving some comfort gave me hope. I knew that once she read my woes, she would write as soon as she was able.

Alfonso would be leaving again in the spring. To be a musician was transient. Though I waited eagerly for him to go, I also found myself dreading being alone.

William Shakespeare and Alfonso were together almost every night. They would go to the pub some nights. William hardly ever spoke a word to me when he came to the door, and he and Alfonso grew closer, almost like brothers. I found it strange. Alfonso was not kind to all men, but William seemed to have a way of understanding him. It was more than I, his wife, ever could.

One time, I was convinced Shakespeare had forgotten me. He came to our house one evening to retrieve Alfonso. The air was freezing. The cold came through the walls of the house and bit my toes, even through my stockings and shoes. I wrapped Henry in a blanket and carried him close to my chest to keep him warm, pulling my cloak tighter. Even though fires had been burning in both the kitchen and the living area all day, it still wasn't warm enough to take off my cumbersome clothing.

I heard a noise outside and turned to see William's figure through the frost covering the window. He strode up to the door with determined steps that reminded me of the day we'd met at court so long ago.

"Master Shakespeare is here," I called to the back bedroom just as I heard William knocking. I placed a hand on the latch, which was cold even through the leather gloves I wore.

Alfonso emerged, pulling on a cap over his ears. He, too, wore a heavy coat and gloves.

"I don't know when I will be back," he said.

I nodded before I opened the door.

William bustled in, his arms wrapped tightly around the rest of his body. He brought a bone-chilling gust of wind with him.

"We had best hurry there," he spoke to Alfonso. "I don't plan to spend any more time in this weather than I have to."

He did not even look at me or greet me as Alfonso passed me and they left, laughing as they went. After closing the door I looked through the window, but it became hard to see them as they continued down the dark streets. How could I have ever thought that William Shakespeare might feel something for me? My heart grew colder than I thought possible as I brought Henry next to the hearth. I tried to keep my mind off my memory of that day at the theater.

On several occasions, the two men came to the house instead of the pub. Alfonso would carry in a new bottle of wine and I would get out the glasses. These were the only times I ever saw Alfonso happy. When he and Shakespeare were together, they laughed about news from court or talked business. They would speak of money, of the queen, of life in general. Most of the time I heard it through the bedroom door, but if Alfonso had had something to drink before he came home, sometimes I could sit in the chair in the far corner and listen to their conversation.

I was glad when spring arrived. We received a letter from the queen. She wanted Alfonso back at court. I was afraid to ask if I could read it, so I watched him throw it in the fire just as he had last time. It burned rapidly and became ash. I held Henry in my arms and watched my happiness go up in flames.

"The queen wants you back?" I asked tenuously.

He nodded and threw another letter into the fire.

I stood up slowly and walked Henry over to his bed. He fell asleep in my arms and went as limp as a doll. I kissed him gently, saying a short prayer, and only then did I rejoin Alfonso.

"I would like to go to court too," I said, trying to make my voice as brave as possible.

"We've already discussed this." His gruff voice almost made me back down.

"I would like to discuss it again."

He breathed in through his nose, and from the flickering light of the fire, I could see his grip tighten on a piece of paper. What was he so afraid of? Was he afraid that I would sacrifice my honor and pride to the next man I laid eyes on?

I waited for his reply. If this hadn't been such an important situation, I would have enjoyed the peacefulness of it and that we were actually getting along. The fire continued to burn, and my eyes wandered to the paper he was holding.

"That has my name on it." I reached for it.

He jerked it away. I stretched out my fingers, trying to snatch the envelope away from his hands. I couldn't reach it. He held it too far away. Who would have sent me a letter? Could it have been Margaret? Or the queen? I had wondered why I hadn't received a reply from anyone at court. I now understood what he had done.

"How many of those have you burned?" I demanded. "Tell me."

His hand gripped the paper harder. The handwriting on it was as familiar as my own. It was Margaret's. Margaret had been writing to me all along, and he had been burning those precious words of comfort that I needed. No doubt when I had given him a letter to deliver to court, he had just thrown them away as well. What if Frances had wanted to see me? What if something had happened to baby Anne?

I was angrier than I had ever been. I jumped at him, my hands shaped like claws, ready to scratch his face and hurt him like he had hurt me. He took hold of my wrists and held me as I flailed about like an animal. I was ready to kill him. I did not care if blood would be spilled. He had lied to me.

He finally pushed me down into the chair. I felt his hand collide with my nose. He slapped me repeatedly while I struggled to kick him. I could not even feel his attacks. My anger numbed them. I was too upset to care that he was hitting me over and over again. I got hold of his hand, and before I could stop myself, my teeth sank into the curve between his thumb and forefinger.

He stopped for a moment to examine his hand and breathed in angrily through his nose. Then he turned to me, more vicious than ever. He hit my face, harder, and this time the agony exploded.

Only once did I cry out in pain. My hands flew to my tender nose to protect it. Otherwise, I let him hit me. I was done fighting with him. The battle had been won, but the war was not over. He would regret this day and the actions that had caused this uproar. Blood spurted from my nose, and he gave me a look of horror. He seemed disgusted with both himself and me.

Once I knew he was done with me, I stood up and strode past him to Henry's bed. I stood in front of it, a barrier. Alfonso's eyes bore into me.

He laughed.

"It is not the baby I have a problem with. I will never touch him."

"Promise me." My voice came out cracked, and I was surprised that my words were so feeble, like I needed something from him. But maybe I did. Maybe I needed to know that I could put that fear to rest and not worry about Henry's safety.

He considered it, his brow wrinkling. Could I trust him either way? I wasn't sure. But at least I would know that I had tried to protect the boy.

Alfonso nodded. "I promise. You will never speak of this."

"Then allow me my letters. The queen should not think so highly of you if word was to get out that you beat one of her ladies."

He glared at me; he knew I was right. His status as her favorite musician would be tainted if my blood was on his hands.

"They are yours to read."

He came a week after Alfonso's departure. I rushed across our tiny house to open the door before he knocked again. Henry was deep in sleep and I didn't want to wake him. Shakespeare's eyes were on everything besides the wood of the door when I opened it.

"Is Alfonso here?"

"No, he's not. He's gone back to court," I replied.

He grinned. "That's too bad," he said and then stepped inside the door. I put a finger to my lips, signaling for him to be quiet, and motioned him in. He nodded and walked past me. I closed the door silently and turned to face him. "It appears I will have to write to him instead." But he made no move to go.

"What do you need, Master Shakespeare?" I whispered.

"So we are on introductory terms again?" He matched my pitch.

"I hardly see you anymore. I do not know if we are on friendly terms."

His eyes laughed. "I see. Once again, I am William, Lady Lanier."

"Very well. Once again, I am Emilia, William."

There was a pause. We did not speak. Finally he pointed at my nose.

"That is some lovely paint they are requiring ladies to wear nowadays. First it was just rouge."

I had forgotten about my face. Alfonso had left his mark, and it was slow to heal. I was a fair alchemist, but this had been quite a challenge.

I did not need to explain. William gently pulled out a chair and gestured for me to sit down. He went into the kitchen, where he took several herbs from their jars and placed them in a cloth, which he then wetted. I could smell lavender and sage coming from the cloth. The scents floated throughout the room.

"You are good with audiences, words, and herbs?"

"A trick I learned in Stratford-upon-Avon."

He placed the cool cloth on my sore face, holding it against my skin as softly as I would have to Henry's. The liquid seeped through the cloth and eased my aching skin and muscles.

His eyes were concentrated on mine, and I looked away shyly because of the intensity.

"This is what my mother did when I fought. She was always concerned about me. I was her only boy, so she did not know that all boys fight." He chuckled. "This heals all sorts of cuts and bruises."

"What's it like there, in Stratford?" I asked. I had never traveled past Essex or Kent, though I would have been happy to.

"It's small, mostly a farming community. Everyone knows others' business."

He smiled fondly. I wondered if he was remembering his childhood.

"Did you go to school there?"

"Yes. I was one of the few in my family who did."

This man was so honest. There was no pride in his voice

or vacillation before he said anything. It was almost as if he were merely reciting lines from one of his plays.

"Your…" I faltered. "Your wife…does she live there?"

He nodded again, and I could feel him tense. He took the cloth from my face.

"She does."

"Do you visit her often?"

"Very little, I'm afraid."

There was more silence, and I scolded myself for presenting the subject of his wife. It was obvious that he did not wish to speak of her. His mind was now clearly on something else, and I watched him look toward my book of writings on the table.

"Have you written recently?" He handed me the cloth and I put it up to my own face.

"Not since Alfonso's been home. I was just going to start when you came in."

He reached over and fingered my little book. The leather was more worn, since I had written religiously before Alfonso had come home, and he could probably see that I had made some progress. He opened it up, flipping through the pages.

"You really should think of publishing this."

"It is but a child's tale."

"Yet you keep writing."

He had me looking for an answer there. It was true that I believed that it was only a book for Henry, but perhaps I had actually absorbed his words. Maybe I secretly wished that it would be published. That was the reason I continued to spend so much time huddled over that book.

"Here"—he pointed to my tiny script—"is a perfectly charming sentence. 'It was the night of the Midsummer night's dream.' That is beautiful."

I stood up, came around behind him, and placed a hand on his shoulder, peering at the words. He held up the book and pointed at the sentence, showing me where I had written the words.

"But that's what it was," I laughed. "The story takes place Midsummer's night."

"Well, then, it's just fine. What if you used it as the title? Also, the first 'night' should be replaced. 'The twilight of a Midsummer's dream.'"

I sighed. How could I attain his skill? I thought it was a fine sentence before, but now I saw that I could not compare to his talent.

"That is entirely different." I smiled and faced him. "And much better. Now I know I should not write when I cannot think of words such as that."

"On the contrary. This is an excellent first attempt. All writers start with a draft such as this. Then they go back and revise their work. The real skill is going back and deciding what was good and should be kept and what needs to be left unsaid."

I nodded. It made sense that words could not just be plucked out of the air and placed on a page. The first task was to get them down; the second, to make them worth reading.

"Are you writing another play?" I asked, trying to make him forget about my meager attempts.

"Yes. It's simple, but I do like where it is going."

"Can you tell me about it? Or is it secret?" I gave him a coy smile.

"For you, my lady, it would be an honor," he played along,

dipping into a small bow. "It is about two forbidden lovers from two very different worlds."

There was another pause in our conversation. I scratched my palm. I stood from my seat and took the book from his hands. My hand brushed his, and I wondered if he felt the same jolt go up his arm.

The day at the play felt so long ago. That afternoon, when we were once so close, now almost seemed a day with someone else. Then, we were touching each other without shame; now, it was as if we were children just learning the lessons of love.

"That is very kind," I said. "But perhaps..."

He nodded, as though he knew what I was going to say.

"Of course. I understand. A lady and a playwright in a house with the husband gone might generate some gossip."

"I hate to waste your time when it could be so valuably put to use at the theatre."

"The theatre," he said, and I instantly shushed him. The sound of his voice was big and booming, and it echoed off the walls of the unstable house.

"The theatre," he started again, "cannot compare to being here. It's full of ugly men pretending to be someone else. A lady is a sight for a man's sore eyes," he said.

"Really?" I asked. Part of me believed him truly, but the rest was still unsure. Why was he saying this to me? The words were so beautiful, as if they were out of a sonnet or poem.

"Of course. Why would I say otherwise?"

"I don't know." I shrugged. "You spend your days creating fantasy. You make your own world on a whim. Your words may not reflect reality."

"I would never deceive a lady."

I laughed, but it came out sounding bitter. "Not all men are so kind as you."

William watched me for a moment. He ran a hand through his hair and sighed. "If you don't mind me saying so, Emilia Lanier, I think you are not being fair."

"I think you're wrong."

"Do you remember the day I first met you? You told me everyone said you looked like your cousin and I said that I read souls, not faces? Well, that's true," William explained. "And I am sure you know as well as I that every soul has both good and bad parts. You and Alfonso are as different as the sun and the moon. You are the sun, but even the sun can shine too brightly at times. He is the moon, but the moon can shine as the sun some nights."

I nodded, trying to work out what he was saying.

"So what are you, William Shakespeare? A sun or a moon?"

He laughed. "Neither. I am a simple astronomer, gazing upon the heavenly bodies as an unworthy observer."

"You are hardly unworthy."

"I have been told I am. I can only hope that I will leave my mark in the universe, but who is to say what destiny will bestow on me."

The silence that followed was almost unbearable. I felt almost as if the strength of his gaze was too strong. I could not think of anything worth saying. My eyes drifted to the object in my hands, my book of scratched-out words and phrases.

"So this play you are writing…," I asked, trying to give the conversation a slightly different tone. "What will you do with it when you are done?"

"I will tear every line apart. Come, set the book over here and I will show you." He sat down at the kitchen table and motioned for me to join him.

Hesitantly, I walked over and placed the book in front of him. He opened it up as if it were an old friend. A long, slender finger pointed to a line on the first page, where my characters announced their impending wedding.

"You have a good start for a story here. You introduce your main character right away, and from what I've read, it seems the dialogue flows well."

I nodded and winced. "But…"

He laughed. "But all writing can be improved."

We worked for several hours. He would read my composition aloud and tell me what he thought could be improved. He wasn't always kind in his criticism. Sometimes his suggestions felt like knives. But I knew he was right, and I knew that his additions could be what made my writing publishable.

"Tired?" he asked. The sun was saying its last good-bye through the windows of the house.

"No, just confused. The words never sound good enough when I write them. They only sound fine when you revise them and make them your own."

"That's because you are writing them from here." He placed his hand on my head as a priest or bishop would. "Words come from here." His hand snaked down to my chest, where he indicated my heart. It was beating wildly. Could he feel it?

He looked embarrassed for a moment, his face a dark red, and he was about to take his hand away…until I stopped him. I felt my own hands reach his and hold it against my chest. Something had overcome me. I did not care what the queen thought or what Alfonso thought or what the lady next door thought. I wanted something for me. I wanted to be selfish and delight in what I loved.

I could not help that I was attracted to William Shakespeare. I could not help that every time I heard his name I felt the feeling of butterflies' wings beating in my stomach. I could not help that every time he touched me, I felt complete. And it was wrong, I knew it was. God would not approve. The queen would not approve. But for once in my life I had made a decision of my own. It may not have been right, but it was mine. For once I had chosen to do what my heart desired. I loved William Shakespeare. I *loved* someone. Had there ever been a time when I could say that?

William's eyes grew wide at first, as if he was surprised that I would be so bold, but then they softened. And then his lips were on mine.

It was just a kiss. It was nothing more than that, but it was so beautiful and so hard to comprehend. It was like the slap of Alfonso's hand against my lips, but it felt right. Good. And I realized what I had been missing.

I kissed him back; I gave myself to the feeling of happiness sweeping over me. We kissed again and again and again.

"You love me?" I asked him.

Another kiss.

"Yes."

Another.

"When?" I demanded.

The next one was on my neck. He made his way up to my cheek. "No sooner had I looked at you than did I love."

His lips were gentle on mine, and I could not pull myself away. My mind was screaming with warnings and reasons I should not be kissing William Shakespeare, but the rest of me wanted him. I could not stop. I just tasted him.

It was only when Henry cried out that we realized what we were doing. I had been disloyal to Alfonso. Not only did I betray him, but I had done it with one of his best friends.

They were just kisses, but it was more than that.

He had said that he loved me.

I pulled away and rushed over to my baby. I was ashamed that I had ever been so bold. I had sinned. William Shakespeare thought me a whore, no doubt. But the taste of his lips was like nothing I had ever experienced, and I could only imagine what giving in to my emotions would bring.

"You?" William Shakespeare asked. "Do you love me?"

What could I say? I did. I loved him more than I thought any woman could love a man. If I said no, I would lose him. If I said yes, what would happen?

"I do, William."

With the baby now quieted and on my hip, I walked back over to him. His eyes were on mine, not where Alfonso's always went when I talked to him. Had he seen as many things in my eyes as I had in his? Had he thought me beautiful that day when I walked the halls to the banquet hall and met him for the first time?

"But this cannot be." I sighed.

Just a few moments ago we were lost in a world of our own, and now it seemed that world had evaporated. There were responsibilities and commitments that we had both made and promised to keep.

"And everything we said, everything we meant, is nothing to you. Why would you say those things to hurt me…?" He trailed off.

"I know." I took the blame for my actions. It was my fault. "And I am ashamed."

My heart continued beating like a steady drum, and I knew the truth. I wanted to be, but I was not ashamed.

"Ashamed? Do you regret loving me, Lady Lanier? Is that just it? Do you look at me and say, 'He is nothing but a playwright. He is not worthy of my love and I am ashamed to have these feelings for him'?"

"No."

"Then what? Are you too proud?"

"No…"

"Really? Because I cannot figure out why you are turning me away after leading me to think that you cared," he said. "You were a mistress to someone decades older than you; did you do the same things to him to ensure his monthly check?"

My mind spun with his words. Had being Henry Carey's mistress been wrong? I had had no choice. What else could I have done?

"Stop," I cried. "Your words hurt."

Henry began to whimper once again. I could feel his body quivering.

"You act as though you have your life—your morals—completely understood," William said. "But do you really?"

He was right. My values were blurred, more than they ever had been. I could not really know what was truthful and what was fair. How could I? Everything that once seemed perfectly reasonable had been turned around by this man.

"We cannot do this," I sputtered. "It is wrong. You spend so much time alone in that world of your imaginings…but this is not that world. This is not a play. This is real life, and we must decide what is decent and good. And this is not—"

"Is this worse than what you have? Am I, a simple playwright who loves you, worse than your husband, who beats you?"

I pulled back. My hand flew to my bruised nose. "What if Alfonso found out? What if the queen found out? I have seen what she has done, William. I have had to live my whole life by what she has dictated."

"The queen? You cannot live your life by trying to please the queen. She is not your mother, your family, or your God."

I hated him at that instant. He knew more about me than I wanted him to.

"Get out of my house."

I was hateful. I was harsh. I did not like myself when I said this, but I did mean it. His words could be beautiful, but some of them were also sharp and hurtful. Those words were more painful than Alfonso's slaps could ever be.

He glared at me with those eyes. He gave me one hard, long look. And then he was gone.

England, 1595
During the Reign of Queen Elizabeth I
London

The year turned, and I couldn't forget William. I would wake up any given morning, sure that I had done the right thing in not seeing him. It was wrong to think about him. I would break my fast, and then the first creeping of doubt would enter my mind. Had what I said been right? Perhaps I went too far. I would try to push it from my mind.

Then, in midmorning, I would think that I had been wrong. I would cry out and realize what I had done. I burned our food and spilled the wash water. Henry was in his cradle much more than he should have been while I thought about what I had done—what I should have done.

By midafternoon I was ready to travel to his home and tell him that he was right and I was wrong. I was ready to give up everything and find him. I imagined jumping into his arms and kissing him over and over again. I did not care what anyone thought of me by midafternoon.

By dinnertime, I had it all planned out. I would knock on his door the next day and speak elegant words of apology until he took me back. If he didn't, I would continue to do it every day until he did. By this time, cooking seemed pointless and I would do as little as possible, ignoring my groaning stomach and only feeding Henry when he cried out.

I would go to bed, sure of my course for the morning, and sleep soundly, for tomorrow the nightmare would be over and I would once again have William Shakespeare to myself. I would love him until the end of time, and we would always have each other.

And then the cycle would repeat.

It went on for several weeks. I could see the pattern I was living, but I couldn't change it. I didn't write. I didn't eat. I wondered if I was slowly losing my mind.

I neglected Henry during that time. I would carry out the motions of motherhood halfheartedly. I would feed him and change his diapers and rock him to sleep, but my mind was on someone else. I finally made up my mind. I was going to go to him and apologize. I could not stand to leave things on these terms. I wanted my life to be normal again The very day I planned to don my nicest dress and journey across London, I received a post.

At first I thought it might have been a letter from William, so I opened it with a haste I did not know was possible. But as I began to read, I recognized Alfonso's rough handwriting. He would be returning just after Twelfth Night. My heart dropped to my toes. My husband was coming home.

My deepest wish was that Shakespeare would come back to me—and now he would be back, but for Alfonso. The thought of having him in our home without first making amends horrified me. When Alfonso was home, I was just the wife. Now I would be the hated hag of a wife who had turned him down. How could he ever stand to look at me again? I needed to ask his forgiveness.

That day, as my hands held the small bit of paper with Alfonso's messy handwriting, I realized what I needed to do. I would only have one chance to change my circumstances, and that day, well, that was it. Before Alfonso returned home, before I became that vision in William's eyes, there was a chance to change what I had done wrong. I could give William Shakespeare—and myself—a new chance.

I placed Henry on my hip and made my way over to the widow's house next door. I thumped on it sharply.

"Do you want me to watch the child?" she asked. Her eyes judged me instantly.

"I will pay you," I replied. I handed her my baby boy—no, he was easily a child now.

"The playwright?" she nosed. "Aye, I would leave my boy and husband behind for him too."

Her words caught me off guard, and I did not know what to say to her. She was right. How could I deny that what she assumed I was doing was true? I looked away.

"How long should I keep him? Or do you know?" She was smug.

"It won't be long," I said, though there was no way of knowing. I could be turned away before I even got the opportunity to tell him that I was sorry. What if he threw me out onto the street and called me a witch? I wouldn't be surprised. I felt like one.

I thanked her and began down the crowded streets. Wagons and carts pushed by, eager to go around me, as I tried to figure what to do and where to go. The smells of the people and the animals distracted me for a moment. My stomach mocked me as I passed a stand emitting the aroma of freshly baked bread. I should have eaten that morning.

I hoped I could find my way to the theater. I cursed my forgetfulness. I had been thinking so much about how exhilarating his hand felt in mine that I did not pay attention to street names.

Eventually, after asking several people, I was pointed in the general direction of the Rose Theatre. I felt lost, but I kept on going. I even caught myself praying that I would find him. I stopped myself. Should I really be praying to be led to something that was sinful? It didn't seem proper, but I didn't know what else to do.

When I finally stepped inside the theatre, I felt more lost than I had on the streets of London. The pageantry and colors surrounded me in the form of costumes and scenes, and I found myself in a world that was not my own. I looked for something, anything, familiar. My shoes were soaked with mud, and the cold London air filled the large room. Actors and musicians paraded around, and I was confused and frustrated. Finally I approached a well-dressed gentleman.

"Sir," I said, "is William Shakespeare here?"

"Ah, you're the lady he brought here the day *Henry the Fourth, Part One* premiered." He smiled, twisting his beard with his fingers. He looked the same, an expensive ring on each finger and a polished cane in his right hand. "And why would you need him?"

He suddenly looked as suspicious as my widow neighbor. I wondered how many women had been in my position before.

"I need to find him," I simply replied.

He nodded. It amazed me to find that I did not care whether or not he admired me for what I was doing. For, surely, reconciling with a lover would be the only reason for a young lady to walk the crime-ridden streets of London alone.

"One always wants to find Shakespeare." He spoke as if he

himself had attempted it once. "If you are the one who can, then I will tell you."

"You see it too?" I asked, surprised. "I thought only I could."

He laughed and sighed at the same time, a strange but fitting sound of hopelessness.

"That is my point. I can't. But if you can..." He trailed off and it was a moment before he resumed. "Then you are no ordinary musician's wife."

So he knew. He knew who I was. I wondered if William had told him or if it was now common knowledge. I should turn back to my house, take Henry back and put him to bed, and recognize that my life was the way it was. But I couldn't do it.

"He lives not far from here, about two or three miles west and south," he answered. "Would you like me to come? It is not right for a woman to be walking by herself."

When I realized how close he lived to the theatre, I remembered the day he came to my door after the explosion. Truly, he had come to see me that day. Why else would he cross London when he lived so close?

"No. This is something that can only be accomplished by one."

"If you need me, I will be here. I am Henry Wriothesley, his benefactor, and I would be happy to assist you."

"Thank you."

"He is a good man with a good heart."

I set off in the direction he indicated. Was I the only person in this world who could feel Shakespeare's frustrations? Was I the only one that understood his pain?

I dodged around several carts and looked ahead to see where I was going. London was all around me, yet I had not even noticed. I felt as I had when I saw William Shakespeare for the first time—excitement, surprise, and anger because my emotions controlled me so greatly.

I stopped in front of the house where Henry Wriothesley had directed me. It stood solid on a narrow street. It had been well kept. There was no dirt or mud on the exterior, and dark green shutters hung on either side of his front window. The house was small but just right for one person. A second of doubt crept into my mind like a dark shadow.

My feet urged me to run back to my home, but my heart had other plans. I allowed it to take me a step closer, and another, and another, up the steps, until I waited at the looming door. My knuckles tapped the wood five times.

There was silence, and my mind raced. Did he know it was me? And if he did, was that why I heard nothing on the other side of the door? Was he gone? Had I come at the wrong moment?

Then the door opened and there he was. His eyes met mine; his hand gripped the latch tightly. His face was blank. It was as if I were looking into a mirror at myself, with my mind far, far away.

And then he started to smile.

THE MOONLIGHT POURED THROUGH the window that night like milk from a pitcher. It covered his whole chest and my face, and I could almost taste its silkiness. I had never noticed it before that night—how easy the moonlight was to taste. It was creamy, delicious.

I thought of Henry and how he would be sound asleep inside the old woman's home. He would be curled up in warm blankets—ignorant of what his mother had done.

William's bed was smaller than the one Alfonso and I shared. I was closer to him. This was the way it should be. His house was smaller than mine but better kept. There were hardly any lines on the ceiling.

I watched his breaths rise and fall and his lips quiver in deep sleep. I watched the way he always moved toward me when he rolled over; I could see his face, touch it. I noted how his hand would twitch a tiny bit. Even in his sleep, all he could think about was creating new lands and characters.

His eyes opened. He wasn't asleep after all.

"Did we ever have a choice, William?" I asked him.

He closed and opened his eyes again, still trying to wake up. I shouldn't have asked that, for I knew the answer.

"A choice of what?" He kissed my cheek, still lost in his dreams.

"A choice to wait until we knew"—the words floated from my mouth—"knew that we had found each other? The people we wanted to be with."

He observed me for a time, and then he sat up slowly and placed his head in his hands. The covers formed a soft pool around him, and it was as if I wasn't in the bed with him. He was thinking about something else.

"What about your wife?" My lips touched the painful subject like it was burning, but I felt it was fair to ask.

"Does it matter?"

"Of course it matters," I exclaimed.

He cocked his smile sideways, as though what he had to say about her could only hurt me. I knew it would, but I needed to understand. I needed to know why he never saw her...and why I was here.

"It was an accident," he said. "Anne said she loved me. I admired the idea of falling in love. I wanted to be a writer and an actor, and I wanted to know what love felt like...."

He sighed. As he ran a hand through his hair, I noticed a tear forming in his eyes. It was like a piece of glass reflecting the moonlight. I gave him a moment, and he began again.

"She became pregnant. I did the honorable thing and married her. For a while I was angry and resentful. She wanted me to stay home, become a glove maker like my father. She wanted me give up all my hopes, my dreams. I didn't."

He stopped for a moment and smoothed out the thin bedsheets with his hand. He was having difficulty telling these things to me. I wanted to say he could be finished if he wanted, but I was also curious.

"I would say I loved her. Then I would leave for the theatre and I would act so I could leave that town, so I could leave Anne. I would come home at nights, and she would tell me that I was a fool. That what I was doing was hurting her. I didn't care. She couldn't see beyond what was right in front of her," he continued. He looked at me, his small smile cocked to the side.

"When she looked into my eyes, she didn't see anything but a glover. All she saw was a man she'd tricked, a man who wasn't worth her time. One day I got an opportunity to leave Stratford, and I went to tell her, praying that she would be happy for me. I would be making more than a glove maker ever could, and that was what she worried about most—money."

I placed a hand on his shoulder. I felt the presence of his wife among us, though she was miles away.

"She glared at me. And then she said something that I will never forget. She said, 'William, God knows who you are, and God knows you are nothing more than a glove maker's son who was crude enough to put me in such a position. God knows you can pretend to be an actor, use fancy words, leave your wife, and think you are great, but you will never be anything more than what you are right now.' "

The moonlight grew sour in my mouth. I had never met Anne, but somehow I could see her standing in the corner of the room, observing and judging us.

"And?" I asked. I stood up and wrapped a blanket around me before walking over to the window. I needed some distance. I needed to hide from his wife's eyes.

There was no one outside. The streets were bathed in soft light. Only the moon looked at me, with its round, quiet face. I fingered the rough blanket with my free fingers.

"I left. I go back once in a while and stay for a week or two. Then I come back here."

"How many children do you have?" I asked.

"Three. The firstborn, Susanna, is like her mother but wiser. Then there are the twins, a boy and a girl."

"Does Anne love you now?"

He shrugged. "I could not say, but I could not really say from the beginning, either. She says she does, but words are just words. A person can say fine words and mean them, but love is not love unless it's shown."

"She probably means well. She probably wants you home."

"What about me?" His eyes darted to my face. "Maybe I want to live. Maybe I want to fall in love on purpose. She deceived me."

I sighed and pulled the blanket tighter around me. It was suddenly cold, and my body trembled.

He watched me shiver and smiled sadly at me. He patted the bed for me to rejoin him. After I sat back down, the bed sinking under my weight, he placed an arm around me, and it provided some warmth. I was sorrier than he for asking such questions, but I had needed to know.

"Are you sorry you came?" he asked, his voice lower.

I shook my head, but in reality I wasn't sure. What we had done was wrong, but just as I couldn't go back and change that day when we were alone in my house, I couldn't change what I had done now. It was there forever, like a scar, and I wasn't sure I would change it if I could.

"I love you, William."

"And I, you. Are you worried what people will say?"

I shook my head again, but I was. There was so much more to it than just love. Lovers were foolish. William and I weren't. We wanted each other, but we also understood that there were so many things at risk. The world around us judged, and I could not separate myself from that. Perhaps it was partly the way I was raised, but it was more than that. It was this desire I had. I wanted to please everyone. I wanted to please God, the queen, Margaret, and even Alfonso. I hated the widow's disapproving stares. All I knew was that I gave all that up to get what I wanted. I had William Shakespeare.

"What if we just left?" I said. "What if we went to France or Spain? I've always longed to go to France. We could run away—"

"Emilia, oh, Emilia." William chuckled sadly. He took my face between his hands and kissed me gently. "What would that accomplish?"

"I don't want to be here." A tear rolled down my face. "I want to be alone with you and get away from here. I want to see the court of France and be with you. I want to go to Spain and be with you. I'll go to Rome with you. Anywhere. Anywhere but here."

He took me in his arms and held me not like a lover, but like a brother. My tears flowed freely, and I found myself choking and sobbing. It had been some time since I had cried, and the hurt that was bottled up now released. It was not only the pain from the last few weeks that came out; it was also all that I had hidden from Alfonso during those endless days of matrimony. It was missing Margaret. It was not being who I wanted to be. It was being lonely and finally finding someone who understood me and knowing that it could never result in anything more than what we were doing right here and now.

"Would you really leave your only son in the hands of your husband? Would you leave the Countess of Cumberland? Could you actually leave the queen?"

I did not answer. I just continued to weep. His arms fit so nicely around my shoulders. His face went into my hair, and I could feel his breath on my bare skin.

"I just want to hide."

"Why?"

"I worry about when Alfonso comes home and finds out what we have done. I worry for your safety as well as my own."

"He does not need to know."

"How could he not?" I exclaimed. "The man at the theatre knew.

The lady who now holds my son in her arms knows. How could he not learn?"

"He will not harm you."

I laughed through my tears. "You don't know what he's like."

"If he touches you for what you did tonight, whether he finds it out from you or me or the lady next door, I will protect you. I promise."

He kissed my forehead, and then my eyes, and then my now-healed nose. I tried to lose myself in the touch of his skin, but I could not.

THE NEXT DAY, WE strode hand in hand around London. His hand in mine felt so different this time. Before, it had been like energy surging through my hand and into my arm. Now it was a more familiar feeling, a sort of security. We wandered through the heart of the busy city, and my steps grew heavier on the cobblestones the closer we got to my home. I did not wish to resume my life. I wanted to be able to love William all the time.

This part of London wasn't as neglected as the section where I lived. Freshly watered flowers poked their heads out of boxes by the windows. Thoroughly swept steps led the way to polished front doors. I enjoyed seeing men in vividly colored doublets and women in furs and silks getting into carriages and speaking in hushed tones. Jewels and gold winked at me from their caps, and I was reminded of life in court. William had done better than my husband.

He wrapped an arm around my waist and pointed to the

different theatres along the streets. The Curtain. The Red Lion. They were tall and proud, and brightly colored flags waved from their tops, reds and blues and greens.

"And there"—he pointed—"that is the Swan." The paint on the sides was clean and white. "She should be ready for business fairly soon."

"Will they perform one of your works there?" I admired the theatre. I could tell it was almost completed; it looked as though it had a similar structure to the Rose. I heard hammers, and the smell of hay wafted toward us as workers thatched the roof from tall ladders. They waved to William as we passed.

"Perhaps." He smiled. "If I actually finish what I am writing."

I smiled in turn. He kissed me on the cheek as we walked.

As we made it farther into the city, the sounds of horses' hooves faded into the distance. Instead of the light, timely carriages, we heard the plodding of the wooden carts. The whispering of the aristocracy turned into the shouts of vendors.

"You see?" William pointed to a dirtied, slight urchin, who snatched a roll from the baker's stand. "Does that not remind you of the fairies you write about?"

I laughed. I had never thought of it in that way before.

"And there." He pointed again to a reluctant donkey burdened with a heavy load. An impatient farmer pulled at his lead. "I see a dawdling husband whose wife only wishes him to carry more of her purchases. Seems as though it's a heavy burden, no?"

When we reached my house, we stood outside—much as I had the day before, in front of his door. He crossed his arms and stared, waiting for me to speak.

“What do we do now?” I asked.

He tapped his foot lightly.

“Wait.”

“For how long?”

“Until he leaves.”

I looked toward the door. That time would be so empty, so lonely. I was afraid I could barely stand it.

“Then,” he added, “we can be together again.”

I kissed him and patted his forearm. He stroked my hair. We both knew we couldn’t be together again until Alfonso was traveling once more.

“I love you.”

“I love you too, William.”

I gave him one last painful smile as he turned to leave me behind. I would see him again soon, only it would be with his friend, my husband. I would be nothing to him.

I went up to the widow’s door and took Henry into my arms. His soft arms curled around my neck.

“Momma go?” he asked.

I smiled. “Yes, Momma went.”

“Where?”

I closed my door behind me and placed Henry on the floor, where he stood uneasily. What should I tell the child? He was too young to understand.

“Momma went to the market.”

ALFONSO CAME HOME A few days later. He strode in with no greeting and immediately demanded a drink. I obeyed, choosing the finest glass I could find in our meager collection of dishes.

Alfonso had a dark beard now, which looked awkward on his face...almost as if he had glued it on. But he treated Henry with a kindness that surprised me. He patted his head and called him his son. If Henry was a good boy, Alfonso picked him up and placed him on his knee.

His first night back, Alfonso was in a better mood than when he left.

"Here," he said, using a tone I had never heard before. Though it was a command, he spoke it softly and gently passed me the bundle in his arms. "Take my clothes and wash them. I will need them for when the queen calls me back."

I took them from him—an obedient spouse. This was a part I played well. I had spent so many years as Henry Carey's mistress. If Alfonso noticed that my actions were not sincere, he didn't say anything. When he was home, he either spent his time hiding in the bedroom or in front of our hearth. He was quiet.

"Do you want anything?" I asked him before quitting to bed one evening.

He sat in the same chair as usual. From behind, I could see only his hands poking out from either side. He gripped the arms tightly, and his knuckles were almost white in the firelight.

"No," he replied.

I wondered what he was thinking. It was hard for me to imagine Alfonso thinking about anything, but perhaps I was wrong. Maybe William was right and there was more to him than there seemed.

Alfonso and William soon worked side by side. Alfonso played the music for the actors, while William either performed or observed. Shakespeare had invited him to work at the Rose. I couldn't help but wonder whether William had used this opportunity to see me more. I hoped he had.

One night, I had just put Henry to bed and was expecting Alfonso to come home with some members of his troupe. I cleaned the house until it was spotless and made sure that our stock of wine was full. I had swept under the table in the dining room. The oak chairs were starting to warp and were becoming rough and uncomfortable to sit on. I dusted the table and set a vase of flowers on it. The room looked much better with the wood floors swept and the cobwebs cleaned out of the corners.

I was startled that it was just Alfonso who came home. Usually he would have brought at least one person. I wondered at this strange development. Had he found out about William? Had William told him? My heart beat rapidly in my chest as I pulled out a glass for him and chose a bottle of wine. Before I could stop it from falling, another glass fell out of the cabinet and shattered on the wooden floor. I knelt down and picked up the pieces carefully so as to avoid cutting myself.

"Do you have to be so careless?" Alfonso asked.

I was silent. I couldn't see his actions, as he was behind me.

I returned to readying his drink. I was his wife. I cared for his house and did his bidding. There was no need to treat me badly. I had done nothing wrong except for—well, William.

This thought clouded my mind for a moment. My heart pounded. Did Alfonso know? Was that why he'd been so pensive these past few weeks? My palms began to sweat, and they became sticky on the glass bottle.

I took this moment to pour his wine. Alfonso looked up at me. His eyes narrowed in thought. He signaled that I had poured enough, and he picked his glass up and swirled the red liquid a few times. He took a drink and nodded, indicating it was satisfactory.

"Be more aware next time I am gone," he said. "I don't want to pay for a new set of dishes."

"Are you going back to court?" I felt brave enough to ask.

"Yes," he replied. "The queen needs entertainment to please that blasted Essex."

"Essex?" Words escaped from my lips before I could stop them.

Alfonso glared at me. I had said too much.

"Yes."

I nodded. Now I would not be allowed to speak for the rest of the night.

Poor Frances. Robert Devereux was still involved with the queen, then. The queen was obviously not worried about Frances—or the fact that he was married.

"Emilia," Alfonso suddenly said.

I looked up in surprise.

"The queen demands you return to court this season. I said you would accompany me."

My heart screamed for joy at the thought of seeing Margaret again. I had imagined our reunion many times and could not believe that my wish for the past few years was about to be granted. I wondered if the person who sat in the chair with his feet on the table was really my husband.

"And," he continued.

I should have known that there would be a price to pay.

"I am taking the boy with me on my tour next season."

I sucked in my breath. He was too young to be without his mother, but a woman was not allowed to travel with the men unless she was a gypsy. I could not send him away to live with the monster I called my husband. I did not want Henry to have the same upbringing I had as a child.

"The boy is three," I dared to whisper.

Alfonso nodded.

"I was that age when I joined my troupe. I followed my father around and did his will. That's all he would need to do."

"He is but a child. It would not be safe to have him around the wagons and horses."

"I will watch him," Alfonso growled. "He will be safe. He's the only good thing that ever came from our marriage; I will not let him be harmed."

Alfonso's words struck me with surprise. I did not know he cared so much for the child...but mayhap it would have been apparent if I'd looked hard enough. Perhaps Alfonso was right. Maybe Henry was a blessing to our marriage.

It would be an exchange. If I let him have Henry, I would be able to see Margaret again.

But Henry was too young to be traveling the English countryside with a band of animals. I worried that my sweet boy would start to resemble his adopted father.

Then William entered my mind. He would be at court, performing for Her Majesty. He would be there. I knew I could not be with

William if Alfonso would not allow me to journey back to court. And the only way I could return to court was if I gave him Henry. I felt my heart tearing in half. How could I choose between the two loves of my life?

"Henry can go with you," I finally relented.

Alfonso nodded his head approvingly, pleased. Why wouldn't he be? I was doing what was being asked of me.

"Very well," Alfonso said. "That is settled."

ONE MORNING, AS I was hanging Alfonso's laundry out on the line in the yard, I heard a soft voice whispering to me. I scanned the area. A large washtub sat by my feet. Steam rose from it. A fog hung over the sky, threatening rain. I looked behind me, searching. I was the only one there. I looked through the thicket close to the fence. The thicket almost came up over the top of the fence, separating us from the old widow's house next door.

A slender, spotted arm reached over the fence and waved a white piece of paper like a flag.

"From your playwright." I recognized the widow's voice.

I reached over the thicket. Thorns poked me through my thin muslin dress. I took the note from her.

"Thank you," I said.

I could not see her but for that long arm. I heard her scuttle back to her house and close the door. No doubt William had paid her well for her services.

I told Alfonso I was going to the market and left him alone with

Henry. I closed the door tightly behind me and shifted my basket on my arm. I was fortunate that the market was on the way to the theatre in case Alfonso was watching me. He wouldn't have any reason to think that I was doing anything out of the ordinary.

I jostled my way through the crowded London streets. The way to the theatre was more familiar, and I was able to make my way there faster and with less confusion than the last time. There were rehearsals going on that day, and actors milled around. They carried swords and wore sapphire-blue costumes. Some were drunk. There were two young men dressed up as women lounging near the back entrance and smiling at me. Their faces were powdered white, and they had rolled their dresses up to their knees. One of them had a wig on the side of his head, as though he had forgotten it was there.

"Look at that one." The smaller one poked the bigger one in the ribs. "Aren't you a dandy?" This time he addressed me.

I ignored him as I tried to pull open the door that led underneath the stage by grasping the door handle tightly. It was locked.

"Oh, come on, sweet," he droned. "Give us a smile, why don't you?"

I remembered what William said about being in the theatre all the time and wanting to see a woman every now and then. Those men must have suffered the same predicament.

I continued to look the other way. I banged on the door. When I realized no one was going to open it, I turned around to make my way to the bustling front entrance. The men eyed me greedily.

"Do you know where William Shakespeare is?"

They laughed.

"The Bard? What do you want with him?" the larger one asked.

"I need to talk to him," I said sharply. I didn't like the way they were making a jest of him.

"I'm surprised he took a mistress. He used to be all about honor, even when women were throwing themselves at him. Didn't even look at them, and there were some pretty ones in the bunch too."

"I'm not his—" I stopped myself. Was I? Did I want to be a mistress again?

The small one raised his eyebrows drunkenly.

"You're not? Want to be mine?"

"Do you know where he is?"

"Haven't seen him. Last I saw him was…" He counted on his fingers. "Three days ago."

I didn't even bother to thank them. I made my way to the front of the theatre and tried to push through the crowd of actors, set builders, and musicians. I needed to get in. Even if what the two drunkards said was true, that he wasn't there, I would have to see it myself to believe it.

Did I have so little faith in my lover? He had called me here. Why would he not keep his word? The inside of the theatre was as busy as the outside. Though there were many people there, I did not recognize any of them. If William was there, why would he make me struggle to find him?

I saw a familiar face and rushed to him. It was Wriothesley, the man who had directed me to William once before. I remembered his condescending expression and I wished not to speak to him, but if anyone knew where William might be, it would be him.

"Ah." He smiled. "The lady once more. Wondering where he is?"

I nodded.

"You are in luck this time." He pointed up to the balcony.

My eyes followed his finger until I could make out William's shape. His own eyes were on me. He waited for me there.

"Thank you." I smiled. "I am afraid to find how many more times I might ask you where he is."

Wriothesley sighed softly, his pointed beard protruding sharply. "We all ask that question. How many more times will we be able to find William Shakespeare?"

I found myself apprehensive at that chilly parting. Did he know something about William that I did not? I flew up the stairs to the balcony and found that William and I were alone. It was as if we were separated from the world; only the voices of the people below us followed us into our own place.

"It's beautiful, isn't it?" he asked, looking out onto the empty stage. The actors and musicians had made their way off the structure, their rehearsal done for the day. "It's a new start. A clean beginning. Each time, you make something new, something much better than what you had before."

I glanced at the wooden stage, noting that, as usual, he was right. It was beautiful—not because there was anything to look at, but because there was nothing.

"Is that what you want?" I said, and my voice echoed in the empty balcony. I was surprised how quiet it was up there. "Do you want to start over—pretend like what we did never happened?"

But his face told me I needn't worry. His reference had nothing to do with me.

"I want to start anew," he answered, his eyes still turned from mine. "I want to start my life over with you. I want you by my side.

You are the closest anyone has ever come to…" He paused before he continued. He opened and closed his mouth several times, as if he was trying to catch the words in his mouth, trying to find the right expression to use.

"Understanding."

He finally looked at me as I said this and gave me an astonished glance, as if what I had said was exactly what he wanted to hear. Then it grew resentful, as if I knew what he was going to say too well.

"Are you mad at me?" I asked.

"No."

"Why?" I asked. He spoke to me so brusquely that I couldn't help but wonder if he was lying.

He shook his head. Placing his elbows on his knees to support himself, he looked down at the floor of the balcony.

"Because I love you. But I do want you to consider something."

I strode over to him, my dress, the simple muslin one, moving with me. I sat down slowly.

"Yes?"

"I wish you would consider leaving Alfonso."

I was amazed that he would even suggest it.

"No."

"I knew you would say that. Even though I have already left Anne?"

He knew me too well, and I feared that fact. He also knew it was impossible. A scandal like this was for queens and kings. They had a divine right. God looked with favor on whatever they did. A musician's daughter, on the other hand, could not count on that.

"I don't think the Church would forgive it," I said.

"You worry so much about God?" William wondered.

"Yes, I do."

"Then why did you come to me? Why are you here? Do think leaving him would be worse than what we have already done?"

I didn't know. I could not answer him. He was right. This was clearly a sin, but so was adultery. I had already gone against what I believed was right. It was unjust that the queen and Henry Carey could dabble in affairs without repercussions while William and I were forbidden to see each other. But that didn't change anything for me.

"A sin is a sin, William."

"So you believe what we have done is a sin?"

"Yes."

"Then why did you do it?"

Again, another question I could not answer. I hated how easily he made his point while I struggled to make mine. I bit my lip as I thought of something I could say.

"I don't know. I pray God will forgive me."

"Marrying Alfonso was the sin, Emilia. Is it worse for you to love me or hate him? Perhaps the real sin is that you were never given any choices in your life." William's forehead wrinkled. "What does your God really want?"

"Is not your God the same as my own?" I turned in the hard wooden chair.

He sighed a deep, long, painful breath, which about tore my heart in two. "For understanding me so well, you sometimes do not understand me at all. Your God...do you think He wants you to be trapped in this marriage? Alfonso hits you...."

It was no longer just about how much we loved and admired

each other. There were now things we didn't agree on, didn't see the same.

"My God is the same," he said. "I call Him by the same name and worship Him in almost the same way." He looked away for a moment, as though he was trying to think of the most delicate way to say what was on his mind. "But I do not believe that a God who created man in His own image would condemn him for doing what he believes is right."

I thought for a moment before I asked him a question.

"You think what we have done was right?" I grasped the arms of the chair with my hands. I couldn't look at him. I was afraid of his answer.

"Did you feel it was wrong?"

"The Bible—," I began to argue with him once again.

"Words, Emilia. It's just words. Do words make things real? You would know."

"What are we going to do?"

"I do not know."

I suddenly wanted to be held by him. I turned in my seat and reached for him. He opened his arms and held me close to his chest. Whether his God was right or mine, or whether they were the same, I required William's strong arms and his steady breathing.

"What are we going to do?"

He chuckled, the breath from his nose moving my hair slightly.

"Do we have to decide?"

I nodded, my face moving up and down his chest. How much longer could I stay there?

"It's the only thing I have control over anymore. What are we going to do?" I asked again.

"I love you."

"I love you," I said, my question unanswered.

WHEN WE RETURNED TO court, Margaret was the first to greet me. Alfonso had hired a carriage to take our things from London to Whitehall. As we passed through the imposing gates of the palace, I could not help but feel as though I was returning home.

The sky was a dark gray color, and it stretched from one end of the heavens to the other. I could hear soft droplets of rain on the roof of the carriage, but it was not raining hard enough that we would get wet. I pulled Henry's cap farther down on his head and wrapped my arms around his middle. The wheels rattled as they came off the dirt roads and onto the cobblestone entrance of the palace.

I saw Margaret's form as we pulled up to the stable doors. She waved and rushed toward the carriage, quickly opening the door for me. We were at once in an embrace. She looked wonderful, her frame as slim as I had ever seen it and her smile wide. She was older, and she looked it, but it became her. She had always been so maternal that she wore it well.

Alfonso did not even greet her. He grunted and placed one of my few bags of clothing on his shoulders before carrying it into the palace. Henry followed him on wobbly toddler legs, eager to help his supposed father with the men's work. I excused my husband's bad manners and immediately asked how little Anne was doing.

"She is well. Four years old already."

My mouth gaped open. "The time does fly. She is already a woman."

Margaret laughed her jolly laugh, which was as familiar as my own.

"And the queen?" I asked.

Margaret's face fell, and I suddenly knew what plagued Her Majesty.

"Essex?"

Margaret sighed, her hands dropping to her side. Even I, who had been away from court for a number of years, had heard of the queen's affairs with Essex. The earl was married and had several children with Frances but was still by the queen's side. My hands went cold as I realized that my situation was not as different from the queen's as I wished it was.

"And Frances?" I asked.

"Lonely. Away. She's still not speaking to me on the rare occasions she is here; I have received no letters."

"Her stubbornness will be the death of her."

"Yes, I pray that won't be the case."

We made our way into the palace of Whitehall, the queen's favorite residence and the place where she spent the most time as she got older and frailer. Not much had changed since my departure, but I liked that. It felt comfortable. Whitehall was decorated better than Greenwich, and the grounds and gardens were better kept in the summer. I liked the cleanliness of the ladies' chambers, and its footprint was better suited to the size of court Elizabeth kept.

"Little Henry..." Margaret pointed to my child, who was holding a small bundle of our things to help his father. "He's adorable."

"He's a good boy," I said.

"He follows Alfonso around. He seems fond of him."

"Alfonso treats him much better than he treats me," I said in a whisper.

We let them get ahead a bit more so we could talk privately. Still, I wondered if my husband listened to our words as I had his and William's.

"Are you all right?" Margaret asked. "Does he not treat you kindly?"

I refused to nod or even look at her then, but it only gave her all the more reason to suspect. Her eyes were sharp and she raised her eyebrow as she always had before.

"Emilia," she said. She glared at me in frustration.

"I am fine," I answered. "I can take care of myself."

She sighed deeply, her brown eyes beginning to water. It must have been difficult for her to hear.

"He is not around much." I shrugged, trying to justify it, though I did not have a reason to.

She wrapped her arms around my shoulders and squeezed me slightly. She cared for not just my happiness but also my safety, and that meant much to me.

"But he is good to you besides that?"

I laughed. "I suppose. I have never had another husband to compare him to."

She chuckled in turn, observing me carefully. "You are different—changed, somehow. You look wiser, and your words have substance behind them."

"I am wiser, though I don't know if for the better."

"Becoming wiser is always for the better, no matter what lesson there is to learn."

I smiled. "You sound like—" I stopped. I couldn't mention

William so soon. Margaret would suspect instantly, and I was not ready to explain my position to her. Not yet, if ever.

"Emilia," Alfonso called at that exact moment. For once I was glad that my husband ordered me around so. We had lingered too far back.

"At least he called me by name this time." I smiled and gave Margaret one last hug before we parted. We promised to meet soon, for we would not be staying in the same chambers as before. I would be with my husband, and she would be with the queen, as always. I wondered if she would ever be free to live her own life.

I caught up to Alfonso and we navigated our way through the passages. Little Henry held my hand and kept close, his childish face taking in his new surroundings. He was so young. I refused to believe that he was ready to become a musician's apprentice. He would be four when Alfonso set off on his travels, but four years old was barely past a baby.

When we reached our tiny apartment, which was even smaller than the house in London, Alfonso started the fire and began to warm it up. Though it was early spring, it was damp, and the fire felt nice on my skin.

I patted the bed and dust flew up. These were most definitely the chambers of a musician and not those of a queen's lady. The tiny room seemed cramped with furniture. Alfonso had to move a chair to make room for our trunk, but there was a desk for writing, which would be useful in filling my time when Alfonso was performing. A window looked out onto the courtyard, as well. I could watch the members of court from there. There were no unnecessary commodities. I was no longer in the position I was before, but the more

I glanced around the chamber, the more I liked it. The room had all I needed, and I was content. The only thing I was missing was William at my side.

"Get dressed," Alfonso barked, eyeing my tattered wardrobe. He stood up from the hearth and walked two steps to the door. "And meet me in the Great Hall."

"But we have just settled in. I need a moment to unpack my belongings."

"I am not the queen's favorite musician because of my tardiness." He stepped forward again, grabbed my wrist, and tightened his grip enough that I could not pull it away.

I didn't have the heart to tell him that the dress I was wearing was the nicest one I owned. I didn't need to have fine clothes when I was at home all the time in London. Court was different.

Once Alfonso left, slamming the door behind him, Henry and I sat alone in the room and I evaluated my miserable dress. The edges of the sleeves were starting to fray. I no longer needed to attract a husband, but members of Queen Elizabeth's court were supposed to be far from average. We were the leaders, the important royalty of England. Our job was to make the queen look glorious.

I changed my dress and unpacked my sewing needles, remembering that the needles were a gift from Frances so long ago, and saw to what repairs I could make in a few minutes.

I had noticed that Margaret's sleeves on her elegant dress weren't as tight as mine were, so I began to loosen them. Henry came and sat with me on the bed, watching as I tore the seams out. He was whimpering, and I knew he needed comforting.

"How's my boy?" I asked and kissed him on top of the head.

He touched my wrist where Alfonso had grabbed it. "Daddy hurt you?"

My heart dropped suddenly. I knew he would eventually ask this question, but I wasn't quite ready to answer him. Could he understand at so young an age?

"Your father and I disagree."

He bobbed his tiny head. His curls bounced.

"William..." He struggled as all children do when trying to find words. He wrung his right hand in his left and furrowed his brow. "William doesn't disagree with you."

The child saw more than I had given him credit for. What would I say about William? If the boy knew how William and I spoke to each other...

"But he's a friend," I said. "Friends only disagree sometimes. And not all parents disagree."

"Then why do you?"

Why did we disagree? It was a good question, but I could not answer. "It is very hard to explain, darling."

He stuck out his little chest. "I would understand."

Could he possibly? I didn't know if I could even comprehend it myself. I had underestimated Henry's intelligence, but I did not want to burden him with problems at a young age.

"When you are older," I promised.

He asked no more questions and stared at the wall. I was not his friend if I did not give him the information he craved.

I pulled and tugged at the dress, trying to rid it of old, yellowed lace. I would make a hundred stitches and pull out half of them. When I realized the dress was as good as it could be, I gathered my needles and put them away and then brushed the top of Henry's head, fingering his curls and breathing in his faint baby smell.

"Come on, dear," I said. "You will get to see your first feast at court. Won't that be exciting?"

WILLIAM WOULD COME TO court in the next few weeks. I waited eagerly for his return. I worried that he had run into problems with his newest play and that those problems would delay his coming.

I met Margaret in the garden later that week. She brought Anne, who had grown much and shyly poked her head out behind her mother's skirts and watched Henry. He acted as though he had never seen another child in his life. He stared at her, his eyes wide, and I could only imagine how much more nervous it made the poor girl.

Eventually we weaned them off us and encouraged them to play in the courtyard where we could see them. They ran in circles in the spring grass and laughed at each other.

Flowers emerged from the cold ground, and the stone bench was cool through my dress. It was not quite yet the full bloom of spring, but the sun peeked at us through some clouds, and I smiled as it warmed my cheeks.

Margaret and I watched the children for a while, laughing when needed and scolding when required. It reminded me very much of a play; we were the actors, reciting what we were supposed to, acting on cue.

"How is George?" I asked her.

"Fine," Margaret answered. "The child helps some. He wants a boy, though. Has Alfonso implied anything of that sort?"

I shook my head.

"No, I think he is willing to accept Henry as his own. I don't know if I would be able to bear another child. It took me so long to become pregnant last time. I am happy with one."

"I am content with a single child as well, but men will be men. They always expect more. Anne, watch your dress," Margaret cried.

Anne looked up from the muddy patch she'd stepped into and shot a worried look at the fabric.

Margaret paused. Her face was pensive, as if she was thinking carefully about something before she asked me.

"Have you heard about the playwright?" she finally said.

"Which one?" I tried to keep my face composed as Henry brushed off Anne's front gently.

"Shakespeare."

I stopped smiling quickly and turned to her. The expression on her face reminded of me when William talked of writing a play for Henry Carey. Her grin indicated that she couldn't wait to share the news biting at her tongue.

"What gossip is there about him?"

She spoke carefully. "There are rumors he has taken a mistress."

My jaw dropped. News had reached court so soon? Did anyone know who she was? Did Margaret know? Or the queen?

"Who…," I stuttered. "Who is it?"

"I don't know. No one does. The lady has been seen at the Rose Theatre several times with him. Besides that, she seems to be a mystery."

Margaret shook her head. "Strange, isn't it? You look so surprised." Her eyes bore into mine.

"I am," I choked out. "Could it not be his wife?"

"Oh, Emilia," Margaret said dearly. "You still think the best of everyone. His wife is much older than the lady he's been seeing. It is definitely not."

"What does the queen think?"

"I don't know if she's heard. I imagine her reaction will depend on her feelings toward the playwright. There are those who have said that since he hasn't been in court for some time, she has tired of him. Others say she fancies him. If the latter is the case, the woman had better be careful." She watched me closely.

If the queen didn't know yet, then I was safe—at least for a little while longer. "Come to think of it, I am shocked you didn't already know," Margaret continued. "Isn't your husband close to Shakespeare?"

"Yes, he is." I answered carefully, letting the words roll slowly off my tongue. "They often go to the pub, though. I do not see him frequently."

It was true; they did often go to the pub...but I also saw William in my own home, at the theatre, in his bed.

"A few years ago a playwright wouldn't dare to take a mistress, but Shakespeare is well-known. The queen is fond of his work, though she is not as entertained by his histories. She loves his work when it is something she does not already know about."

I clenched my teeth.

"A writer should be able to freely express what he wishes," I said. "If William Shakespeare wishes to write about the histories, then he should."

Margaret raised an eyebrow and nodded. "He is a playwright, Emilia. Nothing more."

"He is not," I said. "He is more than a playwright. He is a genius."

"For spending very little time with him, you are quite protective."

"For knowing very little of him, you are quick to judge."

There was an uncomfortable silence as we mused on what the other had said. I had gone too far in defending William, and Margaret saw it. I was not thinking clearly. I felt tangled inside. I did not want William to tear me away from everything I knew. He distanced me from my son, and now he was tearing me from my friend too.

"I am she," I finally resigned.

"What?"

"I am his mistress."

Her brow smoothed and her face showed empathy, hurt for not having told her earlier, and, the most unexpected, admiration.

"I love him."

"Oh, Emilia." She shook her head sadly. "What have you gotten yourself into?"

"'What a terrible trap I have fallen into.'" I quoted what she had said to Frances when she had fallen in love with the Earl of Essex so many years ago.

"Are you sure you are in love with him?"

I laughed, though the situation hardly called for it.

"I may have never experienced love when I was younger, but I know now."

"And Alfonso?"

"Does not know."

Margaret placed a hand to her head, as if to steady her mind.

"You are the last person I would expect this of." Margaret had had to deal with this with Frances and then Lady Bess and now me. I could see that she did not approve. Even I did not know if I approved of my actions.

"For how long?"

"Only a few months."

"And what if the queen discovers this?"

I did not know. Truly, I did not think the queen would be as upset as she was with Frances or Lady Bess, but I had no way to know. William was one of her favorites, and she did not like it when ladies whom she arranged marriages for had affairs. She was the only one who could decide who they loved.

"Emilia?"

"Yes?"

"Why William Shakespeare?"

I thought for a second on her question. A breeze rustled the lace on my dress. Henry and Anne chased each other in circles on the grass in front of us, laughing at their game.

When my answer came, it did not come from my head. It came from my heart.

"I see things in him. I understand him when no one else does. He often doesn't seem to be completely in this world, but that's because he's not. He is in his own world, creating beautiful characters, settings, and stories. I can't see what he sees and I cannot hope to take his attention from them. But every once in a while, I see just me in those eyes. Not fairies, kings, ships, or witches. Just me. I am all he sees. In that moment, I am the most beautiful woman in the world."

Margaret sighed.

"Is it worth the risk, though?"

"Have you ever been in love?" I asked. "I have seen you. You and George would dance and laugh at the balls like there were no other couples in the room. You were once in love with him, Margaret. I saw it."

"That was long ago."

"But surely you haven't forgotten," I protested.

She was silent for some time, fingering her wedding ring.

"No, I haven't forgotten," she said. "But I have learned better. What has love given me? George has not loved me since he has known I cannot bear him any more children. I once wanted to be free from the queen, and now I dread the day when I will have to leave her side and be with him all the time. In my prison, I am free."

I knew she was right in some way. Love was often not what it seemed, and so many times it ended badly. In William's case and mine the only way it could end was badly—yet I could not force myself from him.

"I have never been in love before. When I was here, all I had was Henry Carey. I was not allowed to fall in love with anyone but him, and forgive me, but what kind of man would do those things to a young girl? A child? Forgive me if I can't love the husband who beats me. Forgive me if I have fallen in love with the wrong person. But William loves me for who I am. No one has ever cared for me in that way."

"I admire you for who you are, Emilia."

I looked into her eyes. They held genuine concern, and her

expression was soft and sad. She had seen so many do what I had done, and now she was to watch me, her best friend, fight the same battle as Lady Bess and Frances. There was so much to lose in this fight. I could lose the money I received from the baron, my position in court, my son, my best friend, my soul. William could lose everything as well. William could lose the support the queen had given him. He would have to start his company over again, this time without money or the queen's adoration.

Could I really ruin William's life as well as my own?

The children began to pick flowers from the queen's flowerbed, and we were quick to scold them. It broke the tension of the conversation. The children were getting along well. Anne was slimming down into a child, while Henry's baby fat clung to his little bones. She watched him with exquisite, round eyes. There was no doubt she would be a beauty.

"Do you think less of me?" I asked.

"No," she said. "I understand why you chose this. I just can't understand why reason hasn't gotten hold of you yet. I understand why you would be his mistress, but I can't understand how you could be in love."

"That's the reason I am his mistress."

"I suppose." She shook her head. "Oh, what *will* the queen think?"

I refused to look at her face, choosing instead to look at the bed of flowers next to me.

"Would the playwright understand if you ignored him when he is here?"

I shrugged my shoulders. They seemed heavier than usual. "I suppose he would."

"He will have to understand. He must realize the danger in his being here. It would not be safe to have him publicly courting you."

I wondered if I could stand being so close to him and not acknowledging him. What if I had never agreed to marrying Alfonso and William had courted me? Of course, he would still be married, but his wife was so far away.... Would it really be different?

Loving him had changed everything around us. "Maybe it should end. Maybe it is not worth it," I said very slowly.

Margaret looked at me, surprised. "I thought you loved him."

"I do."

Margaret's eyes drifted to the children, who were now lying on the ground in exhaustion from their game. I could see her thinking, her fingers laced together.

"The queen," she began, "once loved someone with the passion you have for Shakespeare. But she gave him up for the same reasons you face. It was dangerous to love Robert Dudley. He was married; she was young and claimed to be a virgin. They were a beautiful couple. It was a shame how it ended."

I nodded. Everyone knew about the death of Robert Dudley's wife. She was found at the bottom of a staircase, dead. Was it an accident? Or had the queen, in one of her infamous jealous rages, ordered the girl to be killed?

"You need to think about the consequences of what you are doing. Use your head instead of your heart. I have seen so many follow their hearts and fall to ruin. Frances, Lady Bess..."

"It is not the same thing," I argued.

"Is it not?" she said. "Do you really think that love is different for every person?"

I opened my mouth to speak, but I could not verbalize any words. I had no argument. I had seen as well as Margaret what happened to my friends.

A pang of guilt went through my chest. Was I making a mistake, loving William? And could I say good-bye to William when he was all I had to live for?

England, 1596
During the Reign of Queen Elizabeth I
Greenwich Court

Alfonso decided he would leave court right after the New Year's celebrations. The Christmas celebrations at the queen's court would be over, and there were many dukes and earls who wished to hear music through the long winter months. I hated that Henry would be away from me. He was young, and I feared for his life among the other musicians in the troupe, but Alfonso had shown himself to be a good father despite what he had done to me as a husband. I had given him my word, and I vowed to keep it.

One evening, just before Alfonso was to leave, our family walked to the Great Hall. Alfonso held little Henry's hand. Henry had to run to keep up with his adopted father's long strides. The halls were empty except for the few servants hanging holly on the walls; everyone had already made their way to the Christmas feast. I had to convince Henry to wear his scratchy new clothing. I followed behind the two, surprised at Alfonso's care. He would stop every so often to let the boy catch his breath and then urge him on with a steady, kind voice.

We were almost at the large double doors when Henry Carey appeared from the opposite direction. He hurried along, his cane tapping the wood floor in a rhythmic beat. He seemed to be deep in thought, his head lowered. He stared at the patch of ground just in front of him, carefully watching where he was to step next. When he came to us, Alfonso moved to the side and granted him room to pass. I could feel my palms begin to sweat, and I lowered my eyes too.

"Good evening, Baron Hunsdon," Alfonso and I spoke at the same time. Alfonso greeted him clearly. My words were more muffled.

The baron looked up.

"Master Lanier." He seemed surprised. "It's been awhile since I have seen you at court. How do you fare?"

"Well, thank you," Alfonso grunted. "You remember my wife, Emilia?"

Henry Carey's eyes drifted to me. He had looked frail before, but now he looked deathly. His eyes had sunken deeply into his face, and the top of his head was completely bald, dotted with spots of age. I noticed he had not lost his love for dressing finely; he wore a heavy mink coat over a handsome blue doublet. He leaned over his cane, his shoulders hunched.

"How could I forget?" He chuckled, but it sounded more like a cough. "As lovely as ever."

I offered him my hand, which he kissed. I found the old feelings of disgust surfacing as he drooled on my hand.

Then he noticed little Henry, clinging to Alfonso's leg.

"And who is this strapping lad?" he asked, and for a moment, it seemed as though he really did not know. His narrow eyebrows lowered as he glared at the boy. I felt terrible for the child. I could not imagine anything more frightening.

"This is…," Alfonso began. His mouth hung open. I realized how difficult it must be for him to say his name.

"Henry," I finished. "His name is Henry."

At this, the old man's mouth fell open. He looked over to me and then to Henry, waiting for me to confirm the truth. I nodded at him.

"Well, a handsome boy he is." He bent as low as he could with his ancient back and tried to look little Henry in the eye. "You must take good care of your mother and father, you hear?"

Henry eagerly bobbed his head. His curls bounced around his eyes and ears.

"Good," the Baron said. "I think I shall excuse myself for the evening. It was a pleasure to see you once again, Master Lanier, Lady Lanier."

He smiled at me one last time before turning away and starting down the hall. I watched him walk farther and farther away. His cane continued to make that steady beat. I wondered what thoughts were swimming in his head as he walked away from us. From me, his former mistress. From his son.

Henry took Alfonso's hand once again, and we resumed our walk to the Great Hall. It was quiet for a moment before Henry looked up at his adopted father.

"Who was that man?" he asked.

I looked to Alfonso. What would he say? I saw him squeeze the little boy's hand, but he did not glance at him.

"No one that concerns you, Henry."

I STOOD BY THE entrance to Greenwich to say good-bye to my husband and son. The cold winter air bit me with a savageness that made this good-bye even more melancholy. Bare tree limbs stretched over us like unfulfilled lovers reaching to be held. I had been at court for almost a year.

Alfonso packed the top of the caravan, which would hold him and my baby boy for several months. It was painted a bright red, the color of blood when it first spills forth. The color contrasted with the dirty snow on the ground. The other musicians leaned against the carriage, arms crossed and eyes clear. That would only last until they made it to the first inn, where they would rest for the night.

I hugged Henry for the last time and handed him to Alfonso. I felt part of me go with him. He was my reason for living.

He looked so proud to be in his father's arms. He beamed at me and tightened his grip on his father's shirt. When he smiled, there was no doubt whose son he was. The boy's face was an exact copy of his real father's.

Alfonso didn't notice my saddened look as I said good-bye. He was distracted by Henry's surprisingly strong grip and gently tried to loosen the child's fingers. He spoke to him in a calming voice, his dark fingers wrapped around Henry's tiny ones. It was so different from the attitude he had taken from the very beginning of our marriage. I was not complaining. In fact, I felt quite the opposite. I was glad that he had taken such a kind interest toward him. Perhaps there was hope for our little family yet.

"Take care, darling." I kissed my baby on his soft cheek. He puckered his tiny lips and kissed me too.

"I will, Mother."

"You will see your mother soon," Alfonso promised. He shifted the child so he could address me.

"If he needs anything, I will write."

"Thank you," I said.

He wore a blank expression for a moment and then leaned

closer to me. For a second I thought he might kiss me on the cheek as Henry had. He was so close I could smell his breath.

But then he backed away and stared at the ground. I thought I detected a blush creeping up his neck, but it might only have been my imagination.

"Emilia," he said, "take care."

"I will," I agreed.

He then turned away, his back to me as he made his way over to the cart. I watched as the caravan set off, Alfonso on foot with Henry on his broad shoulders, and I couldn't help but mutter a silent prayer and grasp the small cross I wore around my neck. Henry shifted his weight so he could see me, his smile as wide as ever. He waved his small hand at me.

"Good-bye," I whispered to myself.

My son was gone. I prayed that no misfortune would come to him or even his father while he was in Alfonso's care.

The English snow was as white as lace, and I could hardly keep from bending down and taking it into my hands. I wanted to feel the cold wetness sink into my gloves, burn my skin with ice.

I made my way inside, intent on going to our now-empty rooms. Several lords and ladies whispered to each other as I passed by. When I got back to my chambers, I found a letter under the door. On it was Margaret's handwriting, and I opened it hastily.

Emilia,

Come meet me tomorrow. The queen does not seem to know of your situation, but I have heard that William Shakespeare is back at court. Remain as much out of view from the queen as possible, and please don't do something you will regret later.

Margaret

I placed the letter on the small desk. I knew I should burn it to keep suspicion away, but I was distracted by breathing sighs of relief.

William was back. How long had he been at court? How had I not known? I wondered why he had not written to me to tell me of his arrival. Was William having doubts as well?

But then I thought about the way his skin felt on mine. The way his eyes knew me more than I knew my own self and how I could not survive without the touch of his lips on mine. Could I spend an eternity without him? I started the hearth, and the warmth satisfied me. I hadn't realized how cold I was until the warmth from the flames nipped my nose and cheeks. I threw the letter into the fire and watched it crumble and burn.

I SAW WILLIAM FOR only a moment one night while feasting in the Great Hall during supper. The Great Hall was lit with many candles, and they cast a bright light on the members of court. Plates and knives rattled while voices crowded the room, floating throughout the air. The room was loud with conversation. People sat both left and right of me, clinking glasses and toasting for no particular reason. I waved as inconspicuously as possible across the room, hoping to catch his eye, but he appeared to be busy and did not notice me. He strode across the room with papers in his hand, avoiding people walking about the room as he came closer and closer to Her Majesty sitting on her throne.

She took a sip from her wine before leaning over. William bowed and then whispered in her ear. I watched as she placed a jeweled hand on his shoulder and laughed. Over the noise of the room, I could not hear what they were saying. William handed her the papers in his hand. She looked at them with a critical eye before nodding and handing them back. I could not tell what she was saying, but there was a smile on her lips.

I could feel my grip on my knife tighten.

The man on my right elbowed me and laughed. He had a large nose and wore only a simple frock made of muslin. It was stained on the ends of the sleeves and smelled as though it hadn't been washed in a while.

"Spending a lot of time looking at that Shakespeare, are you not, Lady Lanier?"

The people next to him chuckled. I laughed in turn and tried to look as though I was enjoying the joke, but my stomach dropped. Was it that obvious? Did people know about the affair?

I had to look back to the queen, only for an instant. Did she know too?

As I glanced at her, I finally caught William's eye. A small smile crept up the side of his face. When the queen looked away, I gave another wave, which he returned. I was about to motion for him to join me outside the hall, when the queen's eyes darted back to William. Before I knew it, she was looking at me. Her eyes were sharp, and I recognized all too well the narrow line of her lips.

I lowered my eyes as fast as I could, but my heart thumped in my chest. Her Majesty had caught me looking directly at William. I didn't dare glance up to see if she was now focused on something else.

I took my skirts in my hand and excused myself from the table without looking up. I hurried out, ashamed and frightened.

As I walked out of the vibrant hall, I realized that from now on, I would always be avoiding the queen's gaze.

Days came and went. I couldn't lose myself in events that now seemed to be nothing more than distractions. When I had been at court before, the festivities had added interest to my life. Now they only seemed to be covering up things that could not be spoken of.

I missed Henry. I missed his soft body clinging to my own and his little hands playing in my hair. I longed for the days when we went out into the garden to play among the flowers. I missed simple days and dreamless nights. I wrote to Alfonso, knowing I would not receive a reply back. I understood it was difficult to track him down, but I hoped that if he did receive my letters, he might write to tell me how my child was.

And then, a letter appeared under my door. I recognized the perfect, flowing handwriting and tore it open.

Emilia,

I must see you. Staring at you across the Great Hall the other night was torture. The queen watched my every move, and it would have been dangerous to approach you.

However, I shall defy any person to keep me away from you now. Come and meet me at the gate to Whitehall tomorrow after the noon meal is served. I shall be returning from a short trip to the theatre in London.

Forgive me, my love. I was thinking of your protection and my own.

William

I felt my lips curl into a smile as I read the last words. He still loved me; he still cared. I had believed he had forgotten me. But it was not so. He still cared.

I held the letter close to my heart, hoping it might somehow bring him closer to me.

I WAITED FOR WILLIAM, shivering slightly, both from the winter air that lived further into the spring than I liked and also from the nervousness of seeing him again. Should I be frightened? I did not know. Before, I had always felt as though I was enough for him. Now, I was not so sure.

The large oak tree bent from the weight of snow. William came alone. There was no need for him to bring an entourage, as Henry Carey and Alfonso seemed to require. William's horse loped more clumsily than the nobles' horses would, and I could see his small smile more clearly...perhaps in expectation, perhaps because I wanted to. I missed him.

He dismounted swiftly when he reached me. His horse stopped abruptly, and I was caught up in his arms. He held me tightly; I could not escape. I did not want to. His strong arms grasped me both firmly and softly. I fit so perfectly within his embrace. My body burned like fire. How could that be? I knew all that was at stake: Henry, Margaret, my own life…

He kissed me gently. Worries melted away as we stood there. Was it just us? Or were others watching us as well? I prayed no one could see us.

"Emilia," he whispered.

"William." I broke away from his embrace. "Perhaps we should talk in one of the chambers."

He took my hand, made sure his horse was with one of the hands at the stable, and led me to the palace door. Our footsteps echoed as we walked. His were more hurried than mine; I could almost hear both my reluctance and my wanting in those steps.

"I have so much to tell you," he began, speaking as fast as I had ever heard him. I only caught a few of the words that left his mouth. He gripped my hand tightly. I didn't know whether I should keep holding onto his or if I should take my own away. Nothing felt certain anymore.

"William," I tried again.

"This is incredible. I have spent hours with Wriothesley. He is willing to finance it, and we will begin it soon.… Oh, I can't wait to tell you."

I was afraid that faces would start appearing in the doorframes, so I yanked my hand away. He let go and continued down the stone halls to where the musicians', poets', and playwrights' chambers were. It would have been easy for me to turn back, to save face and argue with him some other time. But I couldn't.

He stopped at one of the heavy wooden doors. He opened it

without hesitation, holding it open for me. His face was eager. If it was for the bed, I didn't think I could resist him.

He closed the door briskly behind him and motioned me to sit down in the chair in front of the rickety desk. Our chambers looked essentially the same. Mine was a little bigger to accommodate the baby, but they still held the same necessities. A cozy hearth, the oak desk, and the bed covered with blankets in the center of the room. There was a window looking outside into the Whitehall courtyard. The glass was dirtied, but one could still make out the looming winter's gray.

He sat down on the bed so that he faced me, looking straight into my eyes. His hands fidgeted, tracing along the chair's intricate scrolls with his long, slender fingers, just as he had the day he told me he was going to write a play for Henry Carey.

"Emilia." He smiled. "I have something I need to tell you."

"So do I," I said. The voice that came from me was weak.

"I am building a theatre."

What I was going to say was forgotten. A theatre? Had I heard him correctly?

"What?"

He took my hand, still smiling.

Had he brought this up now to put off what I was going to say? Or did he really care so much about his theatre that it had to come first?

"Yes, a theatre. I am going to call it the Globe."

"What of the Rose?" I asked, my eyes wide.

"It's too crowded." He frowned and waved the question away with his hand. "People keep coming to see the plays. They love them. I can't fit everyone who wants to see them into the Rose or any of the other theatres."

"But..."

"Wriothesley is paying for most of it, and the Baron Hunsdon as well. All we need is the queen's approval and support."

He paused then and cocked his head to one side. His face had changed little, but there was the scruff of a beard growing on his chin, and he had taken his earring out. He looked like an average gentleman now. Not necessarily a wealthy gentleman, but a gentleman just the same. I found my face growing warm as I looked at him.

"That is what I wanted to talk to you about. About the queen," I finally admitted.

"I know all about it, darling. The queen does not like my histories. It is a slight complication, but I have been tiring of them myself. I want to write something impossible, something that will take the queen to her childhood."

"William." I raised my voice. I could not tell whether he was deliberately disregarding my attempts to speak to him.

"Your story would capture her imagination. What if you worked on it with me? It could be the first play performed at William Shakespeare's Globe."

Again he managed to shock me out of what I was going to say. My childish tale, a play? I could almost hear my name spoken as William's, as a playwright. But now wasn't the time.

"William," I tried again.

"Yes?" This time his eyes were on me and not on the fantasy he always seemed to be imagining.

I took a deep breath and forced a halfhearted smile. "How can we continue with this with the queen so close?"

He frowned. "Emilia..."

I recognized his expression. It was complete and utter abandonment. He stood up instantly, ripping his hand from mine. He turned his back to me, so I could not see he was angry at me.

"I did not know…," he started…but he stopped abruptly. It was not often he was at a loss for words.

"The queen will find out someday; that fact cannot be denied," I continued, even though I was positive he knew what I was going to say. "I love you. I will always love you. Yet I feel as though you don't love me. We have to be more careful. You were there when the queen looked at me in the Great Hall. You know what she is capable of."

"You don't think I have been?" he said, his back still turned to me. His eyes were on the ceiling, his head tilted upward. I wondered if he were making maps of the river Thames out of the cracks as I once had. "I'm trying my best. You know how I would rather defy Elizabeth than cower under her power."

I answered honestly and cruelly, dashing his fantasies.

"Yes, but there is nothing we can do."

He turned around to face me, his face contorting in an angry expression I had never seen before. His hands gripped my shoulders. He attempted to kiss me, whether in anger and desperation or distress at being apart for so long, I did not know. I turned my cheek, though I wanted his lips on mine as much as he did.

"I have no choice? I am bound to her too, as we all are? That is not living. What kind of a sad existence is that?" he exclaimed after I denied him.

"We can't do anything," I said sadly.

"Unless if we are truly to love without care. Let us face the queen and admit it. Leave Alfonso and his wrath."

I sighed quietly enough so that only I could hear it. Didn't he know how hard it was for me to begin with? The last thing I needed was him convincing me to give up the life I had.

"What are you afraid of?" he went on. "That you'll be beheaded like the Queen of Scots, or that you will be exiled like Lady Bess? Or are you afraid to look the queen in the eye and tell her that you have found what she could never have? You can pretend you love Alfonso to please her or the Countess of Cumberland or even to convince yourself, but you know the truth, Emilia. Your God knows the truth."

We were so similar and so different. Our truths were both truth and false. I had once seen my life so clearly, and now I could barely understand my own feelings. Since meeting him, I now understood both my reasons and his. It disturbed me that I could be so easily swayed.

"You know I love you," I answered after some thought. "But I have to think of others besides myself. What of my boy? What of Margaret?"

William did not answer. He glanced away from me and to the window, and I wasn't sure whether he was simply refusing to answer me or whether he had nothing to say. When he was quiet, I never knew what to think.

"Don't be ridiculous," I continued. "You should understand. You love Henry as well. We are endangering him and your friend and my husband."

He looked a little defeated, as though he couldn't believe I was attacking him. I wasn't trying to; I just wanted him to comprehend my position. I did not want to hurt him.

"Think of your family," I added.

"You don't think I have?" he replied angrily. "They are far away and not important enough to be hurt by the queen's rage. She would be more interested in hurting you. What do you think she would do? Behead your boy? Torture Alfonso? Or are you more afraid to stand in front of her and tell her the truth? You only married him to make her happy."

I couldn't argue that.

"This isn't about my marriage."

"Of course it is," he said. "It is about every underlying issue in this relationship we have ever had—your marriage, your apprehension, and your friends' thoughts. You love me; I know this. I know you do. I just can't comprehend why what the queen says or does matters so much to you."

The words would not come to me. How could I tell him that I thought of the queen as my family? My supporter? My guide? Someone to take care of me when it seemed that I would have to take care of myself?

"She was someone who seemed she would always be there and who I could always admire and respect," was all I could say.

He shook his head gently, and a sad smile crept upon his face. He held his hands together and eyed them, as though he were contemplating something about them instead of me.

"Do you doubt yourself so much? You are my sun. I wouldn't love anyone who wasn't."

"I know. And I appreciate your support, but William, you must understand. I have never had anyone's approval but yours, Margaret's, and the queen's."

He shook his head and one of his hands flew into the air.

"Why you should need others' approval is beyond my comprehension. You should need no one's but your own."

"The queen helped me in many ways, and I owe her the life I live today, as do you," I continued.

And he would need her support if he were to build his theatre.

"Well, I can see us doing two things," he commented, his anger subsiding. "We could do as you say and forget we ever met each other, forget we ever loved each other. Perhaps you can do that, but I can't. Neither can I continue to be friends with Alfonso if I have to see you. I couldn't stand coming to your home and seeing you smile and laugh. If the queen wanted to torture me, she could think of nothing worse."

I agreed with him completely. I didn't think I could live, seeing him the way I had before. Even when we had just been friends, it had been hard to see him. It was even worse once we committed and had to pretend that nothing had changed, when, of course, everything had.

"The second thing would be to continue as we are, but to be more careful and more understanding of the other. I was trying to protect you. I thought I was doing the right thing. I can't see why the queen would care about our insignificant happiness, but if you really fear Her Majesty, we will be very careful. Very, very careful."

I nodded slowly, biting my lower lip. Could I compromise? I could still be with William, but was it worth it?

"So what do you propose we do?"

He already guessed what my answer would be. He smiled and took my hand again, his thumb gliding across the back of it. He treated me with such delicacy. It was so unlike Alfonso that I couldn't help but enjoy his fingers enclosing mine.

"I was serious about your story, as I always have been. It is a wonderful idea and I am more than willing to help you with it."

I laughed. "William, it is nothing worth helping."

"When are you going to realize how talented you really are?"

I sighed. "Never, probably."

He kissed me softly on the cheek. His lips were so sure; he was so committed to following what he wanted, what he loved. At that moment I was jealous of William. I was jealous of how everything that seemed right to me wasn't what seemed right to him.

"I love you," I whispered.

He smiled and brushed my right cheek with the tips of his fingers. "I love you too. We will be very careful, Emilia. The queen will not even know. We love each other too much not to continue. I do not want to lose you."

"I don't want to lose you either," I said. A part of me screamed in disappointment at myself that I could not stay angry with him, while another breathed a sigh of relief as I realized I would not have to give him up.

He gave a small laugh back and kissed my neck. Once. Twice. "I have missed you."

"Yes," I simply said. "Yes."

The next thing I knew, my lips were on his and we began to lose our surroundings. I saw and felt only him, and he gave me the impression that he was as lost as me. I had missed him. I had wanted him to hold me and kiss me and desire me, and now I felt complete, as the old, familiar, happy feeling overwhelmed me.

We were very careful. We rarely saw each other, and when we did, we spoke only salutations. We did nothing that could be interpreted as love or passion. We would smile and bow our heads slightly and then continue on.

But the evenings we were together were beyond anything I could have ever imagined. It was a relief not to have to worry about Alfonso, or even Henry. It was only William and only me.

He spent much more time with the queen than I would have liked, but it could not be helped. She called him into her chambers to hear his poetry. The poems he had written about me were given to Her Majesty. He sat in the place of honor some nights in the Great Hall. Hot tears boiled behind my eyes as I saw Elizabeth laughing with him or putting a hand on his back, but I could not let them show.

I only got to be with him late at night when everyone in our quarters was asleep. It was uncommon to find people wandering around this part of the palace at night. Mistresses weren't a normal occurrence in the lower classes; only the wealthy could afford to pay for dresses and jewelry for women other than their wives.

Most of the time William would sneak to my chambers; it was easier for a man to be seen in the halls at those late hours than a woman. He would knock five times, just like he always had.

I would let him in. We would talk of his plans for a new theatre and of our days. He always asked me why I wouldn't let him publish my mediocre play. I would laugh and he would laugh. It was not something I would want exposed to the world with my name on it, but he kept bringing it up.

In my tiny chamber, we would sit on the floor, holding hands, while he worked on his play, *Romeo and Juliet*. Darkness waited for light outside my window, and William and I looked for stars shining through the glass panes while the fire warmed our bones. The scratch of his pen became the rhythm of my life. He sat at that old desk, head bent over delicious words. Every now and then he would read them aloud.

"'A rose by any other name would smell as sweet'?" he asked, candlelight shining on the amber color in his brown hair. "How does that sound?"

"Perfect," I'd reply. It always sounded perfect to me.

"Don't you think it could use a bit more...something?"

"No," I said. "I think it is just fine."

"Should it end happily?" He smiled mischievously. He squeezed my hand and planted a kiss on my neck.

"Yes," I said. "We are happy enough, are we not?"

"Seems unfair to deny them what we have found."

When he wasn't writing plays, he was writing sonnets to pass the time. I would sit on his bed or in the musty chair by the hearth. Sometimes my own scratching would match his and we wouldn't speak; we simply worked together. Even then, it was comfortable just to have him near.

Now and then I caught him looking over at me and watching me as I worked. I could feel his stare.

On days he was more rested, we would pull out my little book of writings and cross out lines, write new ones in, and evaluate the work that needed to be done. I put myself into this project halfheartedly; it was William's more than mine now.

I suppose what I adored most about William was his ability to love me without the usual expectations of a mistress. He didn't just want me for the lovemaking or the kisses or to have me on his arm when he went to state dinners. He didn't seem to mind our late-night talks. In fact, he seemed interested in what I had to say. He would even ask me for advice about his plays.

Yet sometimes he kept me at a distance. When he needed something to recite to the queen the next day, I was not invited to his chambers. There were pieces of his world I was not a part of.

During those times, I couldn't help but wonder if I came second to his work and fantasies. He never asked for anything more than what I was willing to give, and I tried to return the favor. I did not want gifts or dresses or anything a mistress would want. They were what I wanted when I was a mistress to Henry Carey…but maybe if I had loved him, things would have been different. Love was a strange thing. It changed my perspective and made me realize all I had been missing. I tried not to think about all I was giving up.

MARGARET REMAINED AT A distance while William was there. She never spoke about him, and I never mentioned him. I knew she was glad that I could fall in love and be content, but she also thought William wasn't worthy of my love. He was a playwright to her, only that, and she did not approve of the time he spent with the queen. She cautioned us to be just as careful during the nights as we were during the days.

I would visit her sometimes, mostly when William was working. We would have our lunch, and I would get to see Anne. She was a striking girl, her face much more like her father's than her mother's. While Margaret's face had a warm, comforting appearance, Anne's face was more angular, with higher cheekbones and altogether a darker look. Her eyes were sharp and saw much; the girl was wise beyond her five years. It seemed only a few days ago I had held her in her baby clothes and walked her around the palace garden.

She would come and sit on my lap sometimes. We liked each other. She didn't ask questions. All she demanded was that I tell her a story once in a while. I was happy to oblige. I tried to tell stories that would please both Anne and her mother. I loved it when I could get a laugh out of Margaret. My situation was weighing on her, and I tried to cheer her up as much as possible.

It wasn't only me who was causing Margaret distress. The queen was a constant worry to her. Margaret spent most of her days catering to Her Majesty, since Anne was old enough to stay in the chambers under the supervision of the other ladies. I sympathized with my friend. It was long past the time when she should return to Cumberland and raise Anne.

The queen was lonely without Essex. It had been months since she had sent him to Ireland and commanded that her ladies stay close to her side during this time. I was sorry for the queen. She was an old woman now, but she was still not content with what she had achieved in her lifetime. She never would be.

Spring turned into summer, and my days alone were simple and pleasant. I wrote and read and spent time outside until my face resembled that of a gypsy's. I received many stares, mostly from children who had always been told that white skin was fashionable. I was the only dark lady in the court. The others all came from noble English families with centuries of white skin. William loved it, calling me a Moor. His own skin was a lovely olive color; he spent more time in the sun than the other gentlemen.

"We must look like quite the pair," he said one night as we sat talking in his room.

I laughed with him. The musician's daughter and the playwright. What an odd couple we must be.

I was so happy then. We kept our secret as best we could. We were blissful. I prayed often, perhaps more than I ever had before. Even then, I thought about forgiveness. I wondered if what I was doing was truly a sin and how God saw it. Everything I had believed about doing the right thing was confused and contorted. It was easier to forget that what I was doing might be wrong. I did not want to believe it could be.

William would come to church sometimes, his hands folded in his lap and his eyes far away. Music filled the high ceilings, and the glass windows reflected on the ground. When we knelt for our prayers, I would peek at him to make sure he wasn't watching me. He never seemed to pay attention to what was going on, but when I asked him about it, he would always say he liked most of it.

"I don't like the sermons," he would say. "But I love the music. It's all some grand play for God, is it not?"

I nodded. In a way, it was. "The Good Lord is watching us from above," I said. "All the world is a stage, and we are but the players."

William laughed.

William was very happy during this time. I think he saw things he hadn't before, tasted things differently, and finally loved something that was not completely made in his head. I saw myself in his eyes more often now, though I was still competing with witches, kings, and ghosts. In some ways, I was almost a character of his—a person occupying his mind and his plays. Maybe this character was more beautiful than the reality, but I was excited to be his desire and his focus.

Sometimes he was so wrapped up in what he was writing that he couldn't think about anything else. One afternoon I went to his chambers. I was hoping we could spend some precious time together talking—and not about writing. I knocked on his door, and he opened it in haste. His hair was mussed and ink stained his fingers. The scruff on his face seemed thicker.

"Emilia, darling," he said hurriedly. "What is it you need?"

My brow furrowed. "I just wanted to see you," I replied. "Is now a bad time?"

"No." He ran a hand through his hair and paused a moment before speaking. "Well, yes."

"Oh," I said, taking a step away from the door. "I will leave you alone, then."

"No, you can come in," he said...but with his hands on either side of the doorframe, I could tell he did not want me to.

"It is fine," I said, already turning away. I was surprised to find that I did not want to be around him when he was so flustered. My face grew warm. "I will come by later."

Before he could stop me, I hurried down the hall, confused at the feelings that tumbled inside me.

WILLIAM CAME TO MY chambers one afternoon. The summer heat had made the tiny room almost unbearable, but the queen was out in the garden that day, so I stayed in. I sat with my sewing in my lap, hoping to mend one of my dresses enough to be able to wear it.

He burst in. His eyes darted like a mad man's, and he looked almost lost. His shirt looked like he had put it on in haste—it was wrinkled. His bag was slung over his shoulder.

"William?" I asked, standing up. "What's wrong?" I dropped the dress onto the bed.

He went to me and took my hands. "My son is very sick. Anne fears death." He breathed deeply. His hands were shaking. "I am going to see him as quickly as possible."

My hand covered my mouth. "Is she sure? There's no hope at all?"

He looked away and I could see his concern in his eyes.

"Do you have everything you need?" I asked before he had to say anything. "Do you need food? Is there anything I can get you?"

I did not know what to do, but I felt as though I should do something. Yet what could I do but be there for him? I felt powerless.

He shook his head. His thoughts were far away. He was so worried. Even if he didn't love Stratford or his wife, he loved his children.

"You will understand if I do not write to you?"

"Of course," I said. He could not have any contact with me while he was with his wife.

"I will miss you." He was preoccupied.

"I will miss you too," I said.

He kissed me on the forehead. "Take care."

"You as well."

And then he left. I wasn't sure I would ever see him again.

TIME WAS BOTH FRIEND and foe during this period. The longer he stayed away, the longer his son lived. The longer he was home, the more worried I became. I worried first for his child's health; a child should not die. And I worried for my own reasons. Had news of him having a mistress reached Stratford? Margaret had an ear for gossip, but I worried his wife might suspect more than anyone. My nights were lonely. I had no one to talk to. I imagined the couple breathing in the room next to me. I had often smiled at them when we returned to our chambers after a feast. Did they love each other? Did they have children they could raise without worrying about whether they would live to adulthood? I wished with all my heart that I could have given Henry what a child needed. I felt as though I hadn't done what a mother was supposed to, that I had skipped something important.

I often thought back on the first time I had come to court ten years before. I'd been so young. Things that worried me then now seemed entirely trivial. Would time make my current worries unimportant? I hoped it could.

I barely recognized myself anymore when I looked into the mirror. My eyes were the same, a deep brown. They were the only part of myself I found attractive, but even they had changed. They were noticeably wiser and harder. My jaw was more pronounced, and it gave my face a sharper, distinct look. I was thinner; I did not have much appetite.

I was only twenty-seven, and yet it felt like a lifetime had passed in front of my eyes. Time was what I wished for. I wanted time to enjoy being with William, time to see my child grow, time to be happy. I would relish it. I wouldn't take it for granted. I just needed a bit more time.

I DID NOT LIKE the rift that was forming between Margaret and me, so I asked her to meet me in my tiny chamber. She accepted. I think she was as much in need of my friendship as I was of hers. I loved William, and it was obvious now that I had made my decision about him, but I didn't want to exclude others who were so important to me.

Margaret seemed hesitant when I let her into the room that day. Her eyes were wide, and I could tell she was as just as unsure about where our friendship stood. How could I make it clear that I cared for her as I had before? We used to tell each other everything.

"Come," I said. "Tell me what has happened with you recently."

We sat at the miniature table I had crowded into the room. It had been a gift for my wedding, and I was reluctant to use it. Every time I looked at it I felt guilty.

"The queen is not happy." She lowered herself to the chair slowly.

"Essex?" I guessed.

Margaret nodded, her tight bun still as her head bobbed up and down. "She admits that she is still in love with him, but he is arrogant. I am not surprised he was sent away. He is an intelligent man; he will do well with the Irish rebellion. He is not a man, on the other hand, who lets himself be forgotten."

I nodded in turn. It seemed to me that Essex believed *he* was what the world needed, or at least what the world's women needed.

"I believe the queen is trying her best to dismiss him from her mind, and she is doing a fairly good job of it. She rarely writes to him anymore," she continued. "But she is lonely."

I knew about loneliness. At the moment, I was very lonely. I missed William and his words and his eyes. I missed our talks and our kisses, but I also knew that he could not help being away. He loved his son. The child was dying. Of course he needed to be there.

I glanced over at Margaret. I hoped she did not know that the reason I had invited her here was because I was feeling this way—as if this void would never be filled again.

"She is old." I laughed, but not in a jesting way.

Margaret smiled at me, as if she was expecting me to say that. "Perhaps," she acknowledged. "But that does not stop the effects of being lonely."

I thought on her words.

"There is some other news, though," she said. Her eyes were suddenly very bright. "I think I can go home in the near future."

"To Cumberland?" I asked. "For how long?"

"For as long as I wish. The queen's ladies, the ones who have been here for years, are tired of not being able to visit their families or raise their children at home. I have been here for a long time. The queen fears our disloyalty and that of our husbands. She has finally seen fit to let me go and has given me only a few more months of waiting on her."

"That's excellent," I said, knowing how much she desired to return to her home and have her own household.

She smiled broadly. I had never seen Margaret look so content, and I was happy to see that she had found some peace in her life. She had been a loyal maid of honor for the queen, but she more than deserved to live how she wanted. She had made a simple request, and the queen had finally listened.

"I feel terribly for Frances," I commented. "She must be lonely with her husband in Ireland."

"He is hardly ever home, even when he is in England."

"Do you think he really loves the queen?" I asked.

Margaret shrugged. "Who's to say whether he does or he doesn't? I doubt that he wishes for her money; he has plenty of that nowadays. Perhaps he likes the excitement of chasing after something he cannot have."

"Why would he even try to acquire something he knows he can't have?" I asked.

Margaret laughed. "Because he is a man. Men are always hunting. They always want something they shouldn't."

"Poor Frances," I said.

"She brought it upon herself. She knew Essex might change his mind. She knew he was never really in love with her."

"I do not blame her for hoping. Everyone wants their affections to be returned."

Margaret would know that better than anyone.

"What do you think will happen?" I asked.

Margaret bit her lip again. "I always fear the worst."

"Perhaps you shouldn't."

"Someone needs to in this court," she replied simply.

ENGLAND, 1597
DURING THE REIGN OF QUEEN ELIZABETH I
WHITEHALL COURT

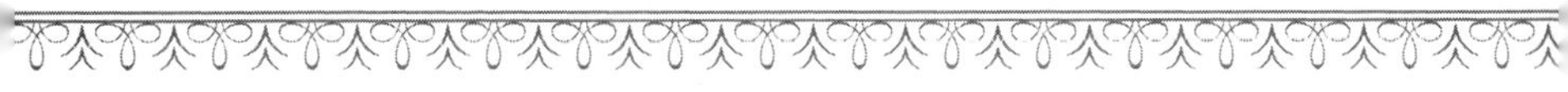

WHEN I DID NOT hear from William, I could only assume one thing. The child had passed away. I imagined William's grief.

I wished he would write to me. I knew it was impossible with his wife so close, but I longed for his words anyway. I wished I could write to him with my condolences. Even though I'd never met the child, I knew how painful it was to lose someone I loved. I could not imagine losing Henry. I regretted sending him with Alfonso. I wanted to hold him close in my arms and know he was all right.

I did receive news about my old master, the Baron Hunsdon. One afternoon a letter arrived for me. His name was on it. What need of me would he have?

My fingers itched as I opened it. I lifted his wax seal.

Dear Madam Lanier,

It is with deep and utter regret that I must inform you of this change in your pension. Looking through my father's books, I see he has been paying you the amount of forty pounds for several years now. I must inform you that this will no longer occur. I am sorry to relieve you of this sum, but I am afraid I have no other choice.

I have sent a letter to your husband as well, hearing he was away from court.

Of most sincerity,
George Carey
Second Baron of Hunsdon

My hands, which once shook so eagerly, now trembled with distress, and I had to sit down on the creaking bed. I knew what this letter meant. Henry Carey had passed away. I placed the letter at my side, and my hands came together. I said a silent prayer for my old master. I couldn't help but think that I was not the person I once was. I was saying good-bye to the girl I once knew.

I RECEIVED A LETTER from Alfonso. He was returning to court.

The day Alfonso came home, I wore my best dress. I greeted him as he appeared at the gate to the palace. His troupe followed him, looking as unkempt as ever. They were dirty, mud staining their boots. Alfonso barely looked at me when he came close. He gave me a simple nod to acknowledge that I was there.

Henry ran up to me, his arms outstretched. I caught him in my arms, pressing him to me as tightly as possible. Oh, how I loved this little boy. I loved him with such a love I could not have thought possible. I loved William for different reasons, and I felt no need to compare these two loves, but I loved Henry because he was mine.

I could feel his little heart beating with excitement. When we finally pulled away, I was astonished to see that he was entirely different than he was a year ago. His hair was curlier than before, framing his tanned face. His eyes were bright. He touched my cheek with his hand, and I could see he was a genuinely caring boy.

He smiled. "Mother, I have so much to tell you."

He spoke with an adult's diction.

"I am sure you do," I said with amazement. He was four now. He was a child, not a baby.

I stood up and took his hand. His hair bobbed as he walked, but even this seemed more a child's trait. We followed Alfonso into the palace.

He was unscathed as far as I could tell; it didn't appear as though any damage had been done. It was so wonderful to hear him talk about life as a musician, a life he had mastered at a young age. He mentioned his supposed father often, and it was clear that he was fond of him.

When we reached the chamber, I started a fire and turned down the bedsheets. I had cleaned the tiny room all day. It looked exactly as it had before they had left. I had even taken out Henry's baby bed for him, although it was obvious now that he would be sleeping with us in ours. His legs and arms were far too long to fit in the cradle.

Alfonso watched me, his eyes following me like a wolf's followed a doe. It was as if he was waiting for something.

"Emilia," he said.

I looked up at him.

"How was court while I was gone?"

I hesitated before I answered.

"It was fine."

Henry ran up to Alfonso and tugged on his shirt. He ruffled the boy's hair. This seemed to remind my husband of something.

"Did you hear about William's son?"

I caught my breath, fearing the worst. What would he do to me if he found out?

"William Shakespeare?" I asked, as if I knew nothing.

"Yes."

I shook my head. "Only that he was very ill."

Alfonso grunted. I wondered how much he suspected. His eyes never left me.

"He died. William is in the greatest grief. I doubt he will return to court in the near future."

He sat down in one of the two chairs close to the hearth. Henry crawled up on the bed, his mood now melancholy. He was a wise child. He knew what kind of an occasion this was.

"I stopped in Stratford before coming here," Alfonso continued. "The poor fellow hasn't even had the heart to write. They think it could be the sweating sickness."

I gave a small gasp. The sweating sickness was a terrible way to die. There hadn't been an outbreak in many years, but every so often it came around again, killing thousands and breaking hearts. If the boy had contracted the disease, it was very likely that it would spread.

I felt for William even more now. His only son was dead, and he wouldn't touch a pen. I wanted to comfort him, but what could I do? I felt weak and hopeless.

"I am very sorry to hear of it." It was all I could say.

Alfonso nodded. He seemed to be thinking of other things now. He turned his chair around to face the fire, while I picked Henry up. He was no longer light, and his taller frame surprised me. He wrapped his arms around my neck, and I could hear him breathing in my scent. It wasn't long before I heard his tiny snores. It had been an exciting day for him. I tucked him in bed and pulled the covers up to his chin.

I went and sat next to Alfonso. The chair creaked when I sat down, but he did not look up. He continued to stare at the fire. The flames reminded me of the night when I had attacked him because he was burning Margaret's letters, but I felt no hostility for him tonight.

It was quiet. There was only the crackling of the fire and Henry's soft snores. Alfonso was thinking again; I could see it. It was as if he were evaluating something. I dared not ask him. Our reunion was going better than I had expected.

"When does a man know what is best for his family?" he wondered aloud.

His words surprised me. I never would have thought something so contemplative would come from his mind. Perhaps this was what William had meant when he said there was more to Alfonso than I realized. I wondered if he was thinking of Henry...or even hoping that we could eventually make a real family.

"I don't think we can know. We are only human," I said.

He nodded, his face grave.

Twelfth Night came and went. The festivities were grand as always. The queen ordered feasts and dancing, though she hardly partook in those pleasures. There was no doubt in anyone's mind—the queen missed Essex.

Alfonso loved working at the palace. When he was called to the queen's side, he picked up his harp and rushed to her throne. He took William's place as her favorite entertainer. Lines of budding sonnets were replaced with lines of music.

I watched him with curiosity one night after Twelfth Night. His fingers nimbly picked at the strings of the harp. He touched them much more softly than he had ever touched me. The melody drifted through the air, and I closed my eyes to hear it better. Alfonso was not the queen's favorite musician simply because of his handsome visage. After the song was over, he laughed, clear and free. I realized that was the only time I had ever heard him laugh because he was happy.

There was a dark side to his felicity, however. As a musician, he was able to eat and drink as much as he wanted, and he used that to his advantage. Wine, beer, ale—he had it all. He would come back to our chambers long after I went to bed. I was always glad Henry was asleep so he could not see his father staggering around like an old man. I wondered if Alfonso had been this relaxed with drinking when Henry and he were away. I certainly hoped not.

One night, he came into our chamber late. Henry was sound asleep in our bed. I had waited up for my husband to make sure he had come home safely. I worked on my story in the dim candlelight. When the sky had been dark for several hours, I heard a knock on the door. I shoved my little book into the wardrobe, hiding it among my dresses.

I crept across the noisy floor as silently as possible, trying not to wake my son. I turned the handle slowly and Alfonso fell into the room, smelling of ale. His vest was loosened.

I pressed a finger to my lips and pointed at Henry with my other hand before shutting the door quietly behind him.

"Where have you been?" I asked. "You should not be out so late."

"Who are you to tell me what to do?"

He appeared as if he were about to fall. He doubled over, putting his hands on his knees, and for a moment I thought he was going to vomit his drinks, but then he straightened up.

"Come here," he ordered, waggling a finger at me.

"Not when you smell of alcohol."

He tripped over to me, a confident half smile on his face. Before I could stop him, he raised his hand and pushed me across the room. I fell on the floor, my knees and the heels of my hands smacking the ground. Blood trickled from my palms where they had scraped across the rough wood.

Alfonso grunted before he crawled into bed like a lumbering animal. He pulled the scratchy blanket over his head. Soon his snores accompanied Henry's.

I sat down in the chair by the hearth. Had I really been so quick to believe in Alfonso? I held my sore hands close to my chest and took hurried breaths. I could not believe I had thought there might be some good in him after all. How foolish I had been to think that things might change.

After the sun slowly began to touch the sky, my eyes began to drift closed. I fell asleep thinking of how I missed William and how I missed being loved.

I knew it wouldn't be long before Alfonso and Henry would have to leave once again. Of course, if the queen wished him to stay longer, he would...but she had plenty of musicians to play for her. Henry was excited to go with him again, and I knew there was no hope of trying to convince him to stay with me for the rest of the year. As long as he was safe, I didn't have a legitimate reason to argue for him to stay. I knew I would face opposition from both my son and husband.

Alfonso didn't once demand I sleep with him after that drunken night. He never said anything to indicate he wanted to. I wondered if he himself were having an affair. I could almost imagine him preying upon the young ladies, as he used to with me. Sometimes I would see him sitting next to one of the queen's ladies. He would play his harp while they clapped and swooned. He would touch one of them on the shoulder or neck or let his hand linger on an arm.

I wondered if he regretted our marriage as much as I did. These thoughts held my mind hostage. I barely noticed that Alfonso had stayed at court much longer than usual. Spring was making itself welcome, and Alfonso departed typically only a few weeks after Twelfth Night. I didn't think the queen had asked him to stay longer.

Eventually, I summoned the nerve to ask him when he intended to leave. I waited until he had just finished playing for the queen. I sat in our tiny room. Henry had been invited to play with some of the other children at court, and I had readily agreed. He spent far too much time with his parents, and I worried he might not have the interaction with children his age that he needed. I picked up my sewing needle and pretended to do something useful. I could hear Alfonso's heavy boots coming down the hall, almost like I could in our house in London.

He opened the door and looked at me without a scowl. He

seemed surprised that I wasn't with Margaret and actually doing something he approved of.

"It's so sunny outside," I said as he sat next to me. Alfonso nodded; he was clearly not interested in my observations.

"Are you planning on touring this year?" I asked. "It is spring."

"Yes," he gruffly answered. My hope for our relationship to grow began to diminish. "I am waiting for William to return to court before I go."

And we didn't talk any more on the matter.

ALFONSO WAITED A FULL month for William to return to court. And then, one rainy spring day, he came back.

Henry and I stayed behind in the room while Alfonso welcomed his friend to court. Although William would have rejoiced at seeing how big Henry had gotten—and would have hopefully been pleased to see me—Alfonso thought it best we stay in the chamber. I agreed. William had suffered a great loss, and maybe at the moment he needed a friend more than a lover.

I wasn't allowed to see him for a week. Those were long days, filled with children's games for Henry. I had plenty of time to think while William and Alfonso were together. What if he had gone back to his wife and realized that he couldn't continue with me? My heart ached at that thought. Maybe he had fallen in love with her again. Maybe his child's death had brought his feelings for his family into sharp perspective. Maybe it was for the best.

I didn't see him until Alfonso and Henry had left. It was a

bittersweet parting. Henry was thrilled to return to work, but I would miss him greatly and not see him for many months. I hoped my kisses and hugs would last that long.

After they had left, I rushed to find William. I was afraid. I didn't know what I would do if William had changed from when I had seen him last. I knocked gently on his door five times. There was no sound from the other side. I wondered if he was out. I was about to turn away when I heard a rustling and the door creaked open.

"Emilia?" he whispered. His voice croaked with a sadness I could not describe. It pained me to hear him so upset.

"Yes."

"Come in." He said the words with such a melancholy ease. It was as if he wasn't even trying to speak and the words escaped his lips anyway.

I prodded the door open a little more so I could inch my way through it. I was hesitant to enter. Would he have aged in such a short time? What would I do if he didn't want me anymore?

He sat on the bed, facing the wall, his hands clasped between his legs as usual. He did not look at me when I entered, but I sensed that he wanted to. He partially turned his head toward me and then went back to looking at the ground. I slowly pulled out a chair so I wouldn't disturb him, tucked my skirts underneath me, and waited for him to say something. I wasn't going to seem as though I needed him, although I needed him desperately.

I waited for several minutes, admiring his profile. I loved him so much, and not just for the excitement of the forbidden or because he saw me as no one else had, but because he was now part of me. I could not think of myself without him. He was as much a part of me as breathing was. Some nights when he was away, I had prayed to God that I could breathe when he did, because it made me feel closer even if we were far apart.

When he finally spoke, his voice came out so softly I could barely hear it.

"The boy...," he said. "He saw things as you and I do. He wanted to be a playwright like his father."

I didn't know what to say. I couldn't imagine his pain. I had never lost anyone that I truly cared about. What could I tell him? I should have come prepared with kind and thoughtful words. Instead, I seemed as thoughtless and as uncaring as my husband.

He looked over at me, and I was surprised to see that his face looked as I remembered it. He looked tired and the lines around his eyes appeared to be deeper, but his eyes penetrated mine in the same way they used to.

"I have missed you," he said.

I knew in that instant that he still cared. The look on his face was one of fear, his forehead wrinkled and his eyes wide. He was afraid of losing me, of losing love, of losing everything.

He stood up and strode over to me, his face focused on mine, and then continued.

"I don't want to lose things. I don't want to go through my life losing the things I love before I get to truly love them. Why are we being so cautious? Because we are afraid of what the queen is going to do? Does it matter? I love you. I don't want to hide it. I don't want to cower behind walls and pretend as though we have never seen each other. I took advantage of my luck once before. What if I do that again and I lose you?"

"But...," I tried to intercede.

"Emilia." He took my hands. "What will the queen do? She wouldn't dare hurt Alfonso or little Henry. She would only punish us. I have been punished more than ever by losing someone I love. My heart broke in two. The only person who could fix it would be you. I can arrange a ship to take us to Venice and we could journey on to Verona...."

"Have you completely lost your mind?"

He shrugged.

"Perhaps. But perhaps in losing my sanity, I have come to see what's truly important to me."

I had dealt with William's strange notions before, but this was entirely ridiculous. I could not think of anything other than my child, who had left only a few hours earlier, and what the queen might do to him when she found out. What would he do without his mother? All his life he would be shamed by the woman who exchanged his happiness and pride for her own.

"William, perhaps you should think about this—"

"What do you think I have been doing?" He laughed, but it sounded sad. "I have spent these months wondering what is left for me. I have hopes for a theatre, but those are only hopes and wishes. I have a wife I cannot live with. I have a friend, but I am madly in love with his wife. What can I lose? My life? That is no excuse. What am I living for? I am living for you. Remember when I told you I wanted to know what love was like? I have found it. It wasn't as it was supposed to be. It wasn't right or ethical. It's the most heart-wrenching, saddening emotion I have ever experienced. And you know what? It's even more heartbreaking when I can't at least let the world know how I feel."

I stood up and walked to the other side of the room so I could look out the window instead of into his piercing eyes. It was a dark day outside, clouds of gray looking as though they might spout rain at any moment. William hadn't lit any lamps in his room, so it was dim inside too.

"What do you expect me to do?" I said. "Parade it around in front of everyone? You think no one will condemn us for it, but they will. Even if you don't care, there are other people who will be affected by our open display. I love you as well. Can you not just be content with this knowledge?"

"Hardly." He threw his hands in the air. "I know you love me. Of all people, I would think you would want to break free of the cage that holds you. You of all people would want to make your own decisions. You have been trapped. Really, I wouldn't be surprised if the only reason you love me is because I gave you that feeling of freedom. You know what you are doing is wrong and you have tried to pull yourself away, but in reality you want that taste of freedom in your mouth."

"Do not turn my reasoning against me," I cried. "You said you were content with being careful. You promised. Now here you are, trying to convince me otherwise."

He grabbed a hold of my shoulders.

"What do you want? Do you want to keep living as you have been for the rest of your life? You may think there is an end to it, but there never is. You may think that when Henry is old enough to take care of himself you can do what you want, but then it will be something else. Alfonso, Margaret, the queen… There is no better time than now. Why shouldn't you be selfish? Why shouldn't you live your life the way it was meant to be lived? You are wasting it away."

His words echoed throughout my body. Their reality made me more hopeless and confused than ever.

"You can't be sure of what the queen would do," I countered. "You say she wouldn't hurt Henry or Margaret, but we would never know until it was too late. I don't want to die, William. Perhaps that is a lack of faith or an understanding I haven't reached yet, but I don't want to leave this world. I need to be here for Henry. The queen is unpredictable."

"The queen has had her own share of affairs," William commented. "Even though she still acts as though her virginity is uncompromised."

I knew he was right. The queen was just as guilty as we were, yet she could do whatever she wished.

"Yes, but we are not royalty."

He paused. His mind was far away. "What do you want? I have asked you this before, and you refuse to answer me. You know what I want. I want you as mine to love. I don't want to hide anymore. We can start something new together—something better," he said more softly than he had earlier.

Here was my chance for acceptance. Here was a man willing to lay down his life for love. Here was what I had wanted forever. Yet I was afraid to take it.

William wrapped his arms around my body. His mouth was next to my ear, and I could hear him breathe a steady, constant breath. He smelled so good and his arms felt strong around me, but I felt as though I was the one comforting him. I let him kiss my cheek, delighting in its gentleness.

"I don't know how much longer I am going to have you," he said.

"Why risk it?" I asked in the same hushed tone. "You will have me longer if we don't risk running away."

"Because I will never have you fully until we can be together for good," he replied. "Who could refrain that had a heart to love and, in that heart, courage to make love known?"

"You are unsound," I said. "Completely unsound."

"I know." He laughed. "And that's why I can't live my life like a normal person. I want to taste life as it was meant to be tasted, and I can't see my life being complete until I have you. Come to Italy with me."

I thought about what he'd said. I thought about finally being able to do what I really wanted. Did I want to spend the rest of my life trapped with Alfonso? Or did I want to be with William?

"What about Alfonso?" I asked.

"He will answer to me."

"Your supporters for the theatre?"

"I will find others."

"The queen?" I saved the most dreadful for last.

"God save her."

I LEFT HIS ROOM promising that I would think over his request—no, his demand. I worried about William. I lay awake that night. My mind raced. Was it worth it? Could we really be open about our relationship?

As I walked the halls, I heard whispers of gossip from the young ladies. They looked at me with their fine dresses and knowing smirks. I could hear William's name on their breath as they snickered at me.

I was afraid of the control William had over me. It wasn't like the control Alfonso had, where I was only allowed to go to the places he wanted me to and see the people he approved of. William controlled my thoughts.

The next day, I was prepared to tell William my choice. I had made my decision, and there was no turning back. My choice burned my lips when I told him what I wanted.

It surprised me almost as much as him.

He looked at me if I were the only thing on earth that could ever matter to him. I was his focus. I was his passion. I looked into his eyes, and my mind went blank but for the thought that now we could really love each other the way we were meant to.

Life was so short; I knew this well. I had seen so much of my life pass before me. When I was old, would I look back and wish we had been more careful? No, I would have wished we had had more time together, more time to be in love.

William couldn't contain his joy at the news. I had chosen him over everything. I had given up my only son, my husband, the security of the queen's favor...my very soul. He began arranging plans for a boat to Italy, a place he had always dreamed of going. Once the Globe was finished, I would never see the queen, Margaret, Alfonso, or Henry again. I would say good-bye to England—the only home I had ever known.

And so William and I began again.

We spent most of our time together. I loved talking to him. I couldn't resist his touch and the feel of his body against mine. I had never felt this way before. I remembered watching the other ladies-in-waiting and feeling their excitement when they fell in love. This time, however, it was me. I still felt anxious in the pit of my stomach, but I tried to ignore it and enjoy his hand in mine and the taste of his lips.

William often let me know how the Globe was progressing. He was contracted to it until it stood high above the London houses, and he also had several plays he needed to finish for the opening. But as soon as it was finished, we were to depart and never return.

We sat in his chambers late at night, trying to finish them in time. He wrote faster than I had ever seen, mumbling lines and rhymes. The smell of ink overpowered the room, and several times I had to ask the maid to bring more for him. The shutters were opened to let in a breeze, and moonlight permeated the room. William ignored the beautiful night and continued to dip his quill into his brass container.

"Could you edit these for me?" he would say as he tossed me *Romeo and Juliet* or *The Taming of the Shrew*.

"Must you make Kat so despicable?" I complained. "She should have at least one redeeming trait."

William laughed while he scribbled in *The Two Gentlemen of Verona*.

"So the shrew should be terrible and likable at the same time? Very well. For you, my lady."

Those days were precious. I couldn't believe this was my life. I didn't want to think about the consequences, even after I received a letter from Margaret. I walked outside to the courtyard to read it, my autumn clothes laced tightly so I would not feel the cool air. Even though the sun shone, the air was crisp with the coming of winter. I opened the envelope with dread.

Emilia,

I thought you were going to be careful. Your apparent secret is on the lips of every lady in the court. If you didn't think yourself popular before this, you most certainly are now. I can only offer one piece of advice. Return to London. If you are to display your affection for Shakespeare, at least do it where only neighbors can see it.

The queen will not look on this with favor. I do not think she knows yet, but she will. She may tell herself it does not bother her, but it will eat at her until her temper boils over. There is no knowing what she will do when this occurs.

Please understand that my words are meant to save you from the same fate as Frances and Bess. They risked it all and gained nothing worth remembering. Remember who you are. Remember what you did to achieve this. I have lost George already; I don't want to lose you too.

I will do my best to make sure the queen does not find out, but I cannot promise that it will escape her ears.

I cannot promise that she will act kindly. I cannot promise anything, which is the danger of it all.

Take care of yourself,

Margaret

I was touched. I would have understood if she had abandoned me and our friendship, but she hadn't. She would continue to protect me.

I considered returning to London. It wasn't a bad idea. William and I could be in peace there, and we wouldn't have to worry about the wandering eyes at court. But I would have to write to Alfonso to make sure I could go, and he might wonder why I wanted to return. I had spent years trying to convince him to let me return to court. And in order to finish his theatre, William needed to earn the support of the queen and several dukes and earls. He needed to be a presence at court.

Nevertheless, I mentioned it to William one evening when we were alone in his chambers. He had had a trying day with the queen, and the lines around his eyes looked deeper than ever. He held his head in his hands as he sat at his desk. I had closed the shutters to avoid a draft, but the last bit of sunlight still poked through the slats. It was light enough that we didn't have to light a candle.

"William," I said, sitting on the bed.

He smiled tiredly. Just the corners of his mouth rose. "Yes, darling?"

"What would you think if we went back to London, just until we depart for Italy?"

He was silent a second before he answered. "London?"

I nodded, noticing the tentative way he spoke. He scratched his head, and I knew he did not approve of the idea.

"We could hide better there. It would be safer than waiting here until the theatre is done. It's only a thought, but..."

"You know I need supporters for the Globe. I can't leave."

His reply was definitive. I searched his face for some way he could be persuaded, but his smile didn't change. After a moment, he reached over and took my hand.

"We'll be all right. Soon we will be free."

I squeezed his hand in return. What he said soothed my nerves a little, but the aching in my heart made me feel as though he was once again choosing his theatre, his work, over me.

But these were some of the best days of my life. William was right. Freedom was all I had ever wanted. It was all I had ever dreamed it would be. Yet Frances's words haunted me: "Someday, you will feel as I do. You will escape as I do."

She had known me better than I'd thought.

England, 1598
During the Reign of Queen Elizabeth I
Whitehall Court

One day William took me to see the growing Globe, just down the river from Whitehall. His arm wrapped around my waist as he led me through the growing structure. It stood like a skeleton, its bones reaching to the sky. I counted how many different rows of seats there would be; planks of wood had been laid down to represent them. I could tell this was bigger than the other theatres I had been in. The Globe would surpass them all.

William stared at it proudly, like a father.

"That's where the upper balcony will go." He pointed. "And here the stage will be built." His voice reverberated back to us, reminding me of the many voices that would crowd this space when it was finished.

He ran his hand over the wood. I placed mine on the wood as well. It felt sturdy beneath my hand. I tried to imagine this shell fleshed out into a great theatre. Hammers and saws lay on the ground, waiting to be picked up and worked with. I imagined the brightly colored flags that would sit on top of the building, waving a welcome to spectators.

"What play will you perform here first?" I asked. The histories would interest his patrons and the commoners, but I found I liked his comedies better. The more fanciful plays reflected what I saw in his eyes, what he really dreamed about. They helped me to escape from what I knew.

He let go of me slowly and shrugged his strong shoulders. He watched me.

"There is a play by a lovely lady I know...," he said.

"Don't start that again." I laughed.

"I'm serious, Emilia. You would be one of the first published women poets in England's history. How could you resist?"

I smiled. "Oh, I can."

He twirled around the wooden beam and caught me in his arms. His breath blew softly on my face. "I am pretty sure that young lady would negotiate."

"And why do you say that?" I whispered.

"Because I know her lover. I hear he knows what is best for her," he whispered in the same tone.

"All men think they know what is best for their ladies."

"What if this one does?"

"What if he doesn't?"

As much as I wanted to see my name in print or my play performed, I could not forget the way Henry Carey had insisted that writing was wrong. I could not disregard the look on his face that day when he told me it was unacceptable. I could only imagine what Alfonso would do if he found out.

William shook his head and kissed me. His lips were so familiar and comforting, yet they still brought an element of excitement with each touch.

"All right, my lady, you win this time."

"I win *every* time," I jested, when he knew as well as I did that it was untrue.

He laughed and kissed me again.

We toured the rest of the theatre. I was awed. It was rounded, like a big sphere. I could see where they were to lay the entrance. Pilings were stacked next to it. It smelled of paint and freshly cut wood. I could hardly believe that, in a few months, these large beams would support the greatest theatre in London. William's plays would be performed here. My play could be performed here.

I HAD TO GO to the tailor's to order some dresses. Money was always an issue, especially since Henry Carey's passing, but I had worn the same few gowns for years and repaired them the best I could, and now they were beyond help. Fabric can only be kept for so long.

I walked into the small shop just off the river. It was clean, painted bright colors, and smelled of ocean salt from fabrics imported from France and Italy. The different colors and patterns lined the walls like colorful soldiers. I ran a hand along them, feeling whisper-thin silks and heavy brocades. Bolts of rich velvets and thick, warm wools were piled high on tables.

Ladies milled around, touching the fabrics and comparing weights and feels. To win the approval of Her Majesty, you chose only the finest. None of the women in the store looked my way when I entered, but I recognized one of them.

I had not seen Frances in years and had assumed she was still in Essex with her brood of children. But today she was here by herself.

She wore a deep forest-green dress with gold stitching. Her hair was pulled back and tucked under a cap. She looked older and more sophisticated than before, but her once-perfect rosebud lips were now tightened into a thin line.

I watched her out of the corners of my eyes, hoping that she might look my way. Her large blue eyes studied a soft silk, and she walked with a steady stride.

The shop was crowded, and I had to pull my skirts away from trampling feet a few times. I was pushed closer and closer to Frances. There was no way I could ignore her.

"Lady Devereux."

She glared at me coldly as I handed the piece of paper with my measurements on it to the attendant.

"Lady Lanier," she spoke in an even, flat tone. "I haven't seen you since your wedding."

"Yes, it has been a long time," I countered. "How is your husband?"

"Missing court," she admitted, but without either a smile or a frown. "He has not taken to Ireland."

"And how are your children?"

"The children fare just fine."

"I am glad to hear of it," I replied. "It is good to know that you are doing so well."

I thought I caught a smile, but it quickly faded and she touched the velvet purse that hung from her belt. She pointed to a length of satin and handed the tailor a few coins. We were silent as he cut the amount she wanted. I played with the cross at my neck while he handed her fabric to her.

"Perhaps you will find this odd...," she began. "But I have heard a rumor about you and the playwright, Shakespeare."

I was taken aback. Frances hadn't even been at court. News had reached the outside so quickly? How could the queen and Alfonso not know?

"I just thought you should know." I could see she was choosing her words carefully by the look on her face.

A long moment of silence stretched out. "How kind of you to care," I finally said. Voices echoed through the room. A man was helping a lady with a spool of French lace. I heard him stride over and, out of the corners of my eyes, saw him reach up and pull down the one she desired.

"Do not disregard Her Majesty so easily," she said. I could hear a touch of worry in her voice.

I paused, thinking about what she said. I wondered what else Frances knew, what else everyone knew. The tailor, sensing a break in our conversation, handed me some fabric samples. I watched her curiously, studying her face to see how she was coping.

Before I could stop myself, I spoke again. "I have missed you."

She did not look at me but nodded her head, as if she had already known. The beginnings of wrinkles surrounded her eyes. She reached a hand toward me, and for a moment I thought she might pat me on the shoulder. But she let her hand fall to her side and turned away, her fabric under her arm. I thought she was going to leave, but a soft, frightened voice carried to my ear.

"Be careful, Emilia."

I heard her hurried footsteps fade behind me, and I listened as the bell over the door rang her exit. I did not turn, but I imagined her walking down the busy street with her bundle before she stepped into the carriage that would take her back to Essex.

Her warning frightened me. I wondered if William and I had made a mistake—one that could cost me my life.

In March, I started to feel strange. I walked around the palace feeling hungry most of the time, even if I had eaten a filling meal only an hour earlier. I was also tired most the time, no matter how well I had slept. I thought nothing of it. There were other things on my mind.

William was busy with the Globe. He spent most of his time with architects and builders, completing the final designs. I wished he would spend less time on the theatre and more time planning his escape with me, but I didn't let it show. His face was tired but he was excited, and I couldn't help but be excited for him.

The plague struck again. Though the wealthy could escape to their estates outside the city, William and I did not have that luxury. Nights when we were together, we heard cries of agony in the room next to us. Doors opened and closed as soothsayers bled victims who had caught the wretched disease.

The number of bodies on the cart just outside the palace gates grew. The wealthier bodies were wrapped in pallid linen, while the poor remained in the clothes they departed this world in.

One day, as I was passing through the halls, I was blocked by a soothsayer coming from the direction I was headed. He held out a hand to block me from going any farther. His eyes drooped with fatigue, and the white shirt he wore was stained with blood and sweat. Herbs dangled from pouches on his belt.

"I would not go that way, my lady," he said. "They are carrying a young woman out of her room, and her husband is coming down with the same symptoms. I would stay far away from here."

"Thank you," I said. "Bless you."

He hurried on, and I went back to my chambers. Every time I heard another moan through the thin walls, I was glad that Henry and Alfonso were traveling the countryside. They would be safer away from the city.

Most of London was locked away, hiding from the unseen enemy, while the rest were buried on the street. I encouraged William not to go out. He laughed, shook his head, and kissed my cheek.

"The Globe is right in the middle of London, dear," he said. "How do you suggest I finish it if I don't go out?"

I couldn't stop him. He was determined to finish his project. I could only watch and pray that he did not contract the disease. I just wanted him to be safe; I didn't want to lose him in that way. I didn't know what I would do if we couldn't be together.

Just as the spring flowers were beginning to bloom, Margaret came to my door.

Her eyes were wide with fear, and I ushered her into my chambers as quickly as possible and closed the door tightly behind her. Her breathing was shallow, as if she had run. I pulled up a chair for her to sit upon.

She lowered herself into the chair and moaned. She wrung her hands together before her right hand flew to her face and she brushed aside a stray hair. Margaret, in all the years I'd known her, had never looked so disheveled and distressed.

"Emilia, I must tell you something," she began, and her voice cracked. She looked as though she really did not want to say the words.

"Of course," I said. "Say what you need."

She swallowed. I feared for her, and I felt dread creeping into my body. Her eyes were red and swollen, as though she had been crying for hours. Not even when her marriage was collapsing or she was with child had I seen Margaret in such a state,

"Perhaps William should join us before I tell you," she said delicately.

It was the first time she had ever called him by his first name. I didn't question her anymore. We waited for William in silence, the burning fire warding off the early spring chill.

She twisted her hands in her lap. I could only think of one thing that would make her so worried for me. I could only think of one reason she would wait for William before speaking. Then the door opened and William burst through. His smile disappeared when he saw Margaret. He closed the door behind him softly.

"I am sorry. I did not realize we had a guest," he apologized.

Margaret nodded curtly, her mind still on what she was going to say.

He sat down on the bed, close to my chair, even though there was a seat for him next to the fire. The mattress creaked stiffly. He looked to me, his small smile just barely visible through the confusion and worry.

"William," I choked out his name, "Margaret has something to tell us."

It was a moment before she collected herself. She turned in her chair so she could clearly see both of us. Her hands shook and she breathed deeply. I gave one last look at William before she spoke.

"The queen knows."

William gasped. It was almost too soft for me to hear, but I could. He reached for my hand, taking it, as if he were trying to hold on to me for as long as possible. He was frightened.

It was some time before he answered.

"What should we do?" His words were clear and slow.

Margaret glanced at me. "She wants to see both of you."

William gripped my hand tighter. "When?"

"Tomorrow."

He sighed. "You could have told us a bit sooner," he grunted.

"Stop," I scolded him. "She did the best she could without the queen suspecting."

He sighed, more deeply and sadly this time. "I am sorry," he said. "It's just…"

Margaret nodded. "I know."

My stomach churned and my hands grew sweaty. What would I say to Her Majesty? I had never been so frightened in my life. My whole body trembled and my heart beat in my chest. It was as if a bird were locked in me, desperately beating its wings to get out.

My right hand, the one that wasn't holding William's, gripped the side of the bed. I was doomed to a fate without William… forever. I couldn't explain the grief and the hopelessness I was feeling.

"Emilia?" Margaret said. "I am so sorry. I tried my hardest to make sure she didn't know."

"I know you did. It is nothing you have done. She was bound to find out." My voice was as an old woman's, drained of life.

Margaret took my other hand, and I was held by two of the most important people in my life. I realized how lucky I was, even in my darkest hour, to have people who loved me and cared about me. If there was one thing I wanted to remember, it was the feeling of wholeness before the feeling of dread came. I grasped this moment like I grasped the hands of my friend and my lover.

"What are we going to say?" I asked William as my mind cleared.

"We are going to tell her the truth. I love you. If she cannot accept this, then we will just have to deal with the consequences."

"And what consequences will those be?" I turned to Margaret. An image of Henry flashed through my mind.

"I do not know," she answered.

I COULDN'T SLEEP. I didn't even try. I lay awake, staring at the ceiling, just as I had so long ago at my little house in London. Images would come to me—of Henry, of Margaret, and of William. I could not control these visions. They greeted me like ghosts. I counted how many times I turned over in my bed, flipping from one side to another.

I remembered coming to court for the first time. I thought of Margaret and Frances and how close they had been and how they were now so far away. I remembered my old master, Henry Carey, and how he was the first to introduce me to William, how he had given me my child. *One.*

I smiled at little Henry's curls and his smile. I admired his devotion to his adopted father and his excitement about becoming a musician. I wondered if I would ever be able to say good-bye. *Two.* The sheets rustled in protest.

I thought mostly of William. He was my one kindred soul. I thought of how much I loved him and how it must come to an end. I would never love anyone the way I loved him. He was part of me. He was who I was, who I cared most about. I would always love him. *Three.*

There was one more soul that haunted me that night. I didn't want to see her. I had spent most of my life hating being compared to her. That night, however, I let her taunt me. I always swore I would never follow Anne Boleyn's example. But I had let her take hold of me and I had let love change me. I wasn't sure if it was for the better or the worse. After that, I forgot to count anymore.

When the first light of morning peeked through my window, I bathed and dressed. My worst nightmare had come true. I would tell the queen the truth, but I didn't know what I would do from there. When she asked me never to see William again, what would I say? What if she threatened a punishment much worse?

I dressed in my newest gown just arrived from the tailor's. I admired the handiwork and the blood-red color. I had never even worn it. I took it as a sign. I would meet the queen in my finest. I pulled my hair away from my face and pinned it. My high cheekbones were pale. I was so afraid.

I took out my cross and clasped it around my neck. If I had ever needed God, it was now.

There was a knock on my door and I knew the time had come. I opened it slowly. A stocky messenger was waiting outside.

"Lady Lanier?" he asked.

"Yes," I replied.

"Her Majesty wishes to see you."

"I suppose she does."

I stepped out of my chambers with my head held high. I would not be known as anything but a lady, even as I was led to my humiliation.

"This way," he said.

The passageways seemed darker and more threatening. I tried to remember everything about them—the carefully woven tapestries, the shine of the suits of armor standing guard, the little bit of sunlight pooling through the windows. It could be the last time I ever saw it like this.

We stopped in front of the two gigantic doors that led to the throne room. They stood like a giant mouth. The intricate carvings mocked me, like large eyes. We waited outside.

"Is someone in there?" I asked.

"The Master Shakespeare," he said. I wondered how many people like me he had shown through those doors.

I was very quiet. I tried to hear William's voice. I could hear muted tones but no words. I could pick out his voice. I wondered if he was thinking of me.

We waited for several more minutes until the large doors finally opened. William stepped out, his face grave. He strode over to me and let me fall into his arms.

He kissed me softly; I could tell he was savoring it. I wrapped my arms tightly around him, never wanting him to let go. He held me for several minutes. We breathed together, and I wondered if it were for the last time. It might be the last time I would feel the strength in his arms and the caring in his touch. It might be the last time I would see myself in his eyes.

"I will be in your chamber," he whispered in my ear.

I nodded so he knew I had heard him.

He squeezed my hand one last time, and then he was gone.

And I had to face the queen.

I entered as slowly as I could, concentrating on the number of steps I took so I wouldn't fall over in fear. I kept my eyes down, like the other times I had met with Her Majesty. I breathed in as deeply as possible and made three curtsies.

The night before, I had thought about how I would address her. I had gone through the list of titles I could use to regain her approval and finally decided on one.

"Your Grace," I said. I dared to look upon her.

Her face was unreadable. Her hawkish eyes seemed to be looking through me, as though I was as transparent as a shard of glass. She looked as if at any moment she would swoop down and devour me. I was and always had been her prey.

Her Majesty wore a gown of satin. Her collar stood high above her shoulders like ruffled feathers. The dress was a creamy white, and it made her red hair seem dark. Curtains were drawn across the window to hide the sun. The room seemed much colder and more frightening than the other times I had been there. I knew what she was thinking. A newcomer at court would have been able to tell what she was thinking. I recognized that hard line where her mouth should have been. It was the line she had worn at Frances's wedding.

"Lady Lanier," she spoke in a cool, even tone. "I have reason to believe that you have been engaging in manners unacceptable in my court. Is that correct?"

She was much older than she had been the last time I had seen her so close. Her paper-thin skin clung to her bones. Her wrinkles had grown deeper.

How could I answer? Even in her old age, she was an imposing force as she sat on her perch above me.

I searched my mind before I replied.

"It would depend on what Your Majesty deems unacceptable."

Her eyes softened. Not enough for the newcomer at court—just enough for the person who idolized her.

"You have spirit. I have always admired that about you. I knew you weren't some average musician's daughter from the moment I inducted you into my court. But...," she continued, "such behavior cannot be present among my ladies. You must tell me the truth, Lady Lanier. Are you Master William Shakespeare's mistress?"

This was the time. I would confess the truth, as I was sure William had done. Why else would he have had such a melancholy look about him when he saw me? It broke my heart to utter the next few words, for I was sure she wouldn't be forgiving after I admitted my greatest sin.

"I am, Your Grace."

"You are married, are you not?"

"I am, Your Grace."

"Do you not know this is a sin against God and His church?"

My mind raced with the thoughts of her with Robert Dudley and Essex. Her words felt like a hundred lies in a single phrase. Was my sin any different from hers? How was being in love with William any worse than what she had done with endless courtiers?

"I do, Your Grace."

She stared at me. I lowered my eyes to the floor. I had never felt so ashamed in my life. I felt as though she were looking inside me.

"And what do you think is an acceptable punishment for one who has ignored the laws of her queen and her God?"

She was not asking my opinion. What would she want to hear? I could not be sure. I opened my mouth, but nothing came out. What would the proper penalty be? When I did not reply, she left the inquiry alone.

She shook her head so delicately I could barely see it.

"I'm afraid I must ask why you chose to deliberately disobey me."

My lip quivered before I could force out what I was about to say.

"I fell in love."

The queen sighed. It was not a sound of acceptance or admiration. It was the sigh I gave if one of my dresses was so torn it wasn't worth wearing again. It was how I knew my cause was lost. The queen had fallen in love too many times and had spent too long worrying about her lovers to care about mine.

"How did a lady such as yourself become attracted to a simple playwright?"

"I am as I always have been, a musician's daughter." It was all I could say.

"That is not the truth," Her Majesty corrected me. "You are a lady of my court. You had everything. " She shifted in her throne. "Who do you think the world will remember more? A lady in my court, or a simple playwright?"

"I would not know, Your Grace."

She nodded. "Very well. You are no longer allowed to see Master Shakespeare, and I must ask you to leave court immediately. I cannot have the other ladies looking to your example. Is that clear?"

"Yes."

"And if I am to hear any more of your relationship with Master Shakespeare, I will have to take"—she coughed—"more drastic measures."

"Yes, Your Majesty."

She waved her hand, my signal to leave.

It was the last time I would ever see Her Highness alive.

I backed out of the hall. An immense sense of relief washed over me. It appeared the queen would not make Henry or Margaret suffer any harm. It was a weight off my shoulders, for I knew I would never have to worry about their safety again.

And yet I could never see William again. There was a pain in my chest I had never felt before, and I felt tears come to my eyes. Now I knew why William had kissed me so. It was a good-bye. He had agreed to the queen's conditions as I had. It was as if a piece of me had been ripped out. Everything I had once been was no longer.

I rushed down through the passageways. My only hope was that William had done what he had said and waited for me. He would be in my chamber for the final time. The final kiss. The final good-bye. People stared. I didn't care. My mind raced. Maybe he was still planning on our escape to Italy. My heart clung to this hope. I could hardly breathe. I hesitated when I reached the familiar door, my hand gripping the handle like a vise. The queen had said I could never see him again. I had disobeyed her wishes before. One last time would not matter. Her Majesty understood the significance of a good-bye. She must. She knew what love was like. It was the most unconscious, hurtful, terribly beautiful experience I had ever lived through. Love was nothing like it seemed in books and poetry. It did not feel the way others had promised. It was not at all the way I'd imagined it when I was young. Falling in love wasn't the right thing to do. The things that mattered rarely were.

I opened the door.

He wasn't there.

My dilapidated desk looked as if it had been rifled through. The drawers were all pulled out of it, and papers were scattered on the floor. The drawer where I kept my story was wide open, and it was empty.

He had taken it.

The rest of the room was untouched except for one thing. I let go of the handle and closed the door behind me. I was abandoned. He had promised I wouldn't be. He had left me without even saying good-bye.

I walked over to the bed as stiff as a corpse. I picked up the rose he had left and let my eyes rest on the sheet of paper he had placed on the bed.

And I read.

Emilia,

I cannot compare you to a summer's day, for you are far more warm and temperate. You may think when you enter this room and see that I am gone that I do not care or love you. You would be very wrong indeed. It may appear that I have left you, but you will never leave me.

You were right. The queen will have nothing of us being together, and I fear things other than times apart. You are as much a part of me as these very words, and you are the reason to write them down, because you have become my passion. You are my inspiration.

I promise you will know of this truth.

William

PART THREE

O, know, sweet love, I always write of you,
And you and love are still my argument;
So all my best is dressing old words new,
Spending again what is already spent:
For as the sun is daily new and old,
So is my love still telling what is told.

—Sonnet LXXVI

England, 1616
During the Reign of King James I
London

I knelt before the tiny memorial stone. I had visited this spot nearly every day for the last seventeen years, faithfully placing flowers and saying prayers. As usual, the words etched in the stone reminded me of him. But then, everything reminded me of him.

She was his child. From the time she was born, there was no doubt. She had his small smile and his enchanting eyes. She was beautiful, as was he. I had named her Odillya, a name similar to his character in *Hamlet*. She was a weak child to begin with, but I'd nursed her as best I could, hoping I would always have her as my most precious reminder.

The iron gate surrounding the perimeter of the cemetery was rusted now, the paths overgrown with stubborn plants. White stones dotted the grass like scattered doves on a tree. Wings sprouted from stone angels, while words beneath them bespoke names no one had ever heard of.

After the queen banished me from her court, I went to live with Margaret in Cumberland. I could not face Alfonso. Not with my shame known throughout all England and a growing child in my belly. He would know it wasn't his.

I wrote. There was nothing else for me to do. I would sit down with a new notebook over my bulging stomach and a pen and write. I wrote of Margaret's home in Cumberland, but mostly I wrote my penance.

I was wiser than I had ever been. Heartbreak had made me stronger, and I knew that I would never make such a mistake again. I wrote poetry in exchange for my forgiveness, to ease my shame, but I wondered if I was ever truly forgiven.

I wanted to publish this work. It would take me thirteen years to finish.

Odillya died at ten months, and everything I had from William Shakespeare was gone. I wrote to Alfonso that day, asking him to accept me back so I could come home. So I could see my son. It was a month before I heard from him, but he accepted. Our relationship was strained for some time. He did not speak to me unless he needed to, and I slept on the hard, wooden floor for a while before I was offered a place in his bed again. But in a way, it was as if nothing had ever changed. Alfonso was still light and dark, but now I had learned I was too.

He and William never spoke again. Their friendship had been lost when we were banished from court. Alfonso never mentioned him again. It was as if William Shakespeare had not existed. I began to wonder if he and I ever had.

There were days when I hated him. There were times when I was angry for falling into the trap of love. I blamed William for the loss of the child; I blamed him for everything. I tried to forget William Shakespeare, but I could not. Little things reminded me of him. When I wrote, I could feel him caressing my skin. When I was lonely, I thought about the times we were really happy. I thought about his kisses and his promises.

There were signs, just as he had promised. He sent me his first book of poetry—direct from his house in London—and I hid it under the mattress for years. It had that fresh smell of new pages, printed and bound together with love and care. When I opened it, its binding crackled as a new book does when it is opened. In his poems he spoke of someone beautiful and dark and mysterious, someone he should not have loved. *"If this error and upon me proved, I never writ, nor no man ever loved."*

His sonnets held me to him. They were the one thing that kept me from denying I had ever loved him. I saw his attempts to win me back through his words. "Hold on," they seemed to say. "I will come for you." *"You shall live—such virtue hath my pen—where breath most breathes, even in the mouths of men."*

Years went by, and I began to accept my life as it was. It would never be as I had dreamed it, but I had given up on dreams long ago. I had given up on everything that seemed to matter.

Life went on. I grew older. I watched my son grow from a child to a man, and I watched as Alfonso handed over the business to him a few years after the queen's death.

We journeyed to Westminster Abbey to attend her funeral. Alfonso played; he had always been one of her favorite musicians. All the ladies-in-waiting were there, the newly widowed Frances included, though she refused to look at me and turned her slender back to me. The abbey was filled with those who had both admired and despised her. I could hear sobs and sniffles in front of and behind me. Pained voices echoed in my ears, and the hymns we sung were loud with grief. The bells rang, as they had so many times before. I did not sing the songs. I did not cry. I stood there with my son, no longer a baby, at my side.

I saw Margaret. She was on the far side of the abbey, and I did catch her eye. She smiled at me sadly and closed her eyes. Even from a distance, I could see she was crying. The woman who had always told her what to do still held a place in her heart. And I hated to think it, but she still did in mine too.

I looked for William in the crowd. Whether he was there or not, I will never know. The mass of people was too large, and I could imagine that he didn't wish to see Alfonso. There was a part of me that could feel him there, whether or not he was.

The country grieved for Elizabeth in many ways, for her intelligence and spirit, her wit and her beauty, but they did not grieve for the harm she had caused. As a final claim of superiority, she had executed her lover, the Earl of Essex, two years before she herself left this world. His lack of respect for the queen's tempestuous nature had been rewarded with the loss of his head.

I was never again happy as I had been with William, but I was never miserable. I lived my life with new wisdom and understanding. The loss of a child and the loss of a lover had brought a new perspective. Every time I felt alone, I would take out the book of sonnets and remind myself that he loved me. He was always on my mind...sometimes hated, yet always loved. Over time, the loathing was not directed at the memory of him, but at the memory of what could never be.

Alfonso grew older. His hair became lined with gray. He no longer felt the need to scorn me. We lived off the money we saved and the small bit of income my newly published book acquired. We rarely spoke to each other as a husband and wife should, and I never loved him. I would never love anyone again. He would sit alone by the old hearth, reading letters or staring into the fire and grumbling when he needed me.

Then, one evening, he spoke of William.

"Emilia," he said, his voice hoarse with age. He had been greatly affected by the recent damp weather.

"Yes," I replied, glancing up from my sewing.

"I need you to do a favor for me."

I nodded. "Of course."

"I need you to go to Stratford."

I wondered what he would be doing in Stratford.

"Why?"

"William Shakespeare is dying."

I dropped my sewing in my lap.

He waited for my answer, his eyes still on the glowing fire and his thoughts on long ago. Did he miss William as much as I did?

It took me a moment to steady my voice enough to reply. I did not want it to seem as though I was too eager or too disheartened.

"Yes, I will go."

I GATHERED MY SKIRTS from around me then kissed my fingers and placed them silently on the stone, feeling the rough rock underneath. I dropped a single white rose at the base. I stood up slowly. I felt as though my body would break with the thought of seeing William again. It had been so long.

I walked through the streets, avoiding people and thinking about what I would say. What could I say? Words I had rehearsed in my mind felt strained when said aloud. A man with a large cart full of fish yelled at me to get out of his way, but I hardly noticed. I let my skirts drag through the mud. It had always been so easy, before, to talk to him. I decided I wouldn't rehearse anything.

When I reached our door, I opened it expecting to see Alfonso in his usual place. Instead, I found him in our bedroom, packing most of my tattered clothes. He looked up at me and grunted.

"You're going to need these," was all he said.

I took the bag from him gently. His eyes looked me over. His face was ragged, and his expression was one of regret, as though he missed his best friend more than he could say. What we all gave up to appease the queen.

"Tell him," he added. "Tell him that I have always thought of him as my friend."

"All right," I said.

"And tell him that if he needs anything in his final hours, I will provide it for him."

I nodded.

He sighed softly and sadly. "Do you know the way?"

I nodded for the second time. It would be about a two days' ride. I would go on horseback; it was faster than taking a carriage. I hoped I could reach him in time.

He handed me two more objects that I had failed to see in his gnarled hand before. They were books. Two books. One was mine, and the other was William's sonnets. Their covers looked as old as he did; I had read through them again and again.

"You never stopped hoping, did you?" he asked.

It was all I could do to keep from weeping. It was the first loving act I had ever received from my husband. I wanted to let him know how much it meant to me that he had never beaten me because of my love for William. I wanted him to know how much I appreciated that he had taken me back after everything I had done.

But all I could do was look him in the eyes and give him a smile. Time had changed everything. I didn't love him any more than I ever had, but I finally knew what William had meant when he said Alfonso, the moon, could shine as the sun.

He smiled back sadly and cocked his head toward the door, indicating that it was time for me to go. I walked down the steps to the door, feeling his eyes on me. I knew how he wished he could go, as well. It was a shame to be an old man with bad health and too much pride. We said our good-byes, and I mounted his horse that was patiently tied outside. I waved once, staring at his figure in the doorway.

And then I kicked the horse lightly and began my journey to Stratford-upon-Avon.

IT WAS EXACTLY AS I predicted; I arrived in the tiny town of Stratford two days after leaving my house. I had stayed a night at an inn along the road and continued on in the morning, my heart pounding with anticipation and fear. I had imagined this scene in my mind over and over again, but I had never imagined it like this.

My entire body shook as I neared the tiny town. Several cattle on a farm just outside the village looked lazily in my direction. I saw only one person on the road and asked him where I could find

Master Shakespeare's home. He pointed to the center of town with his browned hand, saying it was not far from the school.

It had begun to rain by then, fat drops of water landing on the top of my head and shoulders. I rode through the town as quickly as I could so I would not get wet, but I found it hopeless. William would just have to accept me as I was. Now there was more than one reason I was shaking.

I tied my horse outside the small house. I unpacked the few things I wished to bring in to him. The house was nothing like I had imagined. It was kept up nicely, and it was one of the nicer houses in the area. There was a flowerbed not far from the door, and the exterior had been recently painted and tended to.

Holding the two books against my chest, I went up to the door. I knocked on it five times. The world was still for a moment, and I waited to see his face. When there was no answer, I knocked again, this time only twice.

The door opened slowly. A set of eyes peered out into the rainy, dark night. I could tell instantly that they were not William's. I had not known whether his wife would still be living, but now she was before me.

"Who is there?" a shrill voice asked.

"I am the lady Emilia Lanier," I said. "I hear your husband is very ill. He was a good friend of my husband, Alfonso."

She glared at me a little longer before letting me into her warm kitchen. It was shadowy in the room, and the only sound was something boiling in the kettle over the fire.

"Sit down," she offered, indicating a chair facing a round table.

I obeyed, placing the books on the table and sitting as quietly as

I could. I glanced around. The house had little furniture, but there was not a lot of room to put anything. The inside was well taken care of, like the outside. The fire cast shadows on the wall, and I could smell herbs drying.

"Why couldn't your husband come?" She stirred the mixture in the pot, which smelled like stew from where I sat.

"He is ill," I explained. "He is getting older than he would like to admit."

"My husband is dying, Lady Lanier." She spoke sharply. She was of average height, her graying brown hair pulled back under her cap. She wore an apron around her waist, and her nose was wrinkled as if she had smelled something very bad, indeed.

"Yes," I said. "I am sorry to hear it." I hoped that was the proper response.

She sat down across from me, her hard expression unchanging as she studied my face. I could see her peering into every part of me—not only my appearance, but my very soul. She reminded me very much of Queen Elizabeth with her hawkish eyes.

"Do not think I don't know you," she said. "You were his mistress while he was at court. Did you think I wouldn't recognize your name?"

"No." I shook my head. "I knew you would."

She looked at me curiously. I had surprised her. She seemed confused, as though she could not understand why I had come. Her face became tight.

"He still loves you, you know." She leaned toward me. "How would you like to fall asleep by your husband's side each night and wake to hear him saying another woman's name?"

She stopped and glared at me, daring me to speak.

I couldn't. What would I say? I had never thought of her when I was with William.

"He wrote poems to this lady I had never known. He has not written anything for me," she continued. "Not one letter, not one word. I would want to read what he had to say so badly, but he never let me. 'Who is it for?' I would ask. 'No one,' he'd reply. Yet I would read it when he didn't know and find that not one word was addressed to me. How could you understand that?"

She waited for my answer, breathing deeply.

It hurt for me to look at her and speak the truth, because I wanted to lie to her. I wanted to tell her that my relationship with her husband was nothing like she'd thought, but lies always taste like sour milk—they linger long after you've spat them out. I did not want to think about the hurt I'd caused her.

"I could not," was all I could mumble.

She nodded stiffly, as though she was still not sure she could believe me. Her eyes continued to watch me. She ran her hand over the table, feeling the bumps and cracks that came when wood aged. I scratched my palm.

"And you?" she asked. "Do you still love him?"

She surprised me. It was the last question I had ever expected from his wife. I wasn't prepared for it. But the truth had been the best philosophy so far. I might as well say what was on my mind. She could scorn me if she wished.

"I do," I whispered.

She didn't look astounded at all. She nodded curtly, as if all she ever needed to know was in those two words.

"You are different than I thought you would be." She sighed. "You see his imaginings, don't you?"

"I used to," I said. "But sometimes...sometimes I just wanted to see myself in his eyes." I thought about how I always felt the struggle between me and his love of stories.

She gave a little frown. "I have not known one soul who has understood him completely."

"Oh, I never could," I added swiftly. "In some ways he is as much of a mystery to me as he was when I first met him."

She was quiet, her arms crossed in front of her chest and her eyes downcast. I could not read her expression. It was something between empathy and fury—I wasn't sure which it was closer to.

"I wanted to hate you...," she sputtered.

Her face spoke what she didn't say. She loved him as well. I could sense her undying loyalty...and the pain of living every day and night knowing he did not feel the same way.

She had always haunted me, yet I could see how confused and heartbroken we both were. Her face wore lines of sadness.

"You probably want to see him now," she said.

It was all I could do to keep from crying. I nodded gently and gathered my books into my arms. I followed her up the tiny, steep staircase, my heart pounding in my chest. I had never been so lost and scared. What would I say when I met him again?

He wasn't sleeping, just sitting up in his bed with a pen in his hand, writing until the very end. His hair had turned a handsome silver-gray, which only made his olive skin glow even more than I remembered.

Anne Shakespeare cleared her throat.

"William," she said gently, as if speaking to a newborn baby, "someone is here to see you."

He didn't look up. "Tell them I cannot speak to them at the moment." His voice was still musical.

"But, my dear, it is the lady Lanier," she said, her voice cracking slightly.

His head shot up, and he saw me. His lips curled into his small smile, his expression jovial but wise, wiser than he had been before. And his eyes—they were the same as when I had first seen them.

But he was frail, I could tell. Still as handsome as ever, but sick. He looked so very tired, as though he could not take another step. I supposed that was why he was in his bed. I noticed how his hands shook and how thin he was.

"Hello, William," I said softly.

"Emilia? Is that really you?" He spoke as if I was a ghost from another lifetime.

"Yes, it is."

Anne left us alone. I walked over to his deathbed with a smile on my face and a tear in my eye.

"My God," was all he said.

He patted the bed for me to sit down next to him. Still holding my books, I sat carefully. I did not want to disrupt anything or make him uncomfortable.

"Oh, Emilia," he said. "Look at you. You are as beautiful as ever."

I smiled. "He that loves to be flattered is worthy of the flatterer," I said, before laughing.

"Not so, my lady. Did you ever see me flatter any other woman besides yourself?"

I just kept smiling. He was still the same wonderful man I had fallen in love with long ago…and was still in love with after all these years.

He took my hand and held it like a gift. Then he laced his fingers with mine, and the old familiar feeling leaped out of my heart, having been dormant all the time we were away from each another. It was as if we had never left the other's side.

"I bring friendship from Alfonso," I said. "He regrets that he could not make the trip himself. He misses you. He has always missed you."

"Please tell him I have missed him as well. And what is his reason for not coming to see me?"

"He is old. Grows more unlike himself every day."

"If he grows more unlike himself every day, he should be getting better, correct?" He gave a crooked smile.

I laughed, nodding.

"He has been. You were right all along. There was some good in him after all."

"And Henry?"

"He has taken over the family business and is doing a marvelous job."

"I bet he is." William grinned fondly. He touched my cheek with the fingers that weren't holding onto mine.

"And Margaret?"

My heart sank. This was the news I most dreaded telling him.

"She passed on, earlier this year," I replied.

His face dropped, for he knew how much Margaret meant to me.

"Oh. I am so sorry."

"She wouldn't want apologies. She was so happy to return home. I wish you could have seen her. And her daughter has grown to be the loveliest of women."

"I can imagine how much it hurt you," he said.

I nodded, tears once again welling in my eyes. She had been my best friend all those years, caring for me when I needed her and giving me advice when I didn't. I had felt dead myself for days after I got word about her passing, not eating or sleeping. Only time and fond memories had begun to heal my heart.

"Yes, but I know she would not want me to grieve. She lived a full life and will no doubt live happily in the afterlife as well."

William smiled once again. It wouldn't be long before I would have to face death yet another time.

"You cannot know how much I have missed you," he said as he tucked a stray piece of hair behind my ear. "I always believed we would be together."

"We are together." I smiled reassuringly. "We always have been." I showed him one of the books I had brought, the more worn of the two.

It was his sonnets. The pages were tattered, and the cover looked as though it had gone through a war. It had been a fairly nice copy, but that was not evident, the way it was damaged now.

He smiled even wider. "You read it."

"Of course," I said, my words an understatement.

"What is the other one?" he asked, pointing to the next book in the crook of my right arm. I pulled it out and gave it to him.

"Your own book?" he asked, taking his hand out of mine only to hold my work.

"I am a published woman poet without your help, Master Shakespeare," I said.

"I never doubted you would be." He laughed. "This is incredible."

"Oh, I think you doubted me," I gently added. "Why else would you take *A Midsummer Night's Dream*?"

His brow wrinkled. "It was one of the queen's favorites. Did you read the reviews?"

I had indeed. It was the play that brought William back into the favor of Her Majesty, so much so that he was allowed back at court and had received more funding for his work. While I remained exiled, William had regained her respect and trust.

"I did," I said. "I am only joking, William. I honestly didn't care what you did with it. The greatest loss when you left me wasn't that play."

His brow smoothed and he turned to my book in his hands.

"*Salve Deus Rex Judaeorum*," William read the title aloud. "Hail, God, King of the Jews. Incredible." He flipped through the pages, his eyes following them and measuring the length. "What is it about?"

"You will just have to read it," I said.

"I will," he agreed, and I knew he would.

He looked through it one more time before he set it aside and his fingers reached again for mine. He wasn't an old man, and that was why it was so difficult to see him in such a state. He was fifty-two years old. But I recognized the signs, the weakness, and the way he glanced at me. He knew this was the last time he would ever see me.

We talked through the night. Every few hours I would urge him to fall asleep, but he refused. He spoke of our times together, times I had forgotten and times I remembered better than my own name.

We talked of Henry Carey, of Margaret, of the queen. We talked about his theatre, the Globe, which had done so well.

I couldn't tell him of his daughter, Odillya. It would have been too much for him, I believed. Even on his deathbed I would not tell him about the child who had graced this earth for such a short time.

Everything had changed, but then again, nothing had. Our experiences had changed our lives, but they hadn't changed the people we were. And I found myself as deeply in love with him as I had ever been.

Finally, as the morning light began to shine through the upstairs window, William drifted off into a deep, uneven sleep. I had exhausted him, and I could only pray that nothing I had done would change the pace of his decline.

I knew I needed to leave, yet I waited until the sun was rising steadily. It was morning, and William Shakespeare—the greatest writer the world has ever known, a wonderful actor, a remarkable man, my lover—was leaving this world to join the next.

I kissed his cheek, breathing in his scent for the last time. He did not stir, but his unsteady breathing told me what soon would be no longer. I gently placed a neatly folded letter in his hand. I took one last glance at him and then left.

I found his wife asleep in a chair in the kitchen, her face distraught even in her sleep. I hoped that one day she would find the happiness she had searched for all her life. Quietly, I pulled off Henry Carey's ruby ring that I'd worn all those years and set it on the table next to her so she could not miss it when she awoke. It would help to pay for her life when William was gone. It was the least I could do, for she had done what I never could have: forgive a woman for loving the man she had wanted for her own.

When I stepped out into the morning light, I saw that the flowers reached their faces toward the sun, straining to feel the warmth it provided. I too turned my face to the rising sun.

William's death wasn't the end. It was a gorgeous beginning.

I closed my eyes and imagined the day I had first seen him. It had been a wonderful beginning, a moment of quiet beauty, and I felt that today was as well. Death was not the end; it was the start of something better, something that truly mattered.

A great playwright once said, "*Life's but a walking shadow, a poor player that struts and frets his hour upon the stage and then is heard no more.*" I knew the world would never remember me or what I had done, but it would never forget the man I loved.

AUTHOR'S NOTE

EMILIA BASSANO LANIER WAS a real person who frequented the court of Queen Elizabeth I. It is true that she was mistress to Henry Carey, the Baron of Hunsdon, and when found to be pregnant, she was unhappily married to one of Her Majesty's favorite musicians, Alfonso Lanier. She is also one of the first Englishwomen to publish her own volume of poetry. Yet the world seems to have forgotten her. I hope this story will bring more attention to her name.

We know that Emilia Lanier was a favorite of Queen Elizabeth. No one seems to know why she disappeared from the scene at court, so I have created my own reasons for her departure.

I found two dates for Alfonso Lanier's death. I chose the later date in 1616 in order to tell this story, but it is more likely he died earlier, in 1613. After her husband's death, Emilia was said to have opened a school for children. It did not remain open for long. However, from this and other business endeavors, she survived until her death at age sixty-seven.

There is no proof that she was Shakespeare's mistress, but there is no doubt that they would have known each other. As Henry Carey's mistress, Emilia would have met the young William Shakespeare, and they would have been in close proximity to each other often. I imagined a romance between the striking Emilia and the passionate William, but all other events in Emilia's life are true—including her relationship with Henry Carey; the birth and death of her daughter Odillya; her son, Henry; her friendship with Margaret, the Countess of Cumberland; and finally, her published book of poetry, *Salve Deus Rex Judaeorum (Hail, God, King of the Jews).*

I have tried to remain as close to historical fact as possible. William Shakespeare was said to have journeyed to London between 1585 to around 1592. He, too, would have been at court promoting his work and meeting with patrons. All the facts of his life, from his beginnings as an unknown playwright to his development as one of the greatest writers of all time, are faithful.

There is no evidence that Emilia wrote *A Midsummer Night's Dream*. Some scholars have argued that Emilia might actually have been the author of Shakespeare's plays, but there is no decisive proof to support this.

Scholars have long debated the identity of Shakespeare's "Dark Lady," or whether she was only a literary device. Shakespeare dedicated twenty-five sonnets to this mysterious character. Many consider them to be his best, filled with heartache and longing. Shakespeare historian A. L. Rowse felt certain that the Dark Lady would have been Emilia—and that he named one of his characters Emilia (*Othello*) was no coincidence. The Dark Lady, whoever she is, will forever live on.

Emilia Bassano Lanier was a fascinating woman in her own right, whether or not she was a mistress to William Shakespeare. Though there are things we can never know about her life, I hope I have remained true to the essence of Elizabethan history and William Shakespeare's important place in it. As a famous playwright once said, I hope "my words express my purpose."

BIBLIOGRAPHY

Ackroyd, Peter. *Shakespeare*. Anchor, 2005. Print.

Asimov, Isaac. *Asimov's Guide to Shakespeare*. New York: Avenel, 1978. Print.

Bate, Jonathan. *Soul of the Age: A Biography of the Mind of William Shakespeare*. New York: Random House, 2009. Print.

Dunn, Jane. *Elizabeth and Mary: Cousins, Rivals, Queens*. New York: Alfred A. Knopf, 2004. Print.

Greenblatt, Stephen. *Will in the World: How Shakespeare Became Shakespeare*. New York: W.W. Norton, 2004. Print.

Honan, Park. *Shakespeare: A Life*. Oxford: Oxford UP, 1999. Print.

Jenkins, Elizabeth. *Elizabeth the Great*. New York: Coward-McCann, 1959. Print.

Lanyer, Aemilia, and A. L. Rowse. *The Poems of Shakespeare's Dark Lady:* Salve Deus Rex Judaeorum. New York: C.N. Potter, 1979. Print.

Levi, Peter. *The Life and Times of William Shakespeare*. London: Macmillan, 1988. Print.

Neale, J. E. *Elizabeth I and Her Parliaments*. New York: St. Martin's, 19. Print.

Nuttall, A. D. *Shakespeare the Thinker.* New Haven, NJ: Yale UP, 2007. Print.

Picard, Liza. *Elizabeth's London: Everyday Life in Elizabethan London.* New York: St. Martin's, 2004. Print.

Plowden, Alison. *The Young Elizabeth.* New York: Stein and Day, 1971. Print.

Rosenbaum, Ron. *The Shakespeare Wars: Clashing Scholars, Public Fiascoes, Palace Coups.* New York: Random House, 2006. Print.

Rosenblum, Joseph. *A Reader's Guide to Shakespeare.* Barnes & Noble Books, 1999. Print.

Rowse, A. L. *William Shakespeare: A Biography.* New York: Harper & Row, 1963. Print.

Sears, Elisabeth. *Shakespeare and the Tudor Rose.* Meadow Geese, 1991. Print.

Shakespeare, William. *The Complete Works of William Shakespeare.* Ann Arbor: Borders Group, 1996. Print.

Somerset, Anne. *Elizabeth I.* New York: Knopf, 1991. Print.

Starkey, David. *Elizabeth: the Struggle for the Throne.* New York: HarperCollins, 2001. Print.

Weir, Alison. *The Life of Elizabeth I.* New York: Ballantine, 1998. Print.

THE DARK LADY SONNETS

CXXVII

In the old age black was not counted fair,
Or if it were, it bore not beauty's name;
But now is black beauty's successive heir,
And beauty slandered with a bastard shame:
For since each hand hath put on Nature's power,
Fairing the foul with Art's false borrowed face,
Sweet beauty hath no name, no holy bower,
But is profaned, if not lives in disgrace.
Therefore my mistress' eyes are raven black,
Her eyes so suited, and they mourners seem
At such who, not born fair, no beauty lack,
Sland'ring creation with a false esteem:
Yet so they mourn becoming of their woe,
That every tongue says beauty should look so.

CXXVIII

How oft when thou, my music, music play'st,
Upon that blessed wood whose motion sounds
With thy sweet fingers when thou gently sway'st

The wiry concord that mine ear confounds,
Do I envy those jacks that nimble leap,
To kiss the tender inward of thy hand,
Whilst my poor lips which should that harvest reap,
At the wood's boldness by thee blushing stand!
To be so tickled, they would change their state
And situation with those dancing chips,
O'er whom thy fingers walk with gentle gait,
Making dead wood more bless'd than living lips.
Since saucy jacks so happy are in this,
Give them thy fingers, me thy lips to kiss.

CXXIX

The expense of spirit in a waste of shame
Is lust in action: and till action, lust
Is perjured, murderous, bloody, full of blame,
Savage, extreme, rude, cruel, not to trust;
Enjoyed no sooner but despised straight;
Past reason hunted; and no sooner had,
Past reason hated, as a swallowed bait,
On purpose laid to make the taker mad.
Mad in pursuit and in possession so;
Had, having, and in quest to have extreme;
A bliss in proof, and proved, a very woe;
Before, a joy proposed; behind a dream.
All this the world well knows; yet none knows well
To shun the heaven that leads men to this hell.

CXXX

My mistress' eyes are nothing like the sun;

Coral is far more red, than her lips red:
If snow be white, why then her breasts are dun;
If hairs be wires, black wires grow on her head.
I have seen roses damasked, red and white,
But no such roses see I in her cheeks;
And in some perfumes is there more delight
Than in the breath that from my mistress reeks.
I love to hear her speak, yet well I know
That music hath a far more pleasing sound:
I grant I never saw a goddess go,
My mistress, when she walks, treads on the ground:
And yet by heaven, I think my love as rare,
As any she belied with false compare.

CXXXI
Thou art as tyrannous, so as thou art,
As those whose beauties proudly make them cruel;
For well thou know'st to my dear doting heart
Thou art the fairest and most precious jewel.
Yet, in good faith, some say that thee behold,
Thy face hath not the power to make love groan;
To say they err I dare not be so bold,
Although I swear it to myself alone.
And to be sure that is not false I swear,
A thousand groans, but thinking on thy face,
One on another's neck, do witness bear
Thy black is fairest in my judgment's place.
In nothing art thou black save in thy deeds,
And thence this slander, as I think, proceeds.

CXXXII

Thine eyes I love, and they, as pitying me,
Knowing thy heart torments me with disdain,
Have put on black and loving mourners be,
Looking with pretty ruth upon my pain.
And truly not the morning sun of heaven
Better becomes the grey cheeks of the east,
Nor that full star that ushers in the even,
Doth half that glory to the sober west,
As those two mourning eyes become thy face:
O! let it then as well beseem thy heart
To mourn for me since mourning doth thee grace,
And suit thy pity like in every part.
Then will I swear beauty herself is black,
And all they foul that thy complexion lack.

CXXXIII

Beshrew that heart that makes my heart to groan
For that deep wound it gives my friend and me!
Is't not enough to torture me alone,
But slave to slavery my sweet'st friend must be?
Me from myself thy cruel eye hath taken,
And my next self thou harder hast engrossed:
Of him, myself, and thee I am forsaken;
A torment thrice three-fold thus to be crossed.
Prison my heart in thy steel bosom's ward,
But then my friend's heart let my poor heart bail;
Whoe'er keeps me, let my heart be his guard;
Thou canst not then use rigour in my jail:
And yet thou wilt; for I, being pent in thee,
Perforce am thine, and all that is in me.

CXXXIV

So now I have confessed that he is thine,
And I myself am mortgaged to thy will,
Myself I'll forfeit, so that other mine
Thou wilt restore to be my comfort still:
But thou wilt not, nor he will not be free,
For thou art covetous, and he is kind;
He learned but surety-like to write for me,
Under that bond that him as fast doth bind.
The statute of thy beauty thou wilt take,
Thou usurer, that put'st forth all to use,
And sue a friend came debtor for my sake;
So him I lose through my unkind abuse.
Him have I lost; thou hast both him and me:
He pays the whole, and yet am I not free.

CXXXV

Whoever hath her wish, thou hast thy Will,
And Will to boot, and Will in over-plus;
More than enough am I that vexed thee still,
To thy sweet will making addition thus.
Wilt thou, whose will is large and spacious,
Not once vouchsafe to hide my will in thine?
Shall will in others seem right gracious,
And in my will no fair acceptance shine?
The sea, all water, yet receives rain still,
And in abundance addeth to his store;
So thou, being rich in Will, add to thy Will
One will of mine, to make thy large will more.
Let no unkind, no fair beseechers kill;
Think all but one, and me in that one Will.

CXXXVI

If thy soul check thee that I come so near,
Swear to thy blind soul that I was thy Will,
And will, thy soul knows, is admitted there;
Thus far for love, my love-suit, sweet, fulfil.
Will, will fulfil the treasure of thy love,
Ay, fill it full with wills, and my will one.
In things of great receipt with ease we prove
Among a number one is reckoned none:
Then in the number let me pass untold,
Though in thy store's account I one must be;
For nothing hold me, so it please thee hold
That nothing me, a something sweet to thee:
Make but my name thy love, and love that still,
And then thou lovest me for my name is 'Will.'

CXXXVII

Thou blind fool, Love, what dost thou to mine eyes,
That they behold, and see not what they see?
They know what beauty is, see where it lies,
Yet what the best is take the worst to be.
If eyes, corrupt by over-partial looks,
Be anchored in the bay where all men ride,
Why of eyes' falsehood hast thou forged hooks,
Whereto the judgment of my heart is tied?
Why should my heart think that a several plot,
Which my heart knows the wide world's common place?
Or mine eyes, seeing this, say this is not,
To put fair truth upon so foul a face?
In things right true my heart and eyes have erred,
And to this false plague are they now transferred.

CXXXVIII

When my love swears that she is made of truth,
I do believe her though I know she lies,
That she might think me some untutored youth,
Unlearned in the world's false subtleties.
Thus vainly thinking that she thinks me young,
Although she knows my days are past the best,
Simply I credit her false-speaking tongue:
On both sides thus is simple truth suppressed:
But wherefore says she not she is unjust?
And wherefore say not I that I am old?
O! love's best habit is in seeming trust,
And age in love, loves not to have years told:
Therefore I lie with her, and she with me,
And in our faults by lies we flattered be.

CXXXIX

O! call not me to justify the wrong
That thy unkindness lays upon my heart;
Wound me not with thine eye, but with thy tongue:
Use power with power, and slay me not by art,
Tell me thou lov'st elsewhere; but in my sight,
Dear heart, forbear to glance thine eye aside:
What need'st thou wound with cunning, when thy might
Is more than my o'erpressed defence can bide?
Let me excuse thee: ah! my love well knows
Her pretty looks have been mine enemies;
And therefore from my face she turns my foes,
That they elsewhere might dart their injuries:
Yet do not so; but since I am near slain,
Kill me outright with looks, and rid my pain.

CXL

Be wise as thou art cruel; do not press
My tongue-tied patience with too much disdain;
Lest sorrow lend me words, and words express
The manner of my pity-wanting pain.
If I might teach thee wit, better it were,
Though not to love, yet, love to tell me so;
As testy sick men, when their deaths be near,
No news but health from their physicians know;
For, if I should despair, I should grow mad,
And in my madness might speak ill of thee;
Now this ill-wresting world is grown so bad,
Mad slanderers by mad ears believed be.
That I may not be so, nor thou belied,
Bear thine eyes straight, though thy proud heart go wide.

CXLI

In faith I do not love thee with mine eyes,
For they in thee a thousand errors note;
But 'tis my heart that loves what they despise,
Who, in despite of view, is pleased to dote.
Nor are mine ears with thy tongue's tune delighted;
Nor tender feeling, to base touches prone,
Nor taste, nor smell, desire to be invited
To any sensual feast with thee alone:
But my five wits nor my five senses can
Dissuade one foolish heart from serving thee,
Who leaves unsway'd the likeness of a man,
Thy proud heart's slave and vassal wretch to be:
Only my plague thus far I count my gain,
That she that makes me sin awards me pain.

CXLII

Love is my sin, and thy dear virtue hate,
Hate of my sin, grounded on sinful loving:
O! but with mine compare thou thine own state,
And thou shalt find it merits not reproving;
Or, if it do, not from those lips of thine,
That have profaned their scarlet ornaments
And sealed false bonds of love as oft as mine,
Robbed others' beds' revenues of their rents.
Be it lawful I love thee, as thou lov'st those
Whom thine eyes woo as mine importune thee:
Root pity in thy heart, that, when it grows,
Thy pity may deserve to pitied be.
If thou dost seek to have what thou dost hide,
By self-example mayst thou be denied!

CXLIII

Lo, as a careful housewife runs to catch
One of her feather'd creatures broke away,
Sets down her babe, and makes all swift dispatch
In pursuit of the thing she would have stay;
Whilst her neglected child holds her in chase,
Cries to catch her whose busy care is bent
To follow that which flies before her face,
Not prizing her poor infant's discontent;
So runn'st thou after that which flies from thee,
Whilst I thy babe chase thee afar behind;
But if thou catch thy hope, turn back to me,
And play the mother's part, kiss me, be kind;

So will I pray that thou mayst have thy 'Will,'
If thou turn back and my loud crying still.

CXLIV

Two loves I have of comfort and despair,
Which like two spirits do suggest me still:
The better angel is a man right fair,
The worser spirit a woman coloured ill.
To win me soon to hell, my female evil,
Tempteth my better angel from my side,
And would corrupt my saint to be a devil,
Wooing his purity with her foul pride.
And whether that my angel be turned fiend,
Suspect I may, yet not directly tell;
But being both from me, both to each friend,
I guess one angel in another's hell:
Yet this shall I ne'er know, but live in doubt,
Till my bad angel fire my good one out.

CXLV

Those lips that Love's own hand did make,
Breathed forth the sound that said 'I hate,'
To me that languished for her sake:
But when she saw my woeful state,
Straight in her heart did mercy come,
Chiding that tongue that ever sweet
Was used in giving gentle doom;
And taught it thus anew to greet;
'I hate' she altered with an end,
That followed it as gentle day,

Doth follow night, who like a fiend
From heaven to hell is flown away.
'I hate,' from hate away she threw,
And saved my life, saying 'not you.'

CXLVI

Poor soul, the centre of my sinful earth,
My sinful earth these rebel powers array,
Why dost thou pine within and suffer dearth,
Painting thy outward walls so costly gay?
Why so large cost, having so short a lease,
Dost thou upon thy fading mansion spend?
Shall worms, inheritors of this excess,
Eat up thy charge? Is this thy body's end?
Then soul, live thou upon thy servant's loss,
And let that pine to aggravate thy store;
Buy terms divine in selling hours of dross;
Within be fed, without be rich no more:
So shall thou feed on Death, that feeds on men,
And Death once dead, there's no more dying then.

CXLVII

My love is as a fever longing still,
For that which longer nurseth the disease;
Feeding on that which doth preserve the ill,
The uncertain sickly appetite to please.
My reason, the physician to my love,
Angry that his prescriptions are not kept,
Hath left me, and I desperate now approve
Desire is death, which physic did except.

Past cure I am, now Reason is past care,
And frantic-mad with evermore unrest;
My thoughts and my discourse as madmen's are,
At random from the truth vainly expressed;
For I have sworn thee fair, and thought thee bright,
Who art as black as hell, as dark as night.

CXLVIII

O me! what eyes hath Love put in my head,
Which have no correspondence with true sight;
Or, if they have, where is my judgment fled,
That censures falsely what they see aright?
If that be fair whereon my false eyes dote,
What means the world to say it is not so?
If it be not, then love doth well denote
Love's eye is not so true as all men's: no,
How can it? O! how can Love's eye be true,
That is so vexed with watching and with tears?
No marvel then, though I mistake my view;
The sun itself sees not, till heaven clears.
O cunning Love! with tears thou keep'st me blind,
Lest eyes well-seeing thy foul faults should find.

CXLIX

Canst thou, O cruel! say I love thee not,
When I against myself with thee partake?
Do I not think on thee, when I forgot
Am of myself, all tyrant, for thy sake?
Who hateth thee that I do call my friend,
On whom frown'st thou that I do fawn upon,

Nay, if thou lour'st on me, do I not spend
Revenge upon myself with present moan?
What merit do I in my self respect,
That is so proud thy service to despise,
When all my best doth worship thy defect,
Commanded by the motion of thine eyes?
But, love, hate on, for now I know thy mind,
Those that can see thou lov'st, and I am blind.

CL

O! from what power hast thou this powerful might,
With insufficiency my heart to sway?
To make me give the lie to my true sight,
And swear that brightness doth not grace the day?
Whence hast thou this becoming of things ill,
That in the very refuse of thy deeds
There is such strength and warrantise of skill,
That, in my mind, thy worst all best exceeds?
Who taught thee how to make me love thee more,
The more I hear and see just cause of hate?
O! though I love what others do abhor,
With others thou shouldst not abhor my state:
If thy unworthiness raised love in me,
More worthy I to be beloved of thee.

CLI

Love is too young to know what conscience is,
Yet who knows not conscience is born of love?
Then, gentle cheater, urge not my amiss,
Lest guilty of my faults thy sweet self prove:

For, thou betraying me, I do betray
My nobler part to my gross body's treason;
My soul doth tell my body that he may
Triumph in love; flesh stays no farther reason,
But rising at thy name doth point out thee,
As his triumphant prize. Proud of this pride,
He is contented thy poor drudge to be,
To stand in thy affairs, fall by thy side.
No want of conscience hold it that I call
Her love, for whose dear love I rise and fall.

CLII
In loving thee thou know'st I am forsworn,
But thou art twice forsworn, to me love swearing;
In act thy bed-vow broke, and new faith torn,
In vowing new hate after new love bearing:
But why of two oaths' breach do I accuse thee,
When I break twenty? I am perjured most;
For all my vows are oaths but to misuse thee,
And all my honest faith in thee is lost:
For I have sworn deep oaths of thy deep kindness,
Oaths of thy love, thy truth, thy constancy;
And, to enlighten thee, gave eyes to blindness,
Or made them swear against the thing they see;
For I have sworn thee fair; more perjured eye,
To swear against the truth so foul a lie!

CLIII
Cupid laid by his brand and fell asleep:
A maid of Dian's this advantage found,

And his love-kindling fire did quickly steep
In a cold valley-fountain of that ground;
Which borrowed from this holy fire of Love,
A dateless lively heat, still to endure,
And grew a seething bath, which yet men prove
Against strange maladies a sovereign cure.
But at my mistress' eye Love's brand new-fired,
The boy for trial needs would touch my breast;
I, sick withal, the help of bath desired,
And thither hied, a sad distempered guest,
But found no cure, the bath for my help lies
Where Cupid got new fire; my mistress' eyes.

CLIV

The little Love-god lying once asleep,
Laid by his side his heart-inflaming brand,
Whilst many nymphs that vowed chaste life to keep
Came tripping by; but in her maiden hand
The fairest votary took up that fire
Which many legions of true hearts had warmed;
And so the General of hot desire
Was, sleeping, by a virgin hand disarmed.
This brand she quenched in a cool well by,
Which from Love's fire took heat perpetual,
Growing a bath and healthful remedy,
For men diseased; but I, my mistress' thrall,
Came there for cure and this by that I prove,
Love's fire heats water, water cools not love.

An Excerpt from Salve Deus Rex Judæorum ["Eve's Apologie"]

Now *Pontius Pilate* is to judge the Cause
Of faultlesse *Jesus*, who before him stands;
Who neither hath offended Prince, nor Lawes,
Although he now be brought in woefull bands:
O noble Governour, make thou yet a pause,
Doe not in innocent blood imbrue thy hands; 750
But heare the words of thy most worthy wife,
Who sends to thee, to beg her Saviour's life.

Let barb'rous crueltie farre depart from thee,
And in true Justice take afflictions part;
Open thine eies, that thou the truth mai'st see,
Doe not the thing that goes against thy heart,
Condemne not him that must thy Saviour be;
But view his holy Life, his good desert.
Let not us Women glory in Men's fall,
Who had power given to over-rule us all. 760

Till now your indiscretion sets us free,
And makes our former fault much lesse appeare;
Our Mother *Eve*, who tasted of the Tree,
Giving to *Adam* what she held most deare,
Was simply good, and had no powre to see,

The after-comming harme did not appeare:
  The subtile Serpent that our Sex betraide,
  Before our fall so sure a plot had laide.

That undiscerning Ignorance perceav'd
No guile, or craft that was by him intended; 770
For, had she knowne of what we were bereav'd,
To his request she had not condiscended
But she (poore soule) by cunning was deceav'd,
No hurt therein her harmelesse Heart intended:
  For she alleadg'd God's word, which he denies,
  That they should die, but even as Gods, be wise.

But surely *Adam* can not be excus'd,
Her fault, though great, yet hee was most too blame;
What Weaknesse offerd, Strength might have refus'd,
Being Lord of all, the greater was his shame: 780
Although the Serpents craft had her abus'd,
God's holy word ought all his actions frame:
  For he was Lord and King of all the earth,
  Before poore *Eve* had either life or breath.

Who being fram'd by God's eternall hand,
The perfect'st man that ever breath'd on earth;
And from God's mouth receiv'd that strait command,
The breach whereof he knew was present death:
Yea having powre to rule both Sea and Land,
Yet with one Apple wonne to loose that breath, 790
  Which God hath breathed in his beauteous face,
  Bringing us all in danger and disgrace.

And then to lay the fault on Patience backe,
That we (poore women) must endure it all;
We know right well he did discretion lacke,
Beeing not perswaded thereunto at all;
If *Eve* did erre, it was for knowledge sake,
The fruit beeing faire perswaded him to fall:
No subtill Serpents falshood did betray him,
If he would eate it, who had powre to stay him? 800

Not *Eve*, whose fault was onely too much love,
Which made her give this present to her Deare,
That what shee tasted, he likewise might prove,
Whereby his knowledge might become more cleare;
He never sought her weakenesse to reprove,
With those sharpe words, which he of God did heare:
Yet Men will boast of Knowledge, which he tooke
From *Eves* faire hand, as from a learned Booke.

If any Evill did in her remaine,
Beeing made of him, he was the ground of all; 810
If one of many Worlds could lay a staine
Upon our Sexe, and worke so great a fall
To wretched Man, by Satan's subtill traine;
What will so fowle a fault amongst you all?
Her weakenesse did the Serpent's words obay;
But you in malice Gods deare Sonne betray.

Whom, if unjustly you condemne to die,
Her sinne was small, to what you doe commit;
All mortall sinnes that doe for vengeance crie,

Are not to be compared unto it: 820
If many worlds would altogether trie,
By all their sinnes the wrath of God to get;
  This sinne of yours, surmounts them all as farre
  As doth the Sunne, another little starre.

Then let us have our Libertie againe,
And challendge to your selves no Sov'raigntie;
You came not in the world without our paine,
Make that a barre against your crueltie;
Your fault beeing greater, why should you disdaine
Our beeing your equals, free from tyranny? 830
  If one weake woman simply did offend,
  This sinne of yours, hath no excuse, nor end.

To which (poore soules) we never gave consent,
Witnesse thy wife (O *Pilate*) speakes for all;
Who did but dreame, and yet a message sent,
That thou should'st have nothing to doe at all
With that just man; which, if thy heart relent,
Why wilt thou be a reprobate with *Saul*?
  To seeke the death of him that is so good,
  For thy soules health to shed his dearest blood.

DISCUSSION QUESTIONS

1. This book plays with the line between fantasy and reality. How do you see this playing out in the story?

2. Emilia's ideas about purity and morality differ from our own. What do you think about them?

3. Emilia talks several times in the book about not having a choice about how she lives her life. How much do you think this is true?

4. The queen plays many roles in Emilia's life—ruler, leader, mother, and God-like figure. Which do you think Emilia feels most? Needs most?

5. Emilia competes with Shakespeare's plays for attention throughout the story. Which do you think he ultimately loves more?

6. All of the women in this story struggle with duty versus love. How do you see the characters wrestling with this? Which, ultimately, do you think brings them the most happiness?

7. Would you rather be happy or remembered? Do you think Emilia achieved either?